CASSANDRA BROOKE

All My Worldly Goods

POCKET
BOOKS

New York London Toronto Sydney Tokyo Singapore

First published in Great Britain by Simon & Schuster
Ltd, 1994
A Paramount Communications Company

Copyright © Cassandra Brooke, 1994

The right of Cassandra Brooke to be identified as author of
this work has been asserted in accordance with sections 77
and 78 of the Copyright Designs and Patents Act 1988

Simon & Schuster Ltd
West Garden Place
Kendal Street
London W2 2AQ

Simon & Schuster of Australia Pty Ltd
Sydney

A CIP catalogue record for this book is available from the
British Library.

ISBN 0-671-71855-X

This book is a work of fiction. Names, characters, places and
incidents are either the product of the author's imagination
or are used fictitiously. Any resemblance to actual events or
locales or persons, living or dead, is entirely coincidental.

Typeset in 11/12.5 Baskerville
by Florencetype Ltd, Kewstoke, Avon
Printed and bound by
HarperCollins Manufacturing, Glasgow

For Dot

Also by Cassandra Brooke

Dear Venus
With Much Love

1

THERE was no getting away from the water. Most of the garden lay submerged beneath it. From where we were standing the mill-race sounded ferocious enough for a hydroelectric power station. Two drips from the roof performed a duet in the buckets which I'd managed to find in one of the sheds and positioned carefully on the greenish stone flags.

We were gazing out of the window at the incessant rain. Tom's shoulders were hunched up as if he were preparing to do battle with it.

'Who d'you suppose the architect of this place was?' he announced after a while. 'Noah?'

I laughed. Tom didn't.

'And whose idea was this anyway?'

'Yours,' I said.

Tom gave a shrug, and a smile that would have made a Rottweiler cower. He lit a cigarette and blew the smoke thoughtfully at one of the buckets, then at the other.

'So this is it, then,' he went on. 'What we dreamed of. Our country paradise. Our idyll far away from the London smog and the rush-hour . . . Sod it!'

'You might have said that before you signed the cheque,' I suggested.

The reminder of money wiped the smile from Tom's face.

'Jesus!' he said. 'Three hundred thousand pounds. Well, at least you're going to pay half when you've sold your house. *If* you can sell your house.' Tom gave another mournful glance at the rain. 'Three hundred grand – for a shipwreck! Can you believe it? We'll have the salvage boys round any minute, you wait. Look! I can see the buggers already. There!'

I peered out of the window.

'That's the farmer's two boys,' I said firmly. 'They asked to use our field for their cows. Remember?'

'Field! You mean there's real earth under that lake? The cows must be aqualung specialists – or dead.'

Tom started digging into his breast pocket. He pulled out the estate agents' prospectus and began to read it out.

'"A classic Grade II Listed Mill House located on the River Avon." *On* the River Avon? *In* the River Avon. My legs have got rising damp already. "Amidst glorious wooded countryside." Who wrote this crap? Wooded countryside, my arse! The hurricane removed the woods, and the countryside got drowned. It only needs an albatross and I'm the Ancient Mariner. And there *is* one! See?'

'It's a seagull,' I suggested.

'Looks big enough for an albatross to me . . . Now it's lining up to shit all over the car. Piss off, you!'

Tom waved his arms violently at the window. The removals men thought he was waving at them, and waved cheerfully back. I looked at my watch.

'Have you finished?' I asked. 'Because we've got a mountain of unpacking to do.'

But Tom hadn't.

'"The accommodation represents everything associated with a classic mill residence, with a 27 ft. playroom and 4 loose boxes." Well, that's really useful: we've got no small brats and I'm allergic to horses. "Gardens and paddocks extending to approximately 20 acres. A special feature is the rustic arbour." Arbour! What the hell's that, Janice? They must mean "harbour".'

At this point in the performance I thrust an arm through Tom's and began to urge him towards the door. With my other hand I indicated the part of the prospectus which said: 'Adjoining the main residence is a self-contained Guest/Staff cottage.'

'That's what matters right now, Tom,' I said. 'Where we hole up till we get a chance to fix this lot. It's only the first of March and it won't rain for ever.'

'Why didn't we move to France, Jan?'

'Because you don't speak French.'

'I could learn. Peter Mayle did.'

Ignoring this new diversion I went over to the door and stepped outside, hoisting my umbrella. The removals men had finished and were closing up the back of the pantechnicon. One of them was holding up a piece of paper for me to sign. Tom was taking no notice.

'Look,' he exclaimed, stabbing the final page of the prospectus with his forefinger. 'It says we've got "Private Drains". Christ, the whole place is a Public Drain. Everyone in Wiltshire's pissed all over it.' He paused, looked at me, and suddenly he burst out laughing. 'And I love it.'

With that he tossed the prospectus over his shoulder and, ducking under the umbrella, threw his arms round my waist and spun me round and round in the rain.

'And I love *you*, my beautiful Venus. This is happiness – even if we have to swim for it. So let's unpack, provided the first thing we unpack is the wine. I insist. Entre Deux Mers might be appropriate: what d'you think?'

I thought there was a fair chance I might love him too.

There's an old Chinese curse – 'May you live in interesting times.'

I do.

Life was never in danger of being boring with Tom. It had never been boring with Harry either, for that matter, only painful and frequently lonely. The important discovery was that it was much more lonely having a husband who wasn't there than having no husband at all. Loneliness is not a matter of being alone, but of being deprived, without the freedom to adjust to deprivation. 'Twelve years as an old-fashioned wife and mother,' Ruth had pronounced incredulously. 'Not a single affair. Madness!'

Ruth was my oldest friend. We were at school together. She was always everything I wasn't. It was as if somehow she'd stolen a few extra years to give her a lead over everyone else – and certainly over me. She was in full bloom before I'd even budded. She knew all about French letters while I still imagined they were something to do with pen-friends. What Ruth didn't know about life I assumed she'd chosen not to know because it wasn't worth it; and it was years before I stopped feeling honoured to be her friend. She was dark and dangerous. She was also Jewish – not so much lapsed as collapsed: it was one of those trappings she'd discarded long ago, like sweet-papers, or virginity.

The best thing about Ruth was that she liked *me* – even after I stopped being an ugly duckling; even after I married someone she loathed; even after I had a child she could never have. It was impossible to imagine the world without Ruth, however far apart we lived. She wrote. She phoned. She breezed in and out of my life. And, in a kindly way, she mocked.

'Not a single affair. Madness! Thank God you made up for it.'

I suppose I did rather. After I finally booted Harry out, the experience of being available, of making myself available, came as a revelation. Men, after all, make themselves available all the time, or at least when the little wife has her back turned. I could have collected assignations like trading stamps if I'd had a mind to all those years. Blonde. Very pretty. Petite. Sparkly. Good legs. Neat breasts – 'Champagne cups', Ruth used to say. Good God, I needed only to have crooked my little finger: it would have been absurdly easy, like nicking sweets from Woolworths as a child. So easy it never occurred to me I might actually do it. I was married, and that was it. Looking back, it feels absurd: such a triumph of conditioning, when all the time Harry's conditioning was telling him he was entitled to any bit of fluff he fancied provided he wasn't found out too often.

Well, he *was* found out – a bit too often. And in no time *I* was the one who was available. I was free: free to ask men out, free to ask men in. Now I was on an equal footing with all those marriage-weary males who had shaken off the first bonds, or at least were practising for it, testing the waters to see how deep into adultery they dared go, or could afford to go.

There were a few problems. I didn't always learn the right script. At first I didn't realise that it's one thing for a man to lead a woman astray and then murmur on the pillow 'You've got lovely breasts'; but for her to be handy with the zip and say 'You've got a lovely prick' – well, no sooner said than the thing would shrivel back into the Y-fronts. Once, not long after Harry departed, I cooked a cordon bleu dinner for a man I fancied more and more with each course, until I could bear it no longer. I disappeared into the bathroom and returned stark naked. And did he strip off in ten seconds and leap on me with a stallion's erection? Not at all. He turned pale and threw up all over the kiwi fruit sorbet. I never asked whether it was my cooking that had made him ill, or my body.

After that I kept my appetites under wraps, at least until the man made the first move. That was Ruth's advice again. 'Easy, my dear; the first move is always in the groin. You can't miss it. But don't be put off by a mere bulge; it could be a sock put there to impress.

Nothing is worse than finding yourself trying to arouse a Wolsey.'

It was all very well for Ruth: she had a marriage. An 'open marriage' admittedly, so wide open it was a miracle it didn't get blown apart. I had no marriage at all: I was a single mother who had to work at the local deli to supplement Harry's hand-outs, with a twelve-year-old son who took a proprietorial delight in awarding Brownie points to my various men-friends. I'd be installing whoever it might be in the sitting-room with a vodka and tonic when this face would appear through the banisters, eyes flicking to and fro with the conversation like an umpire at Wimbledon. Then a hand would appear with one finger raised, or two, or four; and occasionally a second hand, usually for someone I'd already decided had nothing between his ears and precious little more between his legs.

The one man who got no points at all was Tom. On his very first visit he took his eyes off my breasts for long enough to catch sight of this face grinning between the banisters, and said without the smallest hint of irritation: 'How about telling the little bastard to piss off?' The next time, Tom brought him a cricket bat, the creep, and from then on Clive became his staunchest advocate.

As far as I was concerned Tom was everything I never wanted. He was nearly twenty years older than me – in his fifties – and he'd been married God knows how many times. Whenever I mentioned his name to a girlfriend there'd be this unaccountable silence. It soon became clear that he'd had them all at some time or other, even the most straight-laced of them. They never quite knew what to say to me, though the general message seemed to be that Tom was great in bed and a total louse.

I didn't find it surprising that a man should have picked up some basic skills in the course of so much active service. But Ruth was more sceptical. There was a snort on the telephone, and then 'Tom must be the only man in history to have been divorced five times for being a great lover.' After I put the phone down I wondered how she knew it was *five* times. I rang back. Had she been yet another notch on his bow? I asked. No, Ruth assured me, though it hadn't been for want of trying on his part.

So I kept him firmly at bay, while finding to my irritation that I was enjoying his company more and more. It became something of a sparring match. Tom would play the dandy and dress up in ever more elegant Italian suits. But then at the restaurant there'd be some raven-haired tart, all mascara and cleavage, whom he'd claim hardly to know. ('Honestly, sweetheart, I can't even remember the girl's name.' 'Huh! She seemed to remember yours without any trouble.') Next time round I'd put on my slinkiest Jean Muir outfit in order to upstage whoever it might be: then there'd be nobody there, and Tom would be so turned on all evening. I might as well have been wearing nothing at all as far as his eyes were concerned, and it became a question of how to get home before the charm and the brandy did the work Tom intended them to.

I also grew aware of an uncomfortable weakness in my line of defence. It was impossible not to fancy the idea of being seduced by a dedicated professional: here was a man with an olympian reputation, and wasn't sampling it an experience not to be missed? Could any woman deny that she'd love to have known what it was like to be seduced by Lord Byron? Tom would have liked more than anything to have been Lord Byron: he said so tediously often until I pointed out that if he were Byron, at his age he'd have been a romantic corpse for nearly twenty years by now. 'In that case I'll settle for being his biographer: that's what I'll do when I'm rich, and I'll become even richer.' And he laughed as though he believed it. I was too fond of Tom to suggest that being a lecher didn't necessarily qualify him to be Byron, any more than being a veteran hack on one of the tabloids qualified him to be the great man's biographer. All the same – and there was always an 'all the same' whenever I tried to dismiss Tom's credentials – I did spend an inordinate amount of time wondering if, and when, and what, and what then? I knew none of the answers, but the questions refused to go away.

I finally gave in on election night. Tom was cooking something Moroccan which was filling the flat with the aroma of saffron and coriander. It was a tiny flat, hardly what I'd expected. 'I know,' said Tom in a resigned voice inviting pity. 'London is full of lovely houses I used to own, lived in by ex-wives who don't have the decency to re-marry.' The courts had always granted them the house, he explained sadly. 'Why?' I asked. 'Because you'd always behaved so badly?' 'Probably,' he said casually. I could have throttled him. Jesus! Five wives: what was I doing here? Why was I there, watching him weave his skills as a chef around me? It was at least an hour before the first election results would be announced, and already I was getting pissed. What was more, getting pissed and enjoying being there, curled up like a cat on the sofa. Five wives! There were so many Mrs Tom Brands in and around London that it wasn't so much a title as a brand-name. When I said this, Tom merely laughed; then assured me in that mock-innocent way of his that really he'd never intended to get married so many times. 'Oh, I see,' I retorted. 'It was just out of the kindness of your heart, I suppose.' 'Something like that,' he answered, as if the subject were hardly worth dwelling on. He stopped basting the lamb to refill my glass. 'You're the loveliest woman I know,' he said without the slightest change of tone. Then, as my stomach did a little jump, he turned to gaze at the TV set where pollsters were filling in time contradicting each other. 'So, what's it going to be – a hung parliament?' I took another sip of wine and peered at him over the top of my glass. 'I'd like a well-hung parliament,' I said.

It was a good line, but it was also the end of my defence. He undressed me as though unwrapping a rare orchid, fingers moving softly over the petals. I wanted him more than I'd ever wanted anyone. In the early morning the TV set was still on. Labour had lost. 'You never got your hung parliament,' Tom mumbled, half-awake. 'Never mind,' I whispered, 'it's better this way.'

That was Stage One. Tom moved in. We never discussed it. He belonged in my bed and in my life. Clive was delighted – a bit too delighted. He flicked a lock of hair back from his eyes and looked at me questioningly. 'Mummy, if you don't hurry up and marry

Tom, I suppose he'll go off and find someone else just like Daddy did.'

It was hardly the moment to remind my beastly son that I'd been the one to kick Harry out, and about time too; nor, at the age of thirty-seven, was I exactly the geriatric wrinkly he seemed to imagine.

Did I want to marry Tom? No, I don't think I did. Why are children so conventional about these things?

'I've told them all at school that you're living in sin, and they're frightfully envious of me,' Clive went on. 'Oh, *are* they just?' I said archly, wishing I had the money to send him to boarding-school.

Money, I felt sure, would change a lot of things in my life. The trouble was, whenever I fantasised about what exactly it would change, all I could think of was that having money would stop me worrying about *not* having money, and that seemed rather feeble. 'One thing's certain,' pronounced Ruth, 'you'll never grow rich with Tom. I'd stick to painting.'

But I'd tried that. As a dewy-eyed art student I'd dreamed of world fame with my splashy abstracts unburdened across acres of cotton-duck; though the real reason had been that I was in love with my tutor who was a tiny bit famous for splashy abstracts painted across acres of cotton-duck. I tried hard to make mine as meaningless as his. In the end my mother nobly bought one, and that was that. As for the tutor, he took my virginity and shortly afterwards shot himself – I don't believe there was any connection – and I gave up painting for five years, by which time there was only the space and opportunity for small watercolours of flowers between cooking for Harry and changing Clive's nappies.

True, after my marriage collapsed my career as an artist did enjoy a brief and unusual renaissance. Several wealthy men-friends commissioned me to paint murals for their houses, though it invariably turned out to be for their bedrooms, and instead of making advance payments they merely made advances. Then the recession killed off these skittish enterprises and I was left with serving prosciutto in the local deli, and ultimately with Tom – neither of which offered the smallest prospect of fame or fortune.

Until the day when Ruth was proved wrong about Tom, and we were catapulted into Stage Two.

It happened in an accidental way. Ruth is married to a career diplomat whose career alternately blossoms and withers as a direct result of her influence upon it. Among Ruth's less valuable assets is her cooking. Ambassadors have been known to seek early retirement rather than face another of her dinner parties. After one particularly bowel-testing occasion she remarked to me that someone really ought to compose an *anti*-cookbook, and dedicate it to her.

I repeated this conversation to Tom, and he grinned. Being a gifted cook himself, he took the view that it should be a perfectly genuine seafood cookery book. The recipes would be no problem: he could easily provide these from his long experience as a globe-trotting journalist. But the illustrations (by me!) should adopt a strikingly novel approach. Colour photographs in cookery books, he explained, always made the food look plastic, and in any case what you ended up with never looked remotely like them. No, what we needed to explore, he went on, growing more enthusiastic by the minute, was the fact that food is an oral pleasure – an erotic experience. I was looking doubtful, but Tom didn't seem to notice. 'What shall we call it?' he said. 'What about Ruth's idea?' I suggested. '*Prawnography.*' Tom's face was one of pure joy.

We then spent an enlivening evening thinking of dishes appropriate to this neo-Freudian approach. Tom knew an outstanding recipe from Baltimore for clams. 'How about *Freshwater Clams in Extra Virgin Olive Oil?*' That took his fancy no end. 'We have to think of the American market: that's where the money is.' I came up with *Prawns Soixante-Neuf,* which quite shocked him at first: we'd only recently become lovers. *Winkles with Nuts* had distinct possibilities for a beginner, we agreed. And so it went on until late in the evening. I wanted to acknowledge Ruth as the primogenitor of our master-piece, and Tom promised to find a suitable recipe for *Ruth Amid the Alien Prawn.*

It was one of those ridiculously enjoyable occasions, warmed by much wine, that one expects not to feel like mentioning in the morning. But at midday Tom phoned me at the deli to say he'd found an enthusiastic publisher and, if I'd just do a couple of trial illustrations in order to convince the art boys, we were seriously in business.

And so we were. *Prawnography* was banned in Ireland, a triumph in Japan, a cult in the United States, and taken seriously in Germany. In under a year we'd made a million between us. Suddenly we were confronted by a reality the entire world dreams of: we no longer needed to earn a living. What was more, we'd done it not by the recommended route of sweat and toil, but with a joke. It was impossible to take grindstones seriously after that, and we decided not to. Tom gave up his job. I gave up the deli. Clive decided he'd love to go to Millfield. And Tom and I agreed to build a new life together in the country. We were going to ditch our past and begin again. Fresh fields and pastures new. At last, I was seriously going to be a painter, and Tom was going to spend the last of his golden years bidding a long farewell to Fleet Street, which might or might not include composing the most robust – if not the most definitive – biography of his hero Lord Byron.

There was one final twist. Badgered by the publishers not to hide from publicity, we finally picked our moment to come out of the closet by agreeing to appear on a popular live chat-show whose host sadly lost his job as a result. Perhaps it wasn't really his fault that he produced painting materials and invited me to create an impromptu illustration for a dish of his choice. His mistake lay in opting for one of his personal favourites, which happened to be an unusual method of preparing monkfish. My imagination made it more unusual still. To make it worse, I suggested washing the monkfish down with Blue Nun – a very blue nun, as it turned out. It was an inspired creation in my view, alas altogether too inspired for the Director General of the BBC, Mary Whitehouse and the Cardinal Archbishop of Westminster. Well, ratings soared; so did our sales. If only my tutor at art college could have lived long enough to see how famous his little blonde student had become. But perhaps he would have shot himself anyway.

And that was that. My TV debut was the *coup de grâce* to our London life. The immediate outcome was our departure after a week of torrential rain to Otters Mill, Sarum Magna, Wiltshire, on the first of March. We were now entering Stage Three. A 'good luck' phone call from Ruth expressed joy at our change of fortune, as well as delight that she now had friends whose experience of life's absurdities matched her own in the merry-go-round of Her Majesty's Diplomatic Service.

2

THE floods receded, and our ark settled on Mount Ararat; except that instead of creatures departing two by two, they began to arrive two by two. We were inspected by the village.

There were several faces I recognised from an earlier excursion into Sarum Magna. I had felt an alien: people in the shop lowered their voices. The shopkeeper's wife gave me an uncertain glance. 'Yes, madam?' she asked, as though she meant 'No!'

'I don't think they like the look of me in the village,' I said to Tom.

'I expect it's because you don't wear a bra,' he answered without raising his eyes from the racing results.

'Nonsense. This is England, not Portugal.'

'Janice, it's darkest Wiltshire.'

'It's still nonsense.'

'All right. I'll give you a better reason.' Tom raised his head from the newspaper. 'They're all saying to each other "How come that scruffy little tart has managed to hook the famous and magnificent Tom Brand?"'

He warded off my hand with the newspaper, and went on reading.

'If they only knew we'd bought Otters Mill on the back of *Prawnography*,' I said.

'Oh, they will. They will. You wait. In no time there'll be a 'Local Authors' window display at Waterstone's in Salisbury, and we'll be there on Saturday afternoons signing copies gratefully. And every time we're invited out to dinner there'll be our book nestling between *The Field* and the 90th birthday biography of the Queen Mother. What's more it'll be open at *Prawns Soixante-Neuf.*'

I winced. 'Oh God! I had no idea the country was like this.'

Why did I ever imagine that a village was full of villagers? I suppose it must be the early imprint of Thomas Hardy novels, or school reproductions of Constable. Or perhaps those baleful afternoons in a London basement listening to the Archers while waiting to collect Clive from school, and trying not to speculate on which of Harry's pretty 'researchers' would be unavoidably detaining him this evening.

For so many years the idea of a village had been a reassuring dream, a place where I would one day be – a place where you belonged simply by being there, where you were welcomed or left alone as you chose, but always nourished by an ancient and timeless rhythm of country life and country values. A place where there was peace like the sighing of the trees. The village store. The village pub. The village green. Cricket matches which began with the removal of cowpats and ended with vast consumptions of ale. Church fêtes where you bought homemade scones, green tomato chutney and gooseberry jam which blossomed into mould within a week. And harvest thanksgivings strewn with intricate corn-dollies and vegetable marrows bulging like bolsters. And, above all, villagers: those people who had always been there, whose very names – even if they couldn't actually be found in the Domesday Book – were none the less rooted in the very birth of this place. Names you didn't find anywhere else, or at least not further than twenty miles away, so that two men conscripted into some distant war would know from the first roll-call that both of them hailed from the valley of the Avon. They'd know it from the names, but also from small private words, special meanings and inflections, which struck an immediate chord no one else could hear, and spoke to them of home.

How sentimental it sounded. But it was what I'd always felt in a soggy corner of my heart.

It must have been our second or third day in Sarum Magna – before the visitations began. I decided to slither up the track in my gumboots, leaving Tom poring over a local map of our damp acres which were gradually becoming visible above the flood-waters. The village was a single street threaded between water-meadows and a long buttress of a hill. Hunched on either side of the street were brick-and-flint cottages, deep-browed and low-slung, with windows designed to keep out the sunlight, and roofs of heavy reed-thatch trimmed into neat chevrons at the top. Each roof, I noticed with surprise, was surmounted by a carved pheasant realistic enough to trick the eye, giving the place a distinctly dotty appearance.

As I was gazing at the pheasants I heard a voice.

'Amazing how you never see them fly, isn't it?'

I turned my head to see a grey-haired bun of a woman of about sixty. She was grasping a wicker basket of cut-flowers in one hand, and leading a goat on a length of rope with the other. She was chuckling to herself.

Without waiting for an answer she walked on, followed at a short distance by the goat; then, still looking straight head of her, she added breezily: 'Good morning, young lady.'

Her bottom moved majestically within purple tweeds as she walked. A cleaner's ticket was safety-pinned to her back.

Eccentric local gentry, I thought. Every village has one. I carried on towards the churchyard and began to gaze at the ancestral names on the gravestones. Budden. Creese. Hazzard. Strapps. Gusse. Rumbold. Smeath. Mustard. Studhelme. Watte. Whitty. Penruddocke. Maydenhide. There they were, those true village names, the natural inheritors of this place, the heirs of brawny people who had cleared the forests, planted the first corn, fished the river, set up the water-mills (*our* water-mill!), built those brick-and-flint cottages that flanked the single street. Yes, this was village life: well, actually it was village death, but never mind – their great-great-great-grandchildren still ploughed the fields and milked the cows which I could see grazing beyond the graveyard wall.

Budden. Strapps. Smeath. Whitty. Maydenhide. I found myself wondering if one day my name would be there too. The thought came as quite a shock. 'Here lies Janice Blakemore. Beloved mother of Clive.' I wasn't entirely sure I could count on that. What else? 'Artist.' Well, I suppose so. 'Mistress of Thomas Brand.' They wouldn't allow that in a churchyard, surely. In any case Tom would be long dead by then. All right: what about 'Formerly mistress of Thomas Brand, and subsequently of others who shall remain nameless. RIP'?

This didn't feel quite at one with the spirit of the place, so I wandered into the church. It was small, cold and Gothic. Ogives were everywhere, one of them enclosing a fragment of stained-glass depicting a devil. Sunlight was pouring through his grin like hell-fire. Nearby I noticed a smudge of wall-painting which you could illuminate by means of a switch on the wall opposite. I decided it wouldn't illuminate anything particularly interesting and drifted into the north aisle where I'd noticed a tomb of some reclining knight glistening damply. His legs were crossed, and his feet rested on a woolsack. A marble sheep looked on patiently.

I bent down to try and decipher the Latin name and date, but could only make out irrelevant words like *utque*. I became so absorbed by this useless exercise that I was unaware I was no longer alone.

'Bustard,' came a resounding voice from behind me.

I gave a start and turned round. Leaning on one of the pews, legs firmly apart, was the woman in purple I'd seen in the street half an hour before. Her basket was now empty except for a pair of gardening scissors. She was smiling broadly.

'Bustard,' she said again, walking up to me with a rolling gait. 'Sir Ranulf. Ancestor of my husband. Killed at Agincourt, the silly bugger: almost nobody else was except the French. You're new here, I understand. I'm Emelda. Come and have a drink – very soon.'

We shook hands beside her husband's ancestor. Then she stooped to pick up her basket and we walked together towards the door.

'Well, that's that done.' She explained she always did the flowers in church. 'Can't think why. Don't believe in the bloody thing. But it looks pretty, doesn't it? And it gives me something to do apart from looking after Ayrton.'

Ayrton, she pointed out quickly as if to get it out of the way, was her husband, Lord Bustard. She gave a throaty laugh, with a final glance back at the ancestral tomb.

'Real name's Bastard. Wrong side of the blanket. Some Protestant in the sixteenth century with his eye on a bishopric changed it to Bustard, after the bird, and stuck the creature on the family crest. Only place you'll ever see it nowadays: the bird's extinct.' She gave a giggle. 'Mind you, so might we be if I hadn't enjoyed a little fling in my younger days. Family tradition, after all, with a name like Bastard – so I told Ayrton. He was very good about it, I have to say. Loved the kid, acknowledged him and all that. I wanted to register him as Bastard – true to history, true to life. But Ayrton pointed out he wouldn't inherit the title. Not that I cared a sod. But Ayrton does. You'll like him. Quite mad. But terribly sweet.'

There was a pause in these intimate confidences while we hoisted umbrellas against the drizzle and Emelda untied the goat from a tombstone. I wondered if she talked to every newcomer like this. Village life certainly wasn't turning out the way I'd expected. Emelda paused by a small wooden gate, resting her basket on top of it, out of reach of the goat.

'I haven't introduced you, by the way,' she said, yanking the animal to heel. 'This is Lloyd George, who *was* of course a goat. And he really did know my father, though not quite as well as he did my mother.' She gave a throaty laugh. 'Now look! We're down the end there, by the river. Call round later in the week. And if you don't, I'll phone and insist. Bring your man, of course. I assume you're not married; you look far too happy. It's Tom Brand, isn't it? I always read his stuff. Dead right about the royal divorce. I could have told him a whole lot more. Yes! Tom Brand,' she went on thoughtfully. 'I met one of his wives once. Terrible woman. Rotten with virtue. He seems to have better taste nowadays. Not that you're not virtuous, my dear, I'm sure. Otherwise why would you be burying yourself here. Why are you, by the way? Most people can't wait to get out.'

I told her about wanting to be a painter, and about my dreams of village life and village people. She looked astonished.

'My dear girl – village people! The last one died at Christmas.' Emelda's flesh began to shake with laughter. Then she patted her hand on my shoulder. 'No, of course there must be a few of them left; you can usually tell them by their BMWs. My husband's probably the only true villager there is: his family's been here for three hundred years as Bustard and God knows how many centuries before then as Bastard. Otherwise it's mostly stockbrokers and naval officers. Stiff with them. You know, my dear, Sarum was the original "rotten borough". Well, it still is. Thank God you've arrived. I like you.'

I liked her too. I was still shaken by her knowing Tom's wife. Which wife? I wondered. And I'd imagined that coming down here would be getting away from Tom's women. I began to get a feeling of being pursued by ghosts.

I walked back to the mill in the rain, running the gauntlet of curious eyes peering from beneath umbrellas. Well, Emelda promises to be great fun, I thought, even if not much else is. We'll see.

Ruth held the view that anyone who actually chose to live in the English countryside for pleasure must be losing their marbles. These were almost her last comforting words before she left for Liechtenstein where Piers, due to some whimsical decision from on high, had been appointed ambassador. None the less she insisted I write and tell her who our new rustic neighbours were. This, she explained, was in order to prepare her for the worst when she and Piers descended on us during their next home leave. Her promptings were insistent. Did the hunt come bounding tally-ho through our garden every Saturday? Had the vicar called yet? Had we been awarded our own pew in church? I pointed out in my first letter that, in spite of its name, Sarum Magna was too small to merit a resident vicar, and in any case an itinerant vicar might prefer to give a miss to a household which had already clocked up six divorces between the two of us, and what's more we weren't even married.

So – no vicar. Tom, to make quite sure, put it about at the Wilton Arms that he was a Confucian. Unfortunately the locals he met there were ill-versed in oriental religions, and it soon became known throughout the village that Mr Brand regarded himself as 'confused'. Several of our early visitors remarked on this with solicitude. 'Retirement takes some adjusting to, Mr Brand – I well remember,' said an ex-naval commander by the name of Normington, whose wife was eagerly enquiring if I played bridge. Tom was surprisingly polite.

There were several of that ilk who beat a path to our door through the receding sludge during our first week at Otters Mill. Why so much navy? I wondered. 'All this water: what d'you expect?' Tom suggested, gazing out to where the River Avon was now distinguishable from our garden by a slither of mud on which a gathering of grateful ducks were busy defecating.

Other visitors soon followed: more or less cheerful solicitors and accountants whose children were hyper-active in the pony club and whose wives wore headscarves and sleeveless green Barbours. They arrived, dragged by yelping terriers on the end of extendable leads, and barked cheerful welcomes at us before being dragged away.

Another arrival was an architect with a stutter so pronounced that I was able to count his fillings by the time he got a word out. Eventually he managed to explain that he was designing a lavatory for a London theatre. 'Ah,' said Tom brightly, 'another Crapper!' The man looked indignant, stuttered some more, then departed. 'That was a bit brutal,' I remonstrated. Tom looked surprised. 'I was merely trying to put him at his ease,' he explained. 'Crapper was a famous designer of lavatories. Thomas Crapper of Chelsea. Any architect should know that.'

Tom's display of knowledge at least ensured that there would be no repeat visit.

Then there was a builder or two who kept eyeing the derelict mill-house through the window as they sipped their gins-and-tonic. They made plaintive noises about the recession and left hopeful gaps in the conversation, which we didn't fill. As they departed they presented us with their cards, 'just in case you're in any trouble, madam'.

An early arrival one morning was a large woman in a cerise track-suit who announced that she taught crafts at the cathedral school in Salisbury. Behind her cowered three daughters with dragons' teeth clamped in braces, and long awkward legs. Mother had clearly been prac-tising her craftwork on their hair. They lived 'just down the lane', she explained. We must call. 'Of course,' said Tom immaculately. 'Hypocrite!' I said after they left. 'You didn't even ask the name of their house.' 'Didn't need to, did I?' he answered. 'It'll be called Gawky Park.'

Then there was Mrs Teape whose husband kept the poultry which woke us at dawn each morning. Mrs Teape had clearly taken an inventory of her facial appearance at the age of thirty-nine, and had kept it that way through several decades since. Her hair was ferociously black, lacquered to the skull with the assistance of two combs clamped together to resemble a small man-trap. Her lipstick made generous excursions on to her upper and lower lip, giving the impression that her mouth was vertical instead of horizontal. The bust was unshakeable, and so were her opinions, which flowed generously. There was nothing about Sarum Magna that avoided her eye and her judgments. With the services of Mrs Teape as our cleaner – which she proposed along with a regular supply of free-range eggs – there would be absolutely nothing I didn't know about this village, and precious little the village didn't know about us. I took a chance and said 'Yes'. Tom listened to her spouting and christened her 'Teapot'.

It was through Mrs Teape that I learnt about some of the inhabitants of Sarum Magna who hadn't visited us, and certainly wouldn't. There was Naomi, apparently with no other name, who lived very alone in a wood just across the river and belonged to some pagan sect, explained Mrs Teape with a quick narrowing of the mouth. In the village she was known as Mooncalf, she explained. And if I encountered her it was best not to say 'Good morning'; best not to saying anything at all, because Mooncalf certainly wouldn't either. Tom took the view that he'd get on with the lady perfectly well since he too belonged to a pagan sect, being a tabloid journalist. But Mrs Teape merely tightened her lips.

She was specially concerned to warn me of one further local, since I'd foolishly said I was a painter, and this was a Mr Cash – Winston Cash. She pronounced the name with distaste. He was a painter too, she explained, 'but not like you, I'm sure'. The eyes grew very round. 'Women. Naked women. I've seen them. Disgusting. And he's not even married.'

I prayed that Mrs Teape would never set eyes on *Prawnography*, and after she left I carefully locked away our pile of copies in a cupboard.

Our last visitor of the week was Mr Gant, the neighbouring farmer who was using our field for his cattle. He sat down heavily one afternoon and accepted a mug of tea, the mug disappearing within what resembled a baseball glove rather than a hand. His speech carried a strong Wiltshire burr, but he was dressed in Newmarket tweeds and a flat cap, and his manner of speech had the brisk attack of a racehorse trainer. His eldest son was at Marlborough with a place at Cambridge, he told us early on. Gant was clearly on the way to becoming a gentleman-farmer. 'Soon he'll be Mr Gent,' Tom suggested. 'A small vowel change, that's all.' Gant liked John Major – 'a good man in the saddle'. I noticed how he tended to speak in farming metaphors, robustly, as if his audience were cattle who needed firm prodding to get them going.'

'Met Mooncalf yet, have you?' he asked.

I told him Mrs Teape seemed to disapprove of her.

'Oh, perfectly harmless heifer, Mooncalf,' Gant declared. 'Maiden lady of a certain age. Inherited money. A bit of a hermit. They go like that in the country. It all goes into gardening. And cranky things – she's some sort of Druid. You know, white sheets at Stonehenge.

Solstices. Used to be a wonderful jeweller; you'd never believe it. Gave it up. One of those rich women who always give up whatever they do well. Too much like hard work – ploughing the old furrow. People start expecting things of you, don't they? She'd rather be out to grass.'

'What about Winston Cash?' I asked. 'Mrs Teape thinks his paintings are disgusting.'

Gant gave a bellow of laughter.

'Disgusting? Paints nudes, that's all. Profitable line of business, I'm told – the Japanese market. The name's not Cash for nothing. Perhaps he should change it to Yen.' Mr Gant guffawed at his own wit. Then the red face creased into a leer. 'Mind you, all he can do is paint them. Weedy old capon, he is, Mr Cash. And handsome birds they are, I can tell you. God knows where he finds them – certainly not in the *Salisbury Advertiser*. The present one's South American, I believe. Tinted creature, anyway. Best udders in Wiltshire.'

His hands did the rest: hands that were used to milking. I tried to forgive him the udders.

'You musn't take Mrs Teape's opinions too seriously,' Gant went on. 'Heart of gold. She'll do anything for you if she likes you. The world's divided into saints and sinners for her. Nothing in between. Well!' He rose heavily. 'Got to go now. Thanks for the tea. Anything you need, just call round. Could do with a few more pretty fillies like you in this village.'

I got the feeling that Gant had spotted fillies far beyond Sarum Magna in his day. And if he claimed that Cash's girlfriend had the best udders in Wiltshire, I was sure he had done his research. Tom and he should have a lot in common, I decided.

Tom was rarely present during these early visitations. He didn't take to them particularly well, threatening to set up a drawbridge, complete with portcullis and a cavity for dispensing boiling pitch. Instead he chose to retire into the kitchen with a book he'd managed to acquire called *How to Restore and Improve Ancient Buildings*. I'd be left explaining how my 'husband' was passionate about DIY and couldn't wait to get his hands on the old mill now that the fine weather was approaching – which it wasn't.

One unexpected outcome of these escapes into the kitchen was that in a remarkably short time Tom became genuinely excited by the thought of converting the mill with his bare hands. As a result, I now had the double burden of engaging stockbrokers and retired naval officers in polite chatter, and then having to listen to speeches by the man in my life on the virtues of flitch beams and kingpost trusses. Or else he'd emerge from the kitchen in a radiant mood just in time to be charming to a hirsute lady who'd been sipping cooking sherry for the past hour while urging me to join the Women's Institute.

'She seemed perfectly all right to me,' he'd announce when the woman had finally departed. 'Don't know what you're worried about. Delightful.'

If I didn't love Tom I could have murdered him.

That was the first week.

Unlike Tom, who was like a schoolboy with a new train set, I felt ill at ease, uncertain. I've never been good at readjusting, and there were moments when this place seemed not so much an adjustment as a wrench. I missed London. I missed the streets. I missed the bustle and promiscuity of town life – which one could always retreat from. It began to puzzle me: when I used to retreat to my little house in Chiswick I often used to think about the country, and all those trees and hedgerows, fields, woods, and so much sky. I'd feel starved of all that, and long for it; promise it to myself one day. But now I was actually here I'd gaze out of the window and all I could see were trees, hedgerows, fields, woods – everywhere. And all I could think of was that remark of Max Beerbohm when he left England for Italy: 'Living in England is like living in the middle of a damp lettuce.'

Did I really want to live in the middle of a lettuce? Was it all a terrible mistake? I wished Ruth were close by, and not in her diplomatic gulag. Then she could have assured me how infinitely worse than Sarum Magna was the carousel of embassy life: at least I didn't have to see the Commander Normingtons if I chose not to, whereas an ambassador's wife had to see them all the time, along with leaders of Pakistani trade missions who didn't drink, Greek shipowners who only wanted to fuck you, and the wives of Indian textile moguls whose saris glittered like a million stars and whose minds were a black hole in space.

The first week – it wasn't easy. But at least Tom was galvanised, and we made love a lot.

'Why does this place make you so randy? You're huge!'

There was a breathless mutter in my ear.

'What d'you expect in a place called Sarum Magna?'

So long as that was all right we'd be OK I told myself. I was simply going through an awkward transition from one kind of life to another. Next week things would begin in earnest. Tom had rapidly agreed that he didn't know a great deal about flitch beams and kingpost trusses, and might be more gainfully occupied studying the life of Lord Byron. So we asked Gant about local builders, and he gave us the names of three in Salisbury. 'Don't go near the cowboys here,' he warned. We threw away their cards and made several phone calls to Salisbury. Tom reckoned that £100,000 should make the mill paradise. And the money was sitting there, thanks to *Prawnography*.

'The royalties from America we'll invest as they come in,' Tom suggested, stretching out contentedly on the sofa. 'And we'll never have to work again.' He yawned. 'I love you, Jan,' he said in mid-yawn. 'Now pour me a drink, will you, sweetheart?'

'In a glass, or over you?'

Life was already feeling a lot better.

And it got better still on the Saturday. Emelda Bustard phoned and insisted we come to lunch. We stayed to dinner. During both meals Lloyd George wandered in and out, chewing things that weren't meant to be chewed.

I had a mental picture of English aristocrats which I suppose matched my sentimental image of English villagers. I should have known from my first encounter with Emelda that Ayrton Bustard was unlikely to be the Grand Old Duke of York, or even the Duke of Plaza-Toro.

31

But what I hadn't expected was Toad. It was not just that he looked like one, with slender bandy legs, paraboloid eyes and a tongue that flicked at the air when he was lost in thought – which wasn't very often. He also shared Toad's natural habitat. Lord Bustard was an amphibian. His element was water. He knew everything there was to be known about creatures who live in water, on it, or by it. He was a world expert on the dragonfly. He was enamoured of water-voles. He enthused about ducks. He even had things to say about plankton. And he fished. Bustard had cast for sea-trout in the lochs of Skye, hooked salmon in the Haffjardara River in Iceland, rainbow trout in Patagonia, marlin off Antigua, steelheads in British Columbia.

The conversation before lunch and long after lunch became a fisherman's *Odyssey* as the years rolled back in a celebration of white water and epic encounters of *Moby Dick* proportions. I began to see how Emelda would have found plenty of time to indulge in her youthful fling.

'Did you never accompany your husband?' Tom enquired, a little battered.

'Only once,' Emelda said firmly. 'I fell in the lake. That's why Ayrton married me. He recognised a kindred spirit.'

Bustard also assumed that Tom, who'd borne the brunt of his fishing tales for so many hours, must share his lordship's passion for rod and line; indeed he assumed that Tom could have had no other possible reason for purchasing Otters Mill: what mattered were the fishing rights that went with it and the river-life that swarmed around it.

'Paradise, that place,' he said. 'I'll come and pass an agreeable afternoon with you, young man. I assume you've unpacked your fishing gear by now.'

Tom looked cornered. He wouldn't know a water-vole from a crocodile, and whenever he'd been fishing it had certainly never been for trout. But I could see it pleased him to be called 'young man'.

Eventually I sacrificed Tom to his watery world and accompanied Emelda into the kitchen where she began to pluck a brace of pheasants as though the Furies possessed her.

'You managed to get them down from the roof, then,' I said, smiling.

Emelda gave one of her rumbling laughs.

'You'll stay for supper, of course, my dear. Nothing special. My son shot these. He's away getting divorced at the moment. I could have told him she was a lesbian the moment I first set eyes on her, though I must admit I never expected a transvestite. Went off with the rural dean's wife. Wonderful scandal: I did enjoy it. No brains, my son. Just like his father. God, he was handsome, though – like so many Corsican fishermen. All hair and cock. Strange how I went from one fisherman to another, isn't it? I wonder why. Never thought about it before.'

The pheasants were by now naked. Lady Bustard was humming to herself contentedly.

'I'm the cook,' she went on. 'No servants. Did once when we had the big house. Had to sell it to pay death duties. Ayrton spent the rest on his fishing trips, and financing all those expeditions pursuing dragonflies; as if we hadn't got enough here. I told you he was mad. The most boring man I ever met, and I'm devoted to him. Your Tom must be a saint to listen to all that fish-talk hour after hour. Though he wasn't always a saint, was he, come to think of it? Before your time, of course.'

This gave me a chance to ask about the wife of Tom's whom Emelda had known. 'Which one was she?' I asked.

Emelda severed the neck of one of the pheasants with a cleaver. Then she looked thoughtful for a moment, holding the blooded implement aloft over the other pheasant.

'Let me see. Harriet, I rather think her name was. Would that be right? Did Tom marry a Harriet? Perhaps he wouldn't remember. Ghastly woman, anyway. Big bum – not as big as mine, but then she was a lot younger. Some sort of relation of the Normingtons, and she came down for the weekend. They brought her over. Suppose Tom must have found her good in bed, or something. Not that there was much sign of it. Spent most of her time spitting about Tom and getting plastered, if I remember. Didn't like her at all. Ayrton just went fishing. The trouble was, the silly bitch decided to go swimming naked in the river and got caught up in his line. Ayrton was in an awful state. I told him I bet he'd never landed a bigger flounder than that, but he didn't think that was at all funny. She'd ruined his rod.' Emelda looked up at me and grinned. 'Mind you, his rod never was up to much. That's what took me to Corsica.'

She gave a throaty chuckle and decapitated the second pheasant.

'Saw you on the box a couple of weeks ago, didn't I? Thought you drew quite beautifully. Don't suppose the Papal Nuncio agreed. No sense of humour, Roman Catholics. Everybody knows what monks get up to. I used to get flashed at all the time in Corsica. Here too sometimes. When I told Ayrton he said they were probably just having a little wee-wee. Isn't he sweet?'

Emelda paused to whack the two pheasants into a blackened casserole.

'Now – d'you feel like doing the beans? For God's sake let's have a drink. And take one to Tom as an act of mercy. Ayrton doesn't drink – thankfully – or his tongue would be even looser. I bet he's on to dabchicks by now. Poor Tom. Is *he* good in bed?'

I said he was, and felt rather coy.

'Thought so.'

I didn't like to ask why she thought so.

To my astonishment Tom said he liked Ayrton a great deal. I could only put this down to his extraordinarily good mood. And by the time we'd got through the second bottle of Côtes du Rhône I shared it.

We finally left about eleven. There was sharp moonlight over the village, and frost in the air. Above the thatched roofs I could make out the silhouettes of pheasants against the night sky. There was the distant hooting of an owl.

'Well, how was it?' I asked.

I could hear Tom take a deep breath.

'I can tell you, sweetheart – anything I don't know about the courtship ritual of the Four-Spotted Libellula isn't worth knowing.'

I laughed and put both my arms round him.

'Do you know we can have river-trout any day we want?' Tom was saying. He slid a hand on to my left breast. 'All that and you too, my little Venus. I'm a lucky man.'

'And drunk with it.'

'Yup!'

And as if to prove it, Tom broke into a loud rendering of *There's an Old Mill by the Stream*. By the time he reached the Nellie Dean bit we were at our front door. I freed Tom's hand from my breast and searched in his pocket for the key.

The house felt damp. We really had to do something about the central heating.

Two letters lay on the mat. One was for me from London, formal-looking. The other was an airmail letter for Tom with the address handwritten and a Los Angeles postmark.

'Can't be bothered to read that tonight,' said Tom wearily. 'It's from Scott. He said he might be coming over.'

Scott was a film-agent friend whom Tom had seen a lot when he worked out in California ten years ago or so – between wives, I seemed to remember. My own letter didn't look so interesting, and I left it with Tom's on the shelf.

We slept late. We even slept through the dawn chorus of Mr Teape's cockerels.

It wasn't until after breakfast that I remembered the letters. Tom took his to the loo. I opened mine. It was from a highly classy publisher – the name jumped out at me – and was signed by someone who described himself as 'Editorial Director'. They were launching a new series of children's classics, he said. Might I be interested in illustrating one of them? He suggested *Gulliver's Travels*. Alternatively, he said, how about Roald Dahl, or Hilaire Belloc's *Bad Rhymes for Worse Children*? He hoped I could be persuaded. 'I greatly look forward to hearing from you. Yours very sincerely, Howard Minton.' He'd scrawled a note after that in a rather flamboyant hand – 'Enjoyed *Prawnography* – and your TV *tour de force*. I see from your address that my weekend place is no distance from you. Perhaps we could meet. How about dinner?'

Ah ha! Where had I heard that before? A convenient little cottage. And a handwritten note so that the secretary shouldn't see.

I heard the loo flush. When Tom came into the kitchen he was unusually quiet.

'Hangover, Tom?' I asked cheerfully.

He just handed me the letter.

'I'm being sued. Palimony. Can you believe it? The bloody bitch.'

3

SUNDAY morning in Sarum Magna was no place for a man of Tom's temperament – least of all on this particular Sunday. Journalists are not the most patient of men at the best of times, nor is Tom Brand the most patient of journalists. And this was certainly not the best of times.

He raged.

In Los Angeles it was still one o'clock in the morning. He couldn't decently phone Scott for another seven hours. The prospect of Tom rampaging round the house for a further seven hours almost drove me to take a long country walk.

It was hard to get a grasp on what exactly had happened. I felt bewildered and anxious. I read Scott's letter a second time in case I'd missed anything. It was brief. He'd tried to phone, he said. But until two days ago we'd had no phone. So he was writing hastily to both addresses – Tom's London flat (now sold), and here. The letter simply explained how he'd heard on the grapevine that Samantha (who the hell was she? I asked myself)

38

was about to bring a court action in California claiming half the American royalties for *Prawnography* on the grounds that most of the recipes in the book were hers. Scott stressed that Californian courts were notoriously sympathetic to palimony claims, and that Tom had better get off his arse if he was to avoid being taken to the cleaners. 'Phone immediately,' the letter continued. 'We both know the truth about Samantha. What you've got to do is to make sure the court knows it too. This may not be so easy, but *courage, mon brave.* Yours Scott.'

The last thing I needed was to hear any of this. I looked away out of the window. It was a sharp, bright morning. The river was hurtling past the mill, dragging small trees and rafts of sedge over the submerged sluices to join the Sargasso Sea of flotsam that was spinning downstream in a froth of brown water. Our garden was by now lifted out of the current, laid out exhausted and battered-looking to dry in the sun. A garden? Could anything possibly ever grow there?

It looked like the Thames at low-tide. We'd acquired twenty acres of mud. Suddenly an electric-blue flash shot between the willows, catching a blade of sunlight. It was a kingfisher. As I strained to follow it a pair of swans planed down on to the calmer shallows of the mill-pool.

Kingfishers. Swans. They were magic moments, and at any other time I would have celebrated being here, in a new home, watching the taming of the waters and the birth of spring. I might have decided to do some sketching, assembled my painting things, got into the stride of my new life. This morning could have been the beginning.

Instead, there was this letter.

'What does it mean, Tom? What is it?' I could hear a resigned note in my voice. I handed back the letter. 'Scott talks about "the truth". What *is* the truth? And what are the lies? Tell me both.'

Tom stopped pacing the kitchen and perched himself on the edge of the table, gazing defensively at me. He pursed his lips, then ran his fingers through his mop of greying hair. He glanced at his watch.

'Christ. Seven hours!' He seemed too distracted to be aware of me. 'I can't ring him before eight in the morning his time, can I? Scott's a night bird. And today's Sunday.'

I waited patiently, leaning against the window.

'Well, she's a lying bitch,' Tom went on fiercely. 'It's complete shit.' The venom in his voice had a touch of panic. 'The idea that she taught me anything except how to put up with her fantasies. It's ridiculous. Lunatic . . . OK, I'll tell you.'

He took a while getting started. I went on waiting, feeling numb.

'I worked in California for a year, as you know,' he blurted out. 'Twelve, fourteen years ago; after I'd walked out on Harriet. That was when I met Scott. I stayed with him for a while. A great friend. We were both fancy-free. Bachelors burning up the town, our marriages behind us. Scott gave me a lot of leads on the Hollywood scene. Stories, scandals, exclusives. Everything. The paper offered me a regular column on the strength of it – *The*

Brand Report. I could do anything, go anywhere I wanted. The column was a terrific success for a while. As an agent, Scott knew everyone. I did him favours; he did favours for me.'

'And one of Scott's favours was Samantha, I suppose,' I said.

Tom glanced up at me warily. I could see him getting ready to duck the flak.

'Well, yes, in a way; although it was more the other way round, really.' A likely tale! I thought. 'You see, everyone in LA knew Samantha's face at that time. Much of the rest of her, too.' I could tell from his laugh that he wished he hadn't said that. 'She was a top model. Or had been. Now she was trying to break into films; every model's dream in California. She'd fucked around quite a bit, and that didn't work. So she decided to rely on her talent and persuaded Scott to take her on – which was fatal because Samantha had a great body and absolutely no talent at all. She did a couple of James Bond movies, which revealed both. Chewed up by piranhas in one film, lost in outer space in the other. And that was about it. There are lots of beautiful bodies in Hollywood. They're not rare items, and there's always another one on the conveyor-belt, younger and less trouble than the last. Well, one day Scott rang me and said "For God's sake, Tom, please do something for that girl. I can't!"'

Tom gave me that plaintive look of his. It means 'What else could I do?' I had to admire the performance; the bastard.

'Well, I suppose I did do something for her. We lived together for six months.'

41

'Go on,' I said. There seemed to be an awful lot of convenient gaps in this story. I decided to come to the point. 'Were you in love with her?'

'God, no!' He sounded horrified at the thought.

I decided this probably wasn't true, and I think I was right, because he said, 'It was just that I was alone, and she was lovely.' That gave it away. So, there was my sexy, romantic Tom. I could so easily imagine the scene. Three disastrous marriages one after the other: the first a desert, the second a correction centre, the third a minefield. So there he was, forty-plus, free at last and thousands of miles away from all those disasters. Huge expense account. Glamorous lifestyle. And along comes this gorgeous nymph, this well-fucked damsel in distress: 'Oh handsome Englishman (bat, bat, wiggle, wiggle), you're so masterful. Help me. I'm such a mess.' Tom, you ass, you would fall for that, wouldn't you?

I found myself smiling. Suddenly I felt very possessive. I'd got him now, and there'd better not be any more long-legged damsels in distress, or they would indeed be in distress, and so would Tom for that matter. I'd cut it off.

'What did she look like?' I asked.

I hadn't intended to say that. It just came out. It irritates me, but I can't help seeing myself mirrored in Tom's women. It isn't that I want to scratch their eyes out. Well, not exactly. I just want to dismiss them from my mind. I suppose I want to feel jealous, and then realise I don't need to.

Tom obviously didn't want to tell me what Samantha looked like. Or perhaps he did, but thought I mightn't like it. He gave a cough and poured himself another cup of coffee. Then he gave it to me in shorthand.

'Tall. Dark-haired. Legs. Great body (he meant breasts). Shrill voice – I hated that. A mind that floated in la-la-land – she'd once read *Gone with the Wind.*'

'And you were her Clark Gable?' I asked.

'She might have loved me if I had been.'

'But she didn't?'

'No, certainly not.'

'So, what happened?'

'Nothing happened. My contract ended. And I came home. Bye-bye Samantha.'

'No tears?'

'Oh, for about five minutes. Within a month she went off with a poet, and married him. Scott told me.'

I was still waiting for the point.

'And . . .? How does cooking come into all this?' I asked. 'You're not going to tell me she spent six months in your delicious company teaching you to cook. That doesn't sound like you at all.'

Tom produced a rather thin laugh. 'No, it doesn't. And we didn't. It's just another of the woman's fantasies.'

'So, how does she think she's going to get away with it, then? And how the hell can Scott believe she might?'

The exasperation must have shown in my face. Tom came and put his hands on my shoulders.

'Jan, we're talking about California. There's no such thing as normality in California. The most normal thing is to be a screwball. And that was Samantha. When the movies died on her, she seized on food. She ate – anything she could lay her teeth on. Pizzas. Double-Macs.

43

Fried chicken. You name it. But above all it was seafood. Lobsters. Crayfish. Blue-shelled crabs. Shark-fins. Molluscs by the mountain. She'd have eaten jelly-fish if they didn't sting. I wish she had.'

Now I began to understand.

'And she taught you?'

'Taught me? You must be joking! She never cooked a thing. *I* did that. She just ate like a pig, until after a few months she began to look like one. Now, this was a real crisis. The body beautiful was far too important, and people were beginning to turn their heads in the street for the wrong reason. So – instant conversion. From being a born-again fattie, Samantha became a born-again macrobiotic fundamentalist. It was like discovering God. By the time I left, the apartment had beansprouts and lemon-grass growing out of the taps. It was like living in a test-tube. I didn't mind fucking like a rabbit, but I didn't see why I should have to eat like one.'

'I'm glad you haven't changed,' I said, and ran my hand through his hair.

Tom laughed.

'Jan, I need a drink.'

He took a bottle of white wine from the fridge and began to uncork it while grasping the neck as though it was Samantha's.

Then he told me the rest. After Tom had departed and she'd married her poet she set herself up as a macro-biotics 'expert'. She even managed to get herself a cookery column in some downtown rag. The recipes were crazy enough for LA to take them seriously. So did a publisher.

44

'The book-jacket showed more of Samantha's boobs than her beansprouts. Even so, it bombed – presumably because when you actually followed the recipes the results would have made a hamster go on hunger-strike.'

'Did the poet die of starvation?' I enquired.

'If he had any sense he sneaked out to get hamburgers.'

So the little lady was broke; the poet likewise. Enter *Prawnography*. A massive bestseller. A tip-off revealed to Samantha who the author really was. That was enough. Forget the macrobiotics. Samantha was now a reborn-again sea-queen. This was the book she would have written herself had she not been robbed, she convinced herself. The rest was easy. There are plenty of friendly lawyers in LA, and Samantha could still remember how to be friendly in return. The result?

A case well and truly stitched up. Slap in a writ. Poor abandoned lady, her career and the best years of her life squandered on a thief who stole away in the night, taking with him all the fruits of her genius, as well as her virtue.

'See?' he said, hunching his shoulders with a grimace.

We sipped our wine and gazed out of the window, saying nothing. This was our place. Suddenly I felt anxious lest we lose it.

'It's all right, Tom,' I said after a while. 'We'll get through this.'

I hoped I believed it. He looked at me almost sadly.

'I'm sorry, Jan,' he said. 'Somehow it feels worse hurting you with things that happened years ago than with things happening now – because I can't do anything about them.' He put his arms round me. 'You know, coming here I so much wanted to dump the past. Slough it off. But it hangs around . . . Fuck it!'

I had to laugh. I knew that if Tom couldn't make me laugh when I felt like anything but laughter, I wouldn't be here.

It was still five hours before Tom could ring Scott. And five hours on a Sunday in Sarum Magna is an awful long time.

It *was* an awful long time. But Tom surprised me. He was calm.

'I think I'll spend some of the five hours getting stuck into Byron,' he announced. And he stretched himself out on the sofa with Leslie Marchand's three-volume biography. I imagined he was trying to impress me – perhaps trying to impress himself. 'Jesus, imagine if there'd been palimony laws in Byron's day. The poor bastard wouldn't have been able to reach the front door for writs.'

I went into the kitchen to put a couple of lamb chops under the grill, doubting that I'd find an appetite to eat anything. I heard Tom bellow out.

'Christ, Jan, listen to this. The first Lord Byron followed Charles II into exile, the stalwart fellow. And his reward? According to Samuel Pepys, his wife Eleanor became the king's seventeenth mistress. Seventeenth! Who d'you suppose did the counting? Perhaps they all stood in line and had numbers pinned on them.' Tom stood up and began to mime the scene. '"Nell Gwynne, you're Number Two – tomorrow, nine o'clock sharp. And bring the oranges. Lady Byron, you're Number

Seventeen – not till Monday week. The king needs the weekend off." Are you surprised he needed a weekend to recover, having just had it off with sixteen different women? Oh, to be a king! Well, this could be fun, Jan – the book, I mean. Better than working for the tabloids. Come to think of it, the subject matter's much the same, really. Royal fucks! The only difference is that in those days a king was expected to have as many women as he wanted, and today they're expected not to.'

I loved Tom. Reluctantly sometimes, but I did. He could change so rapidly from rage to laughter. He could be bullish and vulnerable, exasperating and touching, sexy and outrageous, depressed and the next minute on a high. I'd never met anyone so delightfully miscast as Tom – he should have been all kinds of things he never was: writer, politician, teacher, layabout. Yet he'd have done all those things badly; they would have reduced him. Tom had to be the unpredictable creature he was. His own man. *My* man, in a way that Harry never was. Harry was *every* woman's man. Tom, who'd been every woman's man for most of his life as far as I could see, could still be mine, totally mine. I felt sure of that. Mind you, if some busty tart minced past our door right now I knew precisely where Tom's eyes and thoughts would be, and if he ever acted on those thoughts I'd die. Perhaps that whiff of danger was what fuelled my desire for him. I hoped it was the same for him: I noticed how frequently he'd enquire about the men in my life. How many? Who were they? Were they as good as him? Well, actually one or two of them had been: usually the real shits or meatheads I'd taken to bed because I felt like a one-night stand and a quick goodbye. I'd never wanted to say goodbye to Tom, though one day he'll die and I'll have to. Perhaps I'll just go with him. Double exit.

The Samantha business hurt me, outraged me. I wanted to get my hands on the bitch. I pecked at some lunch, then decided to phone Ruth. I looked up the code for Liechtenstein – 010 41 75: it came after Lesotho, Liberia and Libya. I was grateful that Piers' first post as ambassador hadn't been any of those, though Liechtenstein did sound more comic. Ruth was sure to be funny about Liechtenstein. There was one hour's time difference, the code book said. Ruth should have finished her siesta by now. It was a habit she swore by – 'the best time of all to make love'; by which Ruth tended to mean, 'the best time of all to make love if one's husband is away at the embassy'.

She wasn't breathless this time. She was bored. Liechtenstein was like Wall Street drafted into *The Sound of Music*, she complained. Nobody lived there, but everybody had an office there. Diplomatic dinners could have doubled up as board meetings of the Halifax Building Society. It was also very small, like living in a play-pen with no toys. She'd taken Piers' Lotus out for a spin that morning; starting at the Swiss border she had just managed to get into fifth gear when she saw the Austrian border looming ahead. All the same, the mountains were lovely, and she and Piers were going skiing next weekend. Their host was an Olympic silver-medallist she'd met. That would be fun. How was Tom?

I told her about the palimony case, and feared she might laugh. Far from it. Ruth's voice immediately took on an urgent note. 'My darling, you have to get the best lawyer in town. Does Tom have one?' I said I believed he had a solicitor in Epsom. There was a snort on the phone. 'Epsom! Oh, for God's sake, Janice. He probably plays golf and has a Labrador under his desk. You need a real lawyer. I know one.' And she named someone called Kyra Vansittart. 'She's hot. Believe me, as a Jewess I can recognise a good Jewish lawyer. Half-Russian, married to something disgusting like South African mines. You'd like her. Tom'll fancy her, but don't worry about that: she's into younger men. Get him to phone her tomorrow. Here's the number.'

It was Ruth at her most businesslike. I took down the phone number and promised to let her know how Tom got on with the Vansittart lady. 'The point is,' Ruth added as I was about to replace the receiver, 'Kyra used to practise in LA, so she knows all the legal sharks there. She'll find you one with teeth. Real teeth. Tom's going to need them.'

After I'd rung off I stood there feeling angry with Ruth for being so efficient. I wished now that she *had* found it funny, and had laughed it off. Then I could have done the same. But she'd made it sound so grave, as though we really were in serious trouble. I tried to take stock of the situation. What did we stand to lose? Well, half the American royalties; that was half the money we were intending to invest and live on. Plus lawyers' fees. Jesus, in California they'd be astronomical. Perhaps the American publishers might be required by law to withdraw the book. So, no second, third, fourth editions. No follow-up. Tom and I had already talked jokingly about that: we even had a bet as to who could come up with a title even worse than *Prawnography*.

All that would have to go. This place could go. Our new life.

I did what I invariably do when upset – go for an aimless wander. To keep moving chloroforms the mind. I didn't know the walks round here yet, so I just took myself up the track and along the village street. It was 3.30 in the afternoon: still an hour and a half before Tom would be speaking to Scott in LA.

Suddenly a tiny front-garden caught my eye: a cluster of pale-blue crocuses had thrust themselves between stone pavings and opened in the sun. It was the first glimpse of spring, and they lifted my spirits. When I'm low it's the little things that count; sod the ending of the Cold War.

I crossed the road to look at the crocuses more closely. As I did so there was a cry and a screech of brakes. For a split-second I waited to be hit by a car. I froze, and closed my eyes.

Nothing happened. I opened them again, wondering if I was already dead and looking down from the after-life.

A rotund figure in a bright-yellow anorak was performing a one-legged dance in the road about four feet from where I stood. The other leg was still half-astride her bicycle, from the handlebars on which dangled two rabbits and a long string of garlic.

'I don't know who's more dangerous, you or me,' exclaimed Emelda Bustard, retrieving her right leg and pushing the bicycle upright. 'I can see you were never taught to look left and right, any more than I was ever taught how to ride this thing.'

I apologised profusely, explained about the crocuses, and then walked with Emelda towards her gate while she pushed her bicycle. 'I'm safer like this,' she said. The rabbits were leaving spots of blood along the road in our wake. Emelda explained how she'd lost her driving licence last autumn after injuring an American tourist in the Salisbury Cathedral close. She'd pleaded with the magistrate that she'd been late for a fund-raising meeting in aid of the cathedral spire. The magistrate expressed the view that, with respect to Lady Bustard's charitable works, the spire was in greater danger of falling down through such human recklessness than through natural causes. Besides, driving was not permitted in the close, least of all on the grass. Fortunately the tourist, an admirer of English Gothic architecture, had agreed not to sue.

So, now she bicycled.

'God help any tourist in my path.'

Emelda was chuckling.

'You know, we did so enjoy your company yesterday,' she went on. 'Ayrton talks of nothing else but going fishing with your husband. I describe Tom as your "husband" because he doesn't understand about people not being married; but then he's never really understood about being married either, the dear man.'

Two puddles of blood were forming on either side of her bicycle as we stood by the gate leading to the Bustards' house.

'And how are you on your first Sunday in Sarum?' she said in a kindly voice. 'I'm afraid I've interrupted your afternoon walk.'

I explained I was only walking because I was upset. Emelda looked concerned.

'Oh, my dear, why?'

I told her. I said there'd been this letter when we returned home last night. How Tom was waiting to phone California right now. How we needed the very best lawyer. How unjust it was, all because Tom had known this woman years and years ago, and now she was broke – and a fruitcake as well. What was the matter with the law in America that this kind of thing could be taken seriously? Palimony was like blackmail: they hoped you'd settle privately rather than risk the consequences.

'Even the word's a fake – palimony!' I blurted out angrily, and burst into tears.

Emelda leaned over and placed an arm round my shoulders. I couldn't stop crying. It went on and on.

'Oh, my dear child,' she was saying comfortingly. 'It does sound too ridiculous. Come and have some tea.' Then she gazed at me with a puzzled expression. 'But you must tell me, my dear. Palimony. Isn't that something you feed a dog on?'

I knew then that whenever I felt low I would have to go and see Emelda. I refused the tea: I could hardly wait to tell Tom that palimony was really a brand of dog-food and therefore we had nothing to worry about since we had no dog.

'Oh, is that really so, my dear?' said Emelda when I gently corrected her, wiping my tears away and trying not to laugh. 'What is it to do with, then?'

'It's money demanded by someone you used to live with,' I explained.

'Well, I never knew that. I'm sure it never existed in my day,' Emelda pronounced very firmly. 'If it had I imagine I should have had to pay half of Corsica.' She gazed at me impishly, and suddenly I could see exactly how she would have looked thirty years before. 'I exaggerate, of course. But I did try out quite a few men before settling for Aristide. It was a responsibility, I can tell you, selecting a man capable of ensuring the continuity of an ancient line going back to the Norman Conquest. It needed to be someone who could put some spunk back into the Bustards. And my God, he did: it was like being pursued by a petrol-pump. But the thought of having to pay for it years afterwards, as if it was on the never-never. Ludicrous, my dear, don't you agree?'

I was growing accustomed to Emelda's spirals of fantasy. And I was learning how to pretend to take them seriously, which was what she wanted.

'I think you'd have had to take something away from Aristide for him to have a claim,' I said, keeping a straight face.

'But I did, my dear. I took his son. And that's a lot more valuable than a handful of recipes, don't you agree?'

This time I did agree. And looking at my watch, I realised I had to leave. In half an hour Tom would be making his phone call. I thanked Emelda warmly for having cheered me up, and said goodbye. She mounted her bicycle with a wave – which was unwise – and headed erratically towards the Bustards' house, rabbits and garlic swinging like pendulums from the handlebars. Over her shoulder she called out: 'I'll call and see you next week. I promise not to bring any dog-food.'

Her laughter followed her down the drive.

I walked home. It was odd to think of 'home' as being here, to think of this as 'our village'. In London I was used to being anonymous in a place that was entirely familiar. Here I was scarcely familiar with the place at all, yet I wasn't anonymous in the least: everyone I passed on that late Sunday afternoon nodded, smiled sometimes, and presumably knew who I was. This gave me a rather uncomfortable sensation of belonging here; it was like becoming a member of a secret society whose rules no one had troubled to explain.

A skein of mist was drawn across the water-meadows. The light was a chill blue-grey under the bare poplars, the upper branches of which were trapping the last of the winter sunlight. Then I caught sight of a figure walking briskly across the nearby field, making for a cottage by the river. She was partly obscured by the mist, but I could make out a dark-haired woman dressed in what appeared to be gypsy costume, a violent pink shawl round her shoulders and a wicker basket on her arm. She took long, swinging strides, and to my surprise I noticed that she was barefoot.

'That's her,' came a voice from behind me. 'The one I was telling you about. Lives with the old artist bloke.

She's always like that, summer or winter. Never wears shoes. Often not much else either.'

I turned round to see the large, grinning figure of Mr Gant. I hardly recognised him. There were no tweeds or flat cap; he was dressed in shabby corduroys and a woollen shirt that might once have sported a pattern. A pitchfork rested against his left shoulder, and his sleeves were rolled up to reveal forearms the size of York hams, resting massively on the farm gate.

'Good evening, Mr Gant,' I said.

'Evening to you.'

He was still grinning, his eyes steadily following the gypsy-looking woman. I got the feeling he probably watched her quite a lot. From the farmhouse behind him the well-rounded form of Mrs Gant appeared briefly, carrying washing.

'Out strolling then, are you?' he said, at last directing his gaze at me. I assumed the dark-haired woman had gone.

I nodded. Gant lifted up a huge forearm and began to scratch his face in a serious manner. I noticed both arms were heavily tattooed – a merchant navy anchor on one forearm, a naked lady of unlikely proportions on the other. It occurred to me that maybe once, when he'd been a young merchant seaman, she'd been the slim little nymph of Gant's dreams. Only now, after so many muscular years on the farm, she'd grown even larger on his forearm than the real Mrs Gant in the flesh. Unless of course she *was* Mrs Gant, who had once been the slim little nymph of his dreams. A curious double metamorphosis.

He stopped scratching his face and folded his arms, covering the generous lady with the merchant navy anchor.

'I dunno,' he went on, giving me a serious look. 'All you young fillies cantering round the place. Used to be just farming land round here. Becoming a beauty farm, if you ask me.'

'Does that worry you, Mr Gant?' I asked.

He looked at me in surprise.

'Worry me? Course not. I love it. Wakes the place up. Makes me feel young again. Or makes me wish I was young.' He leaned forward over the gate and tapped my shoulder: it was like being struck by a mallet. 'You are – if I may say so – a most lovely woman, Mrs Brand. I didn't feel I could say it in front of your husband the other evening, but you are. Ray of sunlight. The wife likes your book, by the way. Very interesting we find it. Very instructive.'

And he awarded me a wink that would have been visible from Salisbury on a clear day.

What could I say? Did the entire village possess copies of *Prawnography*? Commander Normington? Mrs Teape? What was that about moving to the country to get away from it all? Oh, for the anonymity of London.

Gant gave me another hammer-blow on the shoulder.

'Now, *there's* someone who could have done with your book when she was younger.'

And he pointed an enormous finger in the direction of our mill, where a tall woman in ashen-coloured clothes was making her way at a drifting pace along the right-of-way that passed our door and over the footbridge into the woods.

'That's Naomi – Mooncalf,' said Gant. 'Still not met her yet? Sad lady. Beautiful once, she was. Believe me. Like a ghost now. A pity.'

There was a final hammer-blow on my shoulder, and suddenly Gant grasped his pitchfork and was off across the yard.

'Got to have my tea . . . And later a little dish out of your book, maybe.'

I could hear him chuckling as he strode away.

It was ten to five. I hurried down the track towards the mill. I could just make out the figure of Mooncalf moving slowly through the trees across the river. I found myself wondering where she'd been, and why. And would I really say nothing to her if I met her, as Mrs Teape had advised? Perhaps one day I might pluck up courage and call on her. 'Beautiful once . . . Like a ghost now,' Gant had said. From here she even looked like one, as if she were projected on to the trees through which she passed.

Such a peculiar afternoon. And whatever would the evening be like? The telephone call – Los Angeles talking to Sarum Magna: it sounded the most unlikely of dialogues. The lights were already on in the house. It felt warm. The sound of water gushing beyond the mill was welcoming. I was beginning to feel at last that this was home. And Tom was at home: that was what made it so. Suddenly this gave me a sensation I'd all but forgotten – of realising that the price of loving someone is the dread of it going wrong. In the years when I'd been a free woman I'd felt strong: now I felt small and fragile. Samantha's intrusion was like a wound – and for Christ's sake she wasn't even one of his wives! At that moment I wondered if perhaps I'd committed myself too much. Shouldn't I have been content to enjoy Tom for what he was, left him to deal with his past and preserved my own life intact?

It made me long for the reckless days when I'd wanted nothing more than to follow my star and keep body and soul apart.

4

TOM was looking personally insulted.

'After all that, I get his answer-phone!'

He gave out a few incoherent sounds and glanced at his watch. It was a quarter past five.

'So, all we can do is wait,' he said in a resigned voice. 'Bloody agents: he's probably earning his ten per cent marlin fishing with Robert Redford, and won't be back for a week.' There were further mutterings. 'Well, at least he's got our phone number now.'

Suddenly Tom brightened.

'And he'll be paying for the call! Serve him right for going marlin fishing.'

'Scott's probably still in bed asleep, Tom,' I said. Then, to get a rise out of him I added, 'with Samantha, perhaps.'

He looked at me sharply, but had the grace to smile.

Then the phone went.

Tom passed me the receiver wearily.

'It's Teapot,' he whispered.

Mrs Teape took a great deal of time asking if tomorrow would be all right for her to start cleaning. And would I like some eggs? Had I heard that Commander Normington's dog got drowned? 'Mind you,' she went on without a pause, 'that dog was always a menace. Chasing cattle. Chasing our hens. Quite untrained. I used to say to the commander, "you should get it trained." It was Mrs Normington to blame really: wouldn't curb its animal instincts, she always insisted. "Mrs Normington," I used to say to her, "if my husband allowed our hens their animal instincts they'd be laying eggs all round the village." Discipline, that's what animals need. Human beings too, if you ask my opinion. Now, that foreign girl – lives with the painter, you know. Heaven knows where she was brought up – in the jungle most likely, with the monkeys. You should see her in the summer, Mrs Brand. At least I hope you won't, for your sake. And I'm sure Mr Brand wouldn't like it. Flaunts herself, that's what she does. And there's a lot of her to flaunt. Quite disgusting, I say. No shame. I tell Mr Teape not to look when he goes to deliver the eggs. Got to keep an eye on these men, haven't you? Not that your husband would ever stray, Mrs Brand. Such a lovely man: I can always tell who are the faithful ones. Mind you, he's lucky to have a wife like you, Mrs Brand. And I expect you'll be having children soon; you look the type, and you don't want to leave it too late, do you? I couldn't have any myself. My tubes, you know. Nowadays of course they'd have done something about it. Cleared them out. Makes it sound like Dyno-Rod. Wonderful what doctors can do these days, don't you think? Mind you, my niece . . .'

I jumped in.

'Mrs Teape, we're expecting a rather important phone call.'

'Oh, then I won't keep you. I'll see you tomorrow. It'll be my pleasure, Mrs Brand. And I'll bring the eggs. Lovely brown ones, they are. Morans. Mr Teape breeds them. Says no others taste quite as good. Mind you, some say Light Sussex are better, but my husband won't have any of that. He used to have Rhode Island Reds once, but the fox got them. A menace, they are. You've got to set the wire really deep. Costs so much, too. I can remember the time when you could pick up a roll of wire-netting for . . .'

'Thank you, Mrs Teape,' I managed to say. 'Look forward to seeing you tomorrow.'

Tom was looking at me askance as I put down the receiver.

'Jesus!'

Then the phone went again.

Tom took the early train to London. He was damned, he said, if he was going to drive ninety miles in order to get clamped; so he took the car into Salisbury, preparing to jostle with the morning commuters glued to their *Financial Times*. 'I'll pore over a copy of *Penthouse* and watch their eyes flicker.' The appointment with Kyra Vansittart was at eleven. 'Ruth says she likes younger men,' I warned him as he left, 'so don't sacrifice yourself too much by taking her out to lunch.' 'Oh, I'll convert her,' he said casually, starting up the engine. 'It's experience and maturity that win through, I find. Goodbye, darling.'

'Goodbye, *darling*,' I said, giving him a sharp dig with my elbow.

He laughed.

So did I. Then suddenly I thought – Why am I laughing? I don't feel like laughing at all. I feel irritated and upset. The women in Tom's life seemed to be breeding like maggots. Now here was another one – Kyra Vansittart. And in a few hours time she'd be sitting across the lunch table in her glamorous designer clothes listening to the man in my life telling her all about the other women in *his* life, while I was parked in the country listening to Mrs Teape talking about fowl-pest. I wasn't so much jealous as left out. No one from *my* past was screwing up our life: they'd all discreetly gone away. And why did his bloody solicitor have to be female? Weren't solicitors supposed to be pin-striped and male? It was all Ruth's fault: a conspiracy of tarts. I found myself playing around with the woman's name – Kyra Vansi-Tart, Kyra Fancy-Tart – and decided to dislike her intensely. I decided to dislike all Tom's women intensely. This comforted me a little. But I wasn't taking this at all well, and there was no one to dump my frustration on except Emelda, who thought palimony was a brand of dog-food.

I might have felt less upset if it wasn't so one-sided. From quite early on in our love life I'd wanted to know every detail of every woman Tom had married, fancied, fucked or been pursued by. If he'd written a book about each of them I'd have pored over every page and still insisted he tell me what was hidden in the margins. But not only did Tom have no interest in telling me; he showed even less interest in the men who'd flown in and out of my life. He'd say 'All right! I suppose you'd better tell me!' and then, just as I was preparing to lay my past naked before him, he'd get distracted by the football results or remember something funny he'd forgotten to tell me yesterday. Even now, after we'd been living together for the best part of a year, he still didn't know that I'd once screwed every man in the street to get my revenge on Harry. I had a past, a real past, and Tom didn't even bother to ask about it. And here was I getting upset about Kyra Fancy-Tart whom Tom hadn't even met.

It was seven-thirty, and we'd been up even before Mr Teape's cockerels. Mrs Teape wasn't due for another hour. I hadn't imagined she'd be coming every morning, but clearly *she* had, and I wasn't sure what to do about it. A cottage with just two people hardly created the kind of mess that warranted a daily cleaner, though I noticed how Tom had already taken to leaving dishes, wine glasses, ashtrays and coffee cups lying around in abandon, and if I made a move to put something away he'd wave a hand dismissively with, 'Teapot'll do it, Jan. Give her something to fill her time.' In fact filling time never appeared to be a problem for Mrs Teape. Yesterday she'd laboured for an hour and a half cleaning and polishing our kettle. At five pounds an hour, for the price of two sessions I could have bought a new kettle.

'It'll be so lovely for you when the mill-house is fixed, Mrs Brand,' she'd announced.

Oh God, I realised, that meant she'd expect to be here all day, not just the mornings.

63

'It'll suit Mr Brand to a tee. Such a lovely man, your husband. I bet the women were all after him before you got him.'

'Yes, Mrs Teape. They were.'

They were.

'But I can see he loves you. He'd never look at anyone else now.'

He would.

'All those years, he was really just waiting for the right woman to come along, wasn't he?'

He wasn't.

'And now I expect you'll start having lots of children, won't you?'

We won't.

I began painting, not out of any powerful sense of vocation, but in order to avoid Mrs Teape – or try to. It wasn't so easy.

'I think that's really lovely, what you're doing, Mrs Brand. You don't mind my looking, do you? Now, that must be Mr Gant's house: I'd know it anywhere from the chimneys. He had such a bad fire there, you know, only last year. Terrible! What a mess it made. Mind you, not quite as bad as the fire Commander Normington had a few years before that.'

I decided that when the weather turned warmer I'd have to paint out of doors.

Meanwhile, right now I had an hour of peace – and a number of thoughts to collect. Scott's phone call had clarified what his letter had said, and made matters seem more urgent. It appeared that Samantha had already acquired a shit-hot attorney who specialised in palimony cases. What was more, the bitch was already blathering to the press and anyone else who'd listen. The *Los Angeles Echo* had run a gossip piece about her last Friday. Nothing sensational, Scott said, but certainly enough to have alerted the rest of the gutter press. Ms Parsons – as she called herself now (though Mr Parsons had apparently done a bunk some years ago) – was described as 'beautiful and talented', having 'made a name for herself as a model, then as an actress, and now as one of America's premier experts on seafood cookery'. The piece went on to refer to 'a tasteless little volume now enjoying some notoriety nationwide, due to recipes created (so Ms Parsons claims) by herself, containing illustrations more appropriate to the decor of a house of pleasure than a cook-book'. What pompous language American provincial reporters use, I thought. The article concluded by identifying the two authors of this 'borrowed' work as the English journalist Thomas Brand, a former live-in lover of Ms Parsons, and an English lady-artist (though perhaps no lady, the paper suggested) formerly married to Washington television reporter Harry Blakemore, and now believed to be on 'close intimate terms' with Mr Brand.

Was the phrase 'close intimate terms' to protect delicate American sensibilities, I wondered, or to protect themselves against the risk of libel? I felt like writing to the editor suggesting that my knee would like to be on close intimate terms with his groin.

Scott's view was that the English tabloids would certainly be on to the story very soon. Maybe Tom could use his influence in that area to put the record straight, unless his solicitor advised that any revelations on his part might prove detrimental to his case. No such legal restraints apparently applied to Ms Parsons, Scott added, Californian law being what it was, and Samantha's capacity to gush being what it was.

As to the woman's fame as a seafood cook, the picture of her in the paper – Scott suggested – raised serious doubts as to whether Ms Parsons would even be able to *see* a dish of seafood placed in front of her, let alone prepare one. 'Perhaps,' he suggested, 'lobster could be marketed as a silicone substitute.'

He promised to put the article in the post.

I had troubled dreams that night. I was in court, and Samantha's attorney looked like Frankenstein's monster. He kept wheeling Tom around the courtroom in one of those witness boxes that look like fairground bumper-cars. And the court was packed with women of every shape and size who'd all of them been Tom's wives, and who rose one after the other to shake their fists at him and demand retribution. Then all together they turned towards me and began to laugh their heads off. I woke up in a sweat of fear – and heard the birds singing. The relief was almost worth the dream.

Tom had duly telephoned Kyra Vansittart. I picked up the threads of an awkward conversation in which for a while Tom was clearly taken to be one of Ruth Conway's lovers seeking legal advice about his wife's pending divorce suit.

He turned to me quite indignantly afterwards.

'Do you know what that woman said, Jan? She said: "Please forgive the misunderstanding, Mr Brand, but you must be the first client recommended by Mrs Conway who *hasn't* been one of her lovers.'"

Tom, who had tried for fifteen years to be Ruth's lover, looked quite upset.

'Extremely good for you, Tom,' I said, 'being reminded that there are women around whom you haven't had.'

His feathers still looked ruffled. It was a good five minutes before he admitted that he rather liked the sound of Kyra Vansittart, and had arranged to see her in London on Wednesday.

'You'll love it, Tom,' I added. 'Being asked by one beautiful woman to reveal intimate details of your life with another beautiful woman, while a third sits patiently at home awaiting your return. What more could you ask?'

That cheered him up.

'The down-side', he said, 'is that I shall be paying the second beautiful woman a fortune to avoid paying an even larger fortune to the first, while the third is already costing us an arm and a leg in mortgage payments because she can't sell her bloody house.'

That was Monday. On Tuesday Tom surprised me by apparently forgetting all about palimony cases and devoting the entire day to reading his biography of Byron. I was busy sorting out my studio, and every so often a comment would float through the open door: 'Hard to imagine Byron playing cricket against Eton, isn't it? Harrow lost.' And a while later, 'Think of going up to Cambridge and promptly keeping a tame bear in a tower above your rooms.'

I don't think I was expected to comment.

And now, today, he was in London seeing Ms Vansittart, and I had this place all to myself – at least until Teapot time.

I felt the need to take stock. It was the first time I'd been entirely alone here. It was also – I suddenly realised – the first time in my whole life that I'd been free to do whatever I wanted. It was a bewildering prospect. A year ago I'd been slicing prosciutto in a Chiswick deli. A year before that I'd been sobbing over Harry's latest infidelity, as well as trying to cope with the first of Clive's expulsions from school. Then, winding back the years before that, it seemed to me that my life had constantly been steered by events and necessities external to myself. Even falling in love for the first time had felt prompted by some outside agency: it was as if a burglar had snatched my heart when I wasn't looking, and had given it to some bastard in the Sixth Form who only wanted it as a trophy to display and boast about. That was when I first realised Ruth was a real friend, because she found me sobbing in a corner and went out and kicked the boy in the balls.

And now here I was. All my life was my own: I could do with it as I wished. My God, all this freedom, I thought – it had better be worth it. So, where should I begin? I could hardly spend the rest of my life painting views of Sarum Magna from my window. What should be the next step?

Then it came to me. I needed to work. Work! The very thing I'd earned all this money not to need to do. That was quite a shock. But there was no getting away from it; as an artist I was probably never going to be much more than a Sunday painter, and perhaps not even that – a Bank Holiday Monday painter provided the sun was shining and I wasn't making love with Tom after a particularly good lunch. If it came to a choice between getting randy and a bit pissed with Tom or painting anaemic watercolours of Mr Gant's farm, there would never be any contest.

Now I really was being truthful to myself, and it was more than a little frightening. Should we perhaps have remained in London, where work was easier to find? No, I decided straight away. This place was idyllic, or it would be idyllic once the mill-house was ready and the garden had recovered from being drowned. Already I could make out several miniature spots of purple through the window, where something or other was telling me it was spring. Later I should have to go out and see what they were.

So, the agenda was – work! Then what about Howard Minton of the posh notepaper and his invitation to illustrate one of the children's classics? That could be a beginning – as well as make me respectable in my son's eyes after the excesses of *Prawnography* – which he would have gloated over if it had been by anyone else, but because it was his mum he was shocked, the hypocritical little beast.

I found Minton's letter and read it a second time. Yes, I would write to him at his smart office and express cautious interest. I might even suggest he come over one day when he was at his cottage. The candlelit dinner I'd choose to ignore, for the time being at least, though I had to admit to a certain thrill at the thought of being professionally wooed by an 'editorial director' over a fine bottle of Nuits St. Georges. A year ago I'd have leapt at such an invitation, and put on something entirely irresistible in case he proved to be entirely irresistible. Christ, Janice, you're getting old, I thought. No, I wasn't. I had a look in the mirror and decided I looked good for thirty-seven. Tiny waist. Tight jeans. Blue eyes. Blonde hair. Nipples showing rather too prominently through the blouse perhaps (Mrs Teape wouldn't approve, but Tom certainly does). Altogether I looked pretty sexy, and felt it.

No, it was nothing to do with getting old. It was something else altogether, something quite new to me. It was a determination not to damage what I had with Tom, for that was the most special, the most precious of things – what I had always looked for, never believing it could ever be mine. And it was going to be mine: all these other women would *not* spoil it.

My musings were interrupted by the arrival of Mrs Teape, dressed in her customary armour-plating and bearing two large packages.

'Saw the postman coming, Mrs Brand. Now, I wonder what someone's sent you. Something nice, I hope. A surprise from Mr Brand, perhaps: he's just the sort of gentleman to give his lady a surprise.'

I refrained from saying that he'd already given me rather too many.

'There's just one letter for Mr Brand. From France. Madame Something or Other. A funny name. No doubt she's a well-wisher; I expect your husband gets a lot of those, and I'm not surprised. But I have to say, Mrs

Brand, how can the French put such things on their postage stamps? This one's nice: quite a nice-looking gentleman – I think I'd like him. But look at *her* – disgusting, if you ask me. Fancy going for a swim without a stitch on – in public too. Just like the French. Sex mad, they are; I've always said so. She's all blotchy, what's more, and no wonder, being out in the sun like that. She'll probably get skin cancer; all this trouble with the woe-zone layer.'

She handed me the envelope. The two stamps showed a portrait of Napoleon, and one of Renoir's *Baigneuses*.

'Thank you, Mrs Teape,' I said.

I didn't recognise the name on the back of Tom's letter, which was addressed to his former London flat – written in a childish hand – and forwarded by the post office. I placed it on Tom's desk and turned my attention to the two packages addressed to me. They were fat, almost identical, and I noticed they were from the literary agent Tom and I had recently acquired to deal with *Prawnography*.

There was also a separate letter from the same agent, which I opened first.

'Dear Janice,' it began, 'I'm sorry to burden you with these. The BBC say they vet all viewers' correspondence for obscenities, lewd proposals, explosive devices and the like, and I was informed that quite a few of the letters prompted by your television performance fell into one or more of these categories. I must say, judging by the tone of some of those the BBC thought fit to send on, the mind boggles at what the ones they censored must have been like. I wonder if it would be worth seriously considering offering a selection of these viewers' letters to a book publisher à la Henry Root. I can imagine your talents as an illustrator might be roused by some of them. For your convenience, I have grouped them into general categories, i.e. Outraged Catholics, Smug Protestants, Perverts (Male), Perverts (Female), Courtiers Amorous, Courtiers Artistic, Humourists, Axe-Grinders, Loonies, etc. In case you don't feel like wasting your time reading them all, I enclose a breakdown of the views expressed by your fan club, listing the various suggestions/prophecies/proposals in order of popularity. Some of these may surprise you. They certainly surprised me. Howard Minton, by the way, tells me he has written to you direct with an intriguing proposal for a children's book. He's an exceptionally bright young man, and I shall be interested to hear what you decide. I think we can assume you would be more than adequately paid. Meanwhile – best wishes and happy reading! Yours, Valerie.'

I took the precaution of closing the studio door against Mrs Teape before opening the packages. Valerie had done her job as conscientiously as if she were preparing the agenda for a company board meeting, each sheaf of letters carefully labelled. I had a quick glance at some of them. They all seemed to be written on cheap lined paper, margin to margin, and a high proportion had key words underlined or in capital letters. There were a great number of exclamation marks, and the words 'blasphemous', 'corrupt', and 'disgusting' seemed to recur rather frequently. I felt quite shaken. *Me?* Blasphemous. Corrupt. Disgusting. Did I recognise myself – this sweet little blonde, devoted mother of teenage son, loving wife (well, a sort of wife), guardian of twenty acres of the English shires, painter of tasteful watercolours of the Avon Valley, about to become the illustrator of a children's classic? I pushed the heap of letters to one side and picked up the sheet of paper that was headed 'Breakdown'. Again it was typed like the agenda for a meeting. It read: 'Viewers' Opinions Concerning Janice Blakemore, as follows:

'– Whore of Babylon, 296 viewers;
– Doomed to hell-fire for the above and other reasons, 312;
– In the true spirit of Lutheran reform, 8;
– In breach of public morality, 428;
– Has outstanding artistic talent, 38;
– Has outstandingly good legs, 436;
– Offers of marriage, 73;
– Offers of a less orthodox nature, 374;
– Grounds for not paying the annual TV licence, 29;
– Grounds for increasing the annual TV licence in order to ensure more such programmes, 9;
– Deserves to be hanged, 44;
– Deserves to be flogged in public, 124;
– Deserves to be screwed in private, 13;
– Deserves to be canonised, 3;
– Deserves to be Minister of the Arts, 2;
– Deserves to be Queen of England, 1.'

I was amazed. The statistics seemed to me far more interesting than the letters were likely to be; besides which, there were far too many letters, and I felt I could

73

spare myself the experience of discovering why it was that 124 people wished to flog me in public, and 312 wished to condemn me to eternal hell-fire. All this merely because I had taken an imaginative approach to illustrating a wine called Blue Nun which, quite apart from being a revolting beverage, is a stupid title for a wine since no true nun – blue or otherwise – would ever be permitted to drink the stuff even if she were misguided enough to want to. What did please me was that although a high proportion of viewers considered I had offended public morality, a rather higher number claimed I had outstandingly good legs; and, since we live in a democracy, I reckoned that by popular vote my legs won the day. I could hardly wait to tell Tom this: he might find it quite a turn-on to read the 436 letters on the subject. I would have telephoned Ruth, too, if I'd thought there was any chance she'd be home at this hour – Ruth who had always claimed she had better legs than mine, besides having an undeniably larger bust.

At that moment the telephone did ring, and I hurried out of the studio to answer it, thinking it might possibly be Tom. It was Emelda.

'Just to warn you, my dear, that my tiresome husband intends to visit you this afternoon.'

I explained that Tom was in London, but said that I'd be delighted.

'Oh, I shouldn't be if I were you,' she replied. 'Visits from Ayrton are a trial. I've told him it will be an imposition, but he's quite set on it. The trouble is, my dear, when your family have been lords of the manor since William the Conqueror you fall into the habit of doing as you please. *Droit de seigneur.* Not that you'll be in any danger from *that* quarter, I can assure you. His urges went into hibernation a great many years ago after the briefest of flights – rather like his dragonflies, only a little smaller if my memory serves me correctly.'

Emelda always managed to say the most frightful things about her husband in a tone of such affection that they sounded like compliments.

'And how are you, my dear?' she went on.

I told her about the viewers' letters, and that I'd received seventy-three offers of marriage.

'How very embarrassing for you,' she said. 'I wonder what would happen if you said "yes" to them all – perhaps asked them all to turn up on the same day. Now that *would* make a good television programme. I may suggest it to Marmaduke.'

Emelda was chuckling delightedly. I told her that one viewer thought I should be Queen of England. The chuckling grew louder.

'Oh, what a good idea. The present one's been there far too long. I told her only last month she should let someone else have a go. Not that son of hers who talks to plants. You'd be quite splendid; I think I shall propose it. Stir the Palace up a little, take their minds off divorces. Now, there's something I need to ask you, my dear,' Emelda went on without any pause for breath. 'I'm collecting people's recipes in aid of the Salisbury spire – just a modest little volume, but I wonder if you'd do the pictures for it. You'd be so good. I'm only asking friends, of course, and they've nearly all of them agreed – except Fergie, who offered me a recipe for Plum Tart, but I thought she'd said 'Plump Tart', so she went off in a huff. They're so touchy, these *arrivistes*. The Church isn't any different, I can tell you: George was positively twitchy when I asked him – but perhaps cooking lacks the evangelical touch. Not that Philip was much better; he thinks he may have forgotten how long you give an egg. I said, 'Come, come, what about all those wonderful barbecues at Balmoral?' But he didn't seem to think burnt bangers would be particularly interesting. Anyway, I'm going to send all of them copies of your book to show them what wonderful things you do. So, do please think about it.'

My God, I did think about it. *Prawnography* on display at Sandringham and Lambeth Palace. Thank heavens I used a pseudonym.

I went back to the studio to find Mrs Teape in occupation, duster in one hand and one of my viewers' letters in the other.

'Thought I'd have a quick dust while you were on the phone; and I couldn't help noticing this charming letter. I hope you don't mind my being a Nosy Parker, Mrs Brand. It was just the words 'Cabinet Minister' caught my eye. Such a good idea. I know Mr Major's keen to have more women in his government; it said so in the paper only yesterday. Oh, I shall be so proud, Mrs Brand. Just think of it – a cabinet minister in Sarum Magna.'

I suppose I should have been relieved that Mrs Teape's predatory eye had fallen on the 'Loony' pile, and not on the mountain of outrage at my 'breach of public morality'.

By the time she left at lunchtime I felt I'd had quite enough of this morning and poured myself a very large drink. And how, I wondered, was Tom getting on – or off – with Kyra Vansittart?

The garden of Otters Mill was threaded by so many streams that from the air it must have looked like the Ganges delta. For the first week I'd scarcely set foot in it, since to do so would have been to sink at least to the knees, if not to more intimate parts. Tom took to referring to it as the Dogger Bank, and kept peering from the window each morning to see what Spanish galleon might have surfaced with the receding tide.

But now, after several days of fine weather and drying winds, it had taken on a quite new character. Something that might even have been grass was beginning to stain the mud a fresh green, and by proceeding cautiously it was possible to squelch one's way around it in some safety. The streams all began and ended in the River Avon – above and below the mill – the distance between the two being perhaps five hundred yards. The river itself described a long curve round the edge of our land, running darkly through deep pools overhung with willows and alders, where the kingfisher often perched before streaking low over the water in a flash of lapis lazuli. I called him Halcyon – until Tom, in an unexpected display of classical learning, explained that Halcyon had been a woman, so either our bird was female or I must find it another name. He then made me feel better by informing me that the male kingfisher always offered his beloved a fish before mating, 'and I just happen to have some smoked salmon in the fridge,' he added. Halcyon days!

Then there was the mill-race. This had been diverted from the river to cut straight past the house through a narrow stone gully where the mill-wheel must once have been. Now it was just a thundering torrent that polished the walls on either side as white as marble, and had trimmed the overhanging willow as if it had been savaged with a chainsaw.

All the other streams I could only put down to some gardener's water fancy. They gushed and meandered through the grounds, becoming a swamp here, a miniature waterfall there, and creating an archipelago of small islands, interlinked by wooden bridges that were now perilously slippery with river-mud deposited by the recent floods.

On one of these islands I came across the famous rose arbour so loudly trumpeted in the agents' brochure. It rose, bleak and skeletal above the grey mud, and I tried to imagine it transformed into something worthy of *Homes and Gardens*, with all the perfumes of the Orient wafting across a June evening. Then, on a neighbouring island, I discovered the carpet of silver-grey crocuses I'd noticed from the window. They were open now as if they'd been peeled, their stamens a brilliant orange, and every now and then one of them would bend under the weight of one of Mr Gant's bees. Italian bees, he'd informed me proudly: 'blonde like you, and docile like I'm sure you're not.' I watched them filling up their sacks with pollen, then dipping into the next flower, which would stoop under its weight before springing up again.

My mood of the early morning had quite vanished. I felt enormously happy. I looked around. Everywhere was the gentle sound of water. A heron flapped clumsily across the river with a sharp bark, and settled sentinel-like on the far shore. I stood watching it, the bird's stillness imposing a stillness on me. Then I glanced back at the mill-house and tried to see it as it would look before the year was out. How very beautiful it will be, I thought, with its mellow brick and bright weather-boarding; we'd build a terrace up there on the first floor above the mill-stream, and in the last of the summer we'd drink our evening wine there as the sun went down.

I wished Tom were here to share it all, share my dreams and my happiness. As for the bloody bitch in California, all tits and envy: we'd see her off.

I never noticed Ayrton until a cough made me turn round, and even then it was a moment before I recognised the elderly visitor, standing rather stooped beside the patch of crocuses. He was wearing a floppy hat whose brim sank so low that his eyes were barely visible. A sharp nose protruded beneath, and below that a tongue flicked occasionally between moist lips, while his head performed regular little bobs as if he were attempting to shake a dewdrop from his nostrils. His shoes were hefty brown brogues which pointed outwards at ten to two, and between them he had planted his stick, consisting of a rugged assembly of knots to which his hands, as they rested on the handle, added many more. His tweeds, which matched the mud he was standing on, were of that traditional English cut designed to emphasise the shapelessness of shapeless men. A pair of small kangaroos could have hidden within the bulge of his hip-pockets.

He was pointing at the flowers by his feet with his stick.

'*Crocus tomasinianus*,' he announced. 'Always the first. My favourites.'

Ayrton's tongue gave an approving flick.

'I trust I'm not disturbing you, madam,' he added.

I said, 'Not at all,' whereupon he uttered a little grunt and nodded in the direction of the mill-stream.

'Wanted to see if the trout were rising yet. A bit early, but in this fine weather they might be.'

I accompanied him to the edge of the water. He peered downwards. This time a dewdrop did form on the end of his nose, and I watched it as Ayrton watched for the trout. The dewdrop disengaged itself, causing a minute ring to form in the water. He produced a large red handkerchief – Mr Toad again, I though – and attacked the offending nostril before returning his hand-kerchief to one of the bulging pockets. He was shaking his head.

'Too early. Another week.' He turned to me. 'Your husband will be out here, I'm sure. I'd like to join him. Excellent fishing, this stretch. Good to have another sportsman here. Last occupant was an ignoramus. What about his flies? D'you happen to know?'

I felt a pang of non-comprehension. Then I remembered that flies were used for catching fish. I was afraid I didn't know, I said. I wasn't a fisherman myself – 'alas!' I was wondering if I should tell my lordly visitor that Tom's fishing days had been confined to shrimping with a net in rock-pools as a child; but before I had a chance to say anything Ayrton took a sudden step backwards in apparent alarm.

'Good heavens. I don't believe it.' He was gazing at the sky and pointing upwards with his stick. 'D'you see it?'

He let the stick fall and wrenched a pair of gnarled binoculars from one of the pockets of his jacket, one finger hastily adjusting the focus.

'Got him. What a beauty. First one for five years. Must be on its way to Loch Garten. Grabbing a little snack on the way. So I'm quite wrong about the trout. Better sight than I've got. Better fisherman too. Here, take a look.'

He handed me the binoculars, his face glowing with pleasure. I'd seen nothing at all except a few trees silhouetted against the sky, and now through the binoculars even these were blurred.

'Too late, it's gone,' Ayrton was saying. 'Pity. Hoped he might stay around for a few days. Well, you didn't expect to see one of those in your own back-garden, did you?'

Since I had no idea what 'one of those' was, I agreed.

Ayrton was by now thoroughly animated, his hands agitating the air, his eyes and nose watering with pleasure. Then, as if the rare bird, whatever it was, had unlocked something in him, he placed a hand tenderly on my shoulder with a smile so radiant it endeared him to me from that moment.

'You know, I believe you must be a bringer of good fortune,' he said. 'I shall visit you again, if I may. Who knows what we shall see?' Suddenly his face became serious, and his head nodded gravely. 'I feel deeply sorry for people who understand nothing about the creatures of the wild. You and I are the fortunate ones – you, perhaps, more than me because you understand about human beings too, which I don't. A total mystery to me; always have been. Give me a dragonfly any day – or a trout – or an osprey.'

And as he said 'osprey' he glanced up to where he'd been gazing a few moments before. It was with some relief that I now knew the name of the bird I'd never seen, and felt able to say in half-truth, 'Thank you, Lord Bustard, for pointing out the osprey to me.'

'Not at all. Not at all. And in a few weeks' time the migrants will be here. Special favourites of mine. We'll watch for them together, if you'll allow me. Are you good on warblers?'

I made modest noises and determined that I'd raid Waterstone's in Salisbury for a bird book at the earliest opportunity. I might also do Tom a favour and buy him a manual on fly-fishing. I imagined myself announcing, 'By the way, I saw an osprey this afternoon, Tom,' as he returned from London; except that Tom would have no more idea what an osprey was than I did. More effective, I decided, would be, 'Lord Bustard was enquiring what flies you use for fishing, Tom.' I could see his look of bemused horror, and hear my own laughter.

The stooped and bandy-legged figure gave a final wave of his stick as I left him at the gate. I watched him affectionately as he made his way down our track towards the road, his stick describing buoyant parabolas between stabs at the gravel, his feet splayed generously as he walked, as if he were wearing frogmen's flippers.

I turned away, still smiling. Dusk was beginning to fall, and a low mist was already settling over Mr Gant's fields, adding a chill to the March evening. I shivered and turned to go indoors, wondering how long it would be before Tom returned. And then something caught the corner of my eye. I turned to look, one hand still on the handle of the front door. There, on the footbridge some hundred yards away, stood a figure in grey. She was doing nothing. She was just looking at me. And she went on looking.

It was Mooncalf. For a moment I thought I should go and speak to her, introduce myself as her new neighbour. Then I remembered what Mrs Teape had said, and went indoors. I drew the curtains.

I made tea and waited for Tom. I'm bad at waiting, and the sight of Mooncalf just standing there had ruffled me. What on earth did she want? Had no one ever taught her as a child that it's rude to stare? It was just our luck to find ourselves living next to the village loony.

Perhaps half an hour passed.

Nothing is more silent than a telephone that never rings. Why should I have expected it to? Perhaps because I felt suddenly lonely – one of those moments of doubt when it seemed an act of pure folly to have dumped ourselves here in this swamp. Where were the shops, the pavements, the warm sounds of city life? Where were the transistors turned up too loud, the domestic punch-ups next door, the hysterical yapping of the neighbour's Jack

Russells, the owlish children begging support for yet another sponsored run in aid of their privileged school?

Here there was only the persistent sound of water.

In my studio, viewers' letters littered the place like an emptied ballot-box. I dumped the lot in the laundry-basket I use for waste-paper, and carried it outside to the dustbin. In the last of the light I noticed with relief that Mooncalf had gone. When I came back indoors I placed my own letter to Howard Minton on the table by the front-door next to Tom's letter from France. At that moment I saw the lights of his car through the curtains; and suddenly living in a swamp began to seem the best of all things.

Tom threw down his briefcase and we kissed like lovers. I loved him for coming back safe from the world.

Everything had gone well, he said, Kyra Vansittart was a tough cookie: she'd asked all the right questions, plus a few he'd have preferred her not to ask – 'but then all solicitors have a prurient side, don't they?' What had emerged most clearly was the necessity of finding a witness prepared to swear that Tom couldn't possibly have nicked Samantha's seafood recipes, since at that time she could scarely boil an egg, let alone do exciting things with freshwater clams.

The question was – who might be such a witness?

The obvious candidate was Scott, since he'd been Samantha's agent and certainly a good deal more than that in the early days; but having passed her on to Tom and slipped gratefully out of her life, Scott's testimony might appear woefully out of date – and besides, as a close friend of the accused he could hardly pass as an impartial witness.

'What about the woman's estranged husband?' Kyra Vansittart had suggested: the mysterious Mr Parsons. 'Where was he?' Tom had no idea. Neither apparently did Scott. Perhaps he could be traced. Ms Vansittart proposed she contact a friend and former colleague in Los Angeles, an attorney well versed in the murkier small print of Californian law. His name was Abram Kollwitz. 'You'll need to fly out and meet him. His fees are high, but his strike-rate is higher. It'll be worth it. But let me write to him first,' she had insisted.

They'd then lunched together in Charlotte Street.

'A large lady, Kyra Vansittart,' Tom explained, 'and after that lunch, even larger.'

Tom assured me he'd only nibbled at a salad, which I was inclined to believe, Tom's waistline being an important feature of his *amour propre*.

'Though we did split a good bottle of Pouilly Fumé,' he added, 'which released a few revelations about Ruth.'

They'd shared a lover or two in their time, Kyra had volunteered. Ruth had somehow always managed to have the last laugh – or the last fuck; which rankled, she said.

It must have rankled with Tom too, I imagined, Ruth being the one friend of mine who'd consistently said no to him. She'd never once explained to me why, though I think I knew, Ruth always selected lovers she could never love: it was safer that way. At least, this was what I chose to believe; it made me feel good about both Tom and Ruth. Otherwise I might have lost them both.

The pain of being reminded about Ruth caused Tom to go in search of a drink, and on his return I handed him the letter from France which he'd overlooked. Tom looked puzzled for a moment, then a cloud passed across his face. He opened the letter and read it. Folded inside was a leaflet which he cast an eye over before shaking his head very slowly, as if a great weariness had overtaken him.

'What is it, Tom?' I asked anxiously.

He put down his wine glass along with the letter and its accompanying leaflet, and looked at me.

'It's from Anne-Marie.' The name didn't register for a moment. 'My first wife,' he explained.

Anne-Marie! She was one I'd scarcely heard about – the first of the five. French – I remembered now.

'And what does *she* want?' I said cautiously.

There was a pause. A bemused look came over Tom's face.

'Now, let's take this quietly,' he said. 'It's not palimony. I promise you. It's not a criminal charge. It's not a writ. It's not a declaration of undying love. It's not a threat. But . . .' Tom gave a hesitant cough, 'it *is* money.' Then suddenly he picked up the leaflet and burst out laughing. 'It's money for . . . would you like to know? The Madagascan vampire bat!'

I tried to look serious.

'Of course, Tom,' I said. 'And now perhaps you'd care to explain.'

'I'll try,' he went on. And he cast his eyes over the leaflet. 'Well, apparently the dear little thing's in danger of extinction! And d'you know why it's in danger of extinction?' Tom gave another cough and began to read out from the leaflet. "'All the bat's organs are held to contain magical properties. Its gall-bladder is believed to cure blindness and cataracts. Its spleen overcomes impotence and infertility." Well, well! I always imagined vampire bats reduced the human population, not increased it. But now we know.'

Tom looked at me in disbelief.

'Jesus Christ! Jan, I write a cookery book, and what happens? I'm threatened with palimony in California, and now vampire bats in Madagascar.'

He very quickly poured himself a second glass of wine.

'But I'm afraid that's not quite all,' he went on, picking up the letter. 'It seems my daughter may descend on us shortly. Apparently she's decided it's about time she got to know her father. Or so Anne-Marie says.'

I said nothing for a moment. Tom's eyes were avoiding mine, which was just as well.

'Perhaps you should start by telling me a few things about Anne-Marie, Tom, don't you think?'

He looked at me and nodded.

5

WHEN I first met Tom I never pressed him to talk about his marriages. I knew there had been rather a lot of them, but I preferred to set them aside as a series of unfortunate mistakes which, had he met me, of course would never have happened. I knew this to be naive nonsense, but after my own disasters with Harry I was yearning to cultivate the flames of romance rather than cast myself simply as the potential Number Six, possibly no more likely to survive than the rest of them.

This was made more difficult by the realisation that a man who has already had five wives presents a grotesque challenge. It's like Russian roulette, except that instead of just one bullet in the chamber, the gun is fully loaded *except* for one; and in defiance of suicide you somehow believe you are the woman who'll make it. All this is extremely bad for the male ego, and equally so for the woman's self-respect, since it ignores the probability that the man is a total louse who should never have been loved in the first place, let alone the fourth and fifth.

All these thoughts went through my head during the days after I first slept with Tom and acknowledged reluctantly to myself that I wanted to go on sleeping with him rather than with any man who happened to take my fancy. The sacrifice was considerable, and so were the risks; but the benefits – as I hoped – were greater.

Then the improbable happened. I realised he loved me. What was more, I thought I loved him. That was when curiosity about my many predecessors became aroused. Suddenly I wanted to know everything about them. Tom of course claimed not to remember, and wafted my questions away, so that after a year I still had only the sketchiest idea of who they were and what they were like – which infuriated me, but in the end I gave up and consigned them to the dustbin of Tom's past.

'The point is, my darling,' Tom would say firmly, usually with a bottle of wine in one hand, 'they are none of them anything to do with us.'

How wrong he was. It was becoming clearer by the day that they were everything to do with us. And now that Number One had intruded herself in the form of a vampire bat, I realised I'd better start accepting his old ghosts as part of my life, since they insisted on remaining a part of his. At least the experience of being haunted began to unseal Tom's lips. It was an unnerving experience, suddenly getting to know the man I loved through the eyes of another woman – a woman, what was more, whom I disliked more and more the longer he spoke about her. As he talked about Anne-Marie I began to imagine myself to be a fly on the wall of his past – an extremely inquisitive fly who longed to ask all sorts of intimate and jealous questions. What had attracted him to her in the first place? Was it the same kind of attraction he had felt for me? Had he made love to her in the same way? As often? *More* often? Did she have lots of orgasms, and were they different from mine? I even wanted to ask banal questions, like what kind of perfume did she use? and what did they talk about over breakfast?

The evening might have passed off better had Tom not been so prim and evasive – exasperatingly so: guarding his memories, pushing the past out of sight. I kept having to nudge him.

'What d'you mean, "*and so we got married*"?' I said crossly. 'Only a minute ago you were plucking up courage to buy her a drink in a student bar, and wishing to hell your French was better so you could chat her up. You seem to be missing out an awful lot, Tom.'

There was a shrug and a long sigh.

'Well, I suppose the truth is I couldn't think about anything else but Anne-Marie day after day.'

This was a bit more like it, I thought.

'What you mean is, you fancied her like crazy.'

There was another sigh. Tom wasn't enjoying this.

'Well . . . Yes!'

Squeezing blood out of a stone would have been easier. We could be at this all night.

'So, let me get it right,' I went on. 'There you are on some reporting job in France. Alone. Unmarried. No woman in your life: at least none that I care to hear about. How am I doing so far? OK?' Tom was nodding a little uneasily. 'You happen to be in Aix-en-Provence with time on your hands. It's June. You're lonely and randy, and the place is full of gorgeous students. How unlike you to find yourself in such a place, Tom. Anyway, suddenly there's this girl in the café who looks like the young Juliette Greco, and she's got great tits, wonderful legs and . . .'

By now Tom was waving his hands in front of me and looking flustered.

'Hey! No, no! Wait!' he was exclaiming. 'I didn't say that.' Then he produced one of his private smiles and made a business of putting another log on the fire. 'Although as a matter of fact,' he went on, 'she *did* have great tits and wonderful legs . . . But that wasn't it.'

I laughed.

'Of course not, Tom!' I said. 'It was her mind, wasn't it? I should have realised.'

He ignored me.

'Actually it was her eyes,' he explained. I saw him go quite dreamy at the thought. 'Enormous, dark eyes – like Greek olives.'

I started to behave rather badly.

'Eyes like Greek olives! Good God! Well, one thing's clear: food and sex came together very early in your career. *Prawnography* was being born years before you ever met me.'

Tom gave me a patient look.

'Jan, you asked me. If you don't want to hear . . .'

'I do. I do,' I said. And I put my arms round him. 'I want to hear everything.' I laughed and kissed him. 'Everything. So, she had great tits, gorgeous legs, eyes

91

like Greek olives. Why *Greek* olives, for Christ's sake? Olives anyway. Sorry mine are blue.'

For a moment I thought Tom might be angry. He just looked at me.

'Blue,' he said softly. 'Yes, yours *are* blue. Sapphires. Harder than olives. And far more dangerous – to die for, my darling.' He drew me gently to him, and his lips brushed my eyelids. 'To die for,' he said again. His fingertips began to stroke the outline of my cheek. Involuntarily I raised my head. My eyes were closed, and I could feel myself drifting away, aware of his hands gradually following the line of my chin, then down on to the throat, a touch as light as feathers. 'Anne-Marie's throat was like a baby's,' he was saying, half-whispering, 'all vulnerability. Yours is soft as silk, but strong – like a column.' And he began to kiss my neck, down and down, as if fearful of bruising it. I was shaking. 'Your skin – I've never touched skin like yours. Ever.' I was entirely lost by now: I hoped he would never stop. 'Her skin never had a scent like yours.' He was unbuttoning my blouse – it was as if no one had ever undressed me before; not Harry, not any lover, no one. His tongue was tracing the cup of my breasts, first one, then the other, then the first again. 'Her breasts were heavy; yours are firm, taut.' I seemed to hear his voice resounding through my own skin. 'Hard, like your nipples,' and his lips closed over them, his tongue drawing them into his mouth. I thought they would explode.

Instead, *I* exploded. I had an orgasm, and collapsed. For a long time he just held me, his arms round me, his face buried in my breasts. My thoughts, such as they were, lay scattered around me. I was surprised to see the room still intact. Why wasn't it blown apart like me? Would I ever stop shaking?

It felt like hours before Tom raised his head, and smiled.

'Where were we?'

I blinked, trying to rake my thoughts back together.

'You were telling me about Anne-Marie,' I said, a little breathlessly. 'Remember? You got as far as her breasts.'

'So I did,' Tom said, running his hands over mine, reading them like braille, circling the nipples with his fingers. 'Nothing like as beautiful as your breasts. Perfect.'

I pressed my own hands over his.

'I'm glad,' I said. 'Very glad. They're yours.' I gazed at him. 'All of me is yours.'

He stood up and lifted me to my feet. They didn't feel very steady.

'Me too,' he said quietly. 'You know that.'

I nodded. I did know. It was all I wanted, and I wanted it always to be like this.

After a moment Tom began to laugh, and I knew what he was laughing at.

'And we only got as far as her breasts,' I said. 'Perhaps it's just as well: I might have died.' Then *I* started to laugh. '*Petit mort!* What d'you imagine Anne-Marie would think if she knew? Taking her body in vain? Tell me – seriously – when you touched her, did she ever come like that?'

Tom looked surprised.

'Good God, no!'

'Really?'

'I promise you. She didn't like me touching her breasts.'

'Never?'

'They were private territory. She tried to hide them.'

'That couldn't have been easy.'

'Oh yes it was. Her bras might have been designed by Banham. She had a whole alarm system fitted to them.'

I laughed.

'So, what *did* she like?'

Tom pursed his lips thoughtfully.

'A gap of about five feet between her and me.'

I was shaking my head.

'Why on earth did you marry her, Tom? Tell me.'

I made coffee while he talked. And I listened, fascinated. It was baffling to realise how entirely unsuited to one another they had been from the very beginning, and how grindingly long it had taken both of them to acknowledge it. But then I'd done much the same with Harry, hadn't I? Clinging to the wreckage. Believing we'd make it in the end, somehow. First marriages are storm-rafts. But they're also the storm, aren't they? Oh God, how they are!

The story was a bit like an old romantic novel you might find in a boarding-house, and you wonder who must have left it there. It began in a sadly familiar way. There is our hero, footloose in a hot southern town. He is twenty-seven. He feels he has a permanent erection even when he hasn't. The world is full of women he can't have.

'Then one evening I saw this raven-haired siren across the café tables,' he explained, his eyes beginning to become a little dreamy.

At last this was getting promising. I sat quietly, fearful lest he started forgetting again.

'Well, she was alone.' (I rather imagined that.) 'So I went over, looking wonderfully composed and casual as usual.' (Bloody liar, you had your tongue hanging out.) 'And she said yes to a drink. Then yes to a second one. And finally, yes to dinner. (Jesus! From the way you put it, Tom, I might have thought all you were interested in was her politics.)

He paused and gazed about him as if searching for a way out. But he knew he was trapped, and stumbled on, enjoying it a lot more than he tried to suggest. I found it so easy to picture him at that time: tall, swaggering, a shock of dark hair, suntanned, handsome in a rakish way, already worldly-wise, unlike the girl's fellow biology students who were all reading Marx and cultivating fluffy beards, and who knew about as much of the world as wherever a few student marches had led them. No doubt they all adored her and wrote her predictable love-letters quoting Alfred de Musset. But this Englishman, he was so interesting and unusual, she would have told her girlfriends, all of them as virginal as she; for this was still the age of virginity, especially in Vichy where, apparently, Anne-Marie's family came from.

'Her father owned a factory making metal parts,' Tom said, as if this had some remarkable significance. (Perhaps that was where his daughter got her bras from, I wanted to suggest.)

'Her mother prayed a lot, and prayed a lot for Anne-Marie. Soon she'd have cause to,' he added with a grimace.

After the second date Tom kissed her publicly on the Cours Mirabeau, and soon afterwards kissed her more privately in the park of the Roman baths.

'And I told myself I was in love. And I was, I think.'

Under the night trees she let him undress her just enough for him to be entirely certain that no lovelier creature existed on God's earth.

'I was convinced that life would be quite intolerable if any man possessed her other than me.'

Oh Tom, you really were a romantic, weren't you? Even now, so very many years later, he still described her as though she were some sort of landscape, with certain dominant features to be admired – legs, breasts, lips, and of course eyes (those famous Greek olives). As a person, Anne-Marie was merely the sum of all those desirable parts, and by possessing the entire collection of them Tom assumed he would somehow possess *her*, whoever she might be.

'I didn't know who she was, of course. But then neither did she.'

Tom imagined he would find out, and that it would be wonderful. Anne-Marie imagined he would tell her, and it would be wonderful. Altogether it was a heady time, and the absense of any adequate common language made it even headier. After much fumbling and sighing he proposed within a week.

'It was the only way to get her bra off.'

To his surprise she accepted within a minute.

'It was the only way she could get out of Aix-en-Provence.'

To be airlifted into marriage with so determined a stanger liberated her at a stroke from all those muddled doubts and small anxieties which clouded her brain. Suddenly there were certainties presented to her. Here was a man who would reveal to her who she was. Now she would no longer have to pretend to enjoy biology. Soon they would live in a place called Kilburn. They would travel. They would have children. Tom, for his part, discovered to his surprise that he'd always been a Roman Catholic at heart: consequently a suitable wedding of that kind was arranged in Vichy. On the morning of the marriage her father took Tom aside. In the afternoon her mother wept. In the evening Anne-Marie lost her virginity and wept too.

'No, of course it never worked,' Tom said, looking up from the fire. 'How could it have done? I'd married a shrine.' He took my hand and gave another laugh. 'Besides, she hated Kilburn. Come to think of it, that was about the only thing we had in common.'

He didn't dwell much on their life together. I was rather glad – it sounded so dismal. I made the occasional interjection.

'Was it sex?'

'In a one-sided way, yes!' he said. 'Anne-Marie had orgasms as though she hated herself for having them. Then she worked hard at never having them again, and accused me of treating her like a whore. I replied that a whore might be a lot more fun, which didn't go down too well. After that she always put her nightgown on in the bathroom. You can imagine it all, can't you? Life in the war zone.'

I nodded. I didn't like to admit I used to put my nightgown on in the bathroom when I was with Harry.

'And she was so beautiful,' Tom was saying, shaking his head. 'I wanted to make love to her like a lion.'

'Perhaps lions are lousy lovers,' I suggested.

Tom looked surprised.

'Yes. Perhaps I was a lousy lover,' he said after a moment or two. 'At least, for her. And yet I suspect any man would have been.'

'How sad,' I said. 'Such a waste. What was it that finally ended it?'

He looked suddenly very tired.

'The child . . . strangely enough. Having Solange.' He managed a smile. 'God knows how that happened after six years,' he went on. 'Anne-Marie must have been asleep, or I was thinking of someone else.' Tom gave a snort and threw another log at the fire. 'Anyway, that's what did it. Solange was the barrier she needed. And one day she just left – with the child. Solange was less than a year old. She should be brought up in France, Anne-Marie declared, not in Kilburn. Mind you, I think she had a point there.'

Back in France, Anne-Marie became a changed woman. She even decided she enjoyed biology after all. She became a schoolteacher.

'Passionate about it, judging by her letters,' Tom went on. 'I'd have sworn there were no passions in her. But there you go – frogs discovered something I couldn't.'

He gave a grim laugh.

She never married again, he explained; she never even recognised the divorce, being a devout Catholic. As far as she was concerned Tom remained the absent husband and father, who sent money for Solange – whom he was rarely permitted to see.

'I was a bigamist, after all. A multi-bigamist, what's more. I might corrupt the child.'

'Did it hurt you a lot, not seeing your own daughter?' I asked.

There was a shadow of pain on Tom's face.

'Yes, it did,' he said. 'Then I got used to it – not knowing her, not even thinking of her as mine.'

I asked him when he'd last seen Solange. He said it had been three or four years ago – she'd come to London with her school.

'Fat and spotty she was. Not like her mother at all. And I didn't know what to say to her. She was just another awkward teenager.'

That was all he said. I began to feel quite sorry for the girl: no father, and a mother who rescued vampire bats. Not that I was viewing her arrival with any joy. I didn't even know how long Solange was coming for. Was she planning to *live* with us – making up for all those lost years? These bloody women kept coming out of the woodwork. When was this new life of ours going to begin?

'There's just one more bit you haven't filled in, Tom,' I said. 'What steered your "ex" from teaching biology to rescuing Madagascan bats?'

Tom was continuing to vent his exasperation on the fire, which spat back at him as he prodded it.

'I think Anne-Marie's passions simply moved on,' he said in a resigned voice. 'Having dissected frogs and mice for God knows how many years she decided to start rescuing them. I should have thought it was a bit late myself, but evidently she didn't. It became her life. Anything at risk, she'd save it. I tell you, she'd mount a campaign to rescue head-lice if they were on the endangered list.'

It was all so absurd I couldn't help laughing.

'She can't have thought much of *Prawnography*,' I said. 'Think of all those poor lobsters we're endangering.'

His lips managed a hint of a smile.

'It certainly must have brought on a few Hail Marys. I wonder how she discovered I wrote it. I can just imagine her quaking at all that celebration of fleshly delights. Until of course she got round to thinking about the money.'

I was still laughing.

'Money for vampire bats. I tell you what, Tom. Why don't we let one loose on her? We could send it back with your daughter.'

This time he managed a real smile. He took my hand again.

'I'm sorry,' he said. 'I wouldn't wish any of this on you. Let's make love.'

There were moments when I could forgive Tom most things.

'So long as your harem doesn't join us,' I said. 'Promise?'

His hands banished the vampire bats from my mind. We made love by the fire.

*

'Bore me some more,' said Ruth on the telephone. 'I love it.'

She was laughing.

I did my best. I told her how Commander Normington's wife had invited us to dinner to meet several 'dear friends from the neighbourhood', and how this had prompted Tom to arrange his flight to Los Angeles, 'unfortunately for that very day'. I went on to say that our builders were due to start work on the mill house before the end of the week, and that Clive would be home for the Easter holidays in two weeks. I then hit her with the news of Emelda's cookbook in aid of the Salisbury Cathedral spire, and of Mr Gant's insistence that I call him John even though I remained his 'pretty little filly'. Ruth still hadn't rung off, so I told her about the crocuses and daffodils that were appearing in the garden, about Ayrton and the osprey, about Mooncalf staring at me from the bridge, and about Howard Minton phoning this morning to invite himself over to talk 'business'. I thought Ruth deserved a good finale, so I left until last the invasion of the Madagascan vampire bat.

'Wonderful!' Ruth exclaimed. 'It all reminds me of home. In the diplomatic service one doesn't have a home. Only other people's.'

It was still snowing in Liechtenstein, she complained. Piers had sprained an ankle falling on the stuff, so she and their new skiing friend had gone off at the weekend alone. He was very beautiful and preferred older women – 'Thank God!' she said – and if that was the way he'd trained for the Olympics, it was no wonder he only got a silver medal. 'I've never been made to feel like a piste before.'

Sarum Magna struck me as extremely tame after that. Hearing her talk made me realise how much I wished she wasn't so far away. I loved her full-bloodedness, her excess, her gift for making things happen, however catastrophic those things might be. And I loved her friendship. The only price I paid was that even in my most disreputable days Ruth had always made me feel like a well-trained household pet compared to her.

'And is Tom behaving himself?' she enquired, which immediately caused me to worry about him going to California. OK, he was only going to meet his attorney, the mythical Abram Kollwitz, but who knows what lonesome creature he might meet on the way, now that he was the celebrated author of *Prawnography*? And here was I, stuck in a Wiltshire hamlet among the spring daffodils, and being 'done for' by Mrs Teape. It was not a glamorous life.

'My darling, you should try Liechtenstein,' Ruth retorted. 'The hottest spot in town is the foyer of the Kowloon and Hong Kong Bank.'

After her Grand Slalom with the Olympic silver-medallist, I wasn't convinced. Ruth would find glamour anywhere, even in the Kowloon and Hong Kong Bank.

All week it had been March that felt like May. While Tom was making loud and groaning arrangements for his trip to California, I took to exploring the sheep-paths that meandered along the limestone ridge above the village, taking with me the superzoom camera Tom had given me for my birthday. I never quite understood why he'd done so, or what I was supposed to shoot with it, but I decided this was the moment to try. So I wandered around looking for things to photograph. After a period of frustration I zoomed the lens at several patches of wild flowers before discovering that by taking a couple of paces forward I could have taken exactly the same shot without bothering about the zoom at all. Then I tried it on a hovering kestrel. This looked more promising. I got the bird perfectly at full zoom, but the instant I pressed the button the kestrel dropped like a stone and I took a prize-winning shot of a cloud at a magnification of three. I wasn't doing very well.

But one morning was magic. I'd set off early, and now stood looking down from the ridge towards the straggle of village houses below me. Except that the village wasn't there. All I could see was a lake of mist on which dozens of roofs were floating like upturned ships. And perched on the keel of each ship was a carved pheasant, as if they were survivors from a storm. The mist billowed and washed around them, sometimes threatening to engulf them, sometimes leaving them proudly strutting in the sun. It was unreal and beautiful.

This, I decided, was precisely what my camera was made for. So I zoomed into the rooftop pheasants until my viewfinder gave me shot after shot of the most dramatic kind. Here were pictures worthy of the front page of *The Independent*, perhaps even of a special award. Having always regarded photography as the most banal occupation on God's earth, I was now transported. For the first time I understood the thrill which professional photographers experience. I might even emulate them,

I thought, and have framed enlargements made of my shipwrecked pheasants, to hang proudly on our bedroom wall. Would Tom be pleased? Would he appreciate my genius? Perhaps it would give him a delightful surprise on his return from California.

Then I had a better idea. An inspired idea. I would select two or three of my more dynamic shots of Sarum Magna's carved pheasants, and post them to Anne-Marie. Oh yes! Brilliant! I'd explain carefully that all our financial resources were at present dedicated to rescuing the Wiltshire Carved Pheasant, so called because of its unique habit of conserving energy in winter by retreating into total stillness on the roofs of local villages. Regrettably, I would go on, the extreme cold of our northern climate often overtook them, freezing them solid, whereupon they dropped off their perches and smashed to smithereens. What a tragedy – she would surely agree. So, in order to preserve this unique inhabitant of our locality, we were devising a method of providing the creatures with heated perches. An expensive enterprise, none the less abundantly worth while.

I did wonder if Tom might think I was merely inciting the stupid bitch to further lunacies – or she might of course turn up to inspect the unfortunate creatures – none the less the joke would give me huge pleasure. I would do it. The woman clearly had no sense of humour whatsoever. I would pay her back in kind.

I gazed down on the village in the most cheerful of moods. The mist was evaporating fast. There was the church, carved in sunlight. There was the Wilton Arms. And there, ringed by bright water, lay our mill. Our home. From up here it looked composed and small – like an island nest. The sight warmed me, and I felt I belonged. Our life here would endure and flourish. Tom's past would not encroach. No, it certainly would not!

By now I was thoroughly intrigued by my new toy, I raised the camera again and pressed the zoom button. Our mill rushed towards me. And there suddenly was Tom. He was reading a newspaper in the garden. From its size I guessed it was the *Daily Mail,* in which case he was sure to be poring over the royal infidelities. I'd noticed recently how it takes a declared republican like Tom to slaver over the long-running bedroom farce performed by the House of Windsor; whereas I, who am a closet royalist, take no interest in their affairs whatsoever, beyond wondering if their lovers have 'By Royal Appointment' tattooed on their bums. In any case, the royals strike me as behaving precisely like all other married couples, except that somehow they believe they shouldn't. What they don't seem to understand is that this is the only reason we like them, because we can identify with them. They make our own sordid divorces appear regal.

I went on peering through my superzoom. Tom had turned the page; he was probably reading Keith Waterhouse, whom he admires and invariably wishes he'd written the piece himself. Certainly he seemed to be studying it very intently. Then I saw him throw the paper down and leap to his feet. I couldn't imagine why until I saw Mrs Teape cross the garden bearing a cup of something – probably her speciality, boiled coffee with condensed milk. Poor Tom – the price of being so admired. He was looking quite agitated, as well he might. Yes, I was right. Mrs Teape paused to adjust the jumbo combs in her hair, and reluctantly departed. I saw Tom wait a second or two before carefully tipping the coffee into a flower-bed. Then he picked up the newspaper again, scanned the page and folded it with an angry gesture. This wasn't like Tom at all. Something was wrong. Perhaps it was the racing results after all, and he'd lost. Or won. No doubt I would soon discover.

I watched Tom leave the garden. I guessed it must have been the telephone – people have a particular way of walking when they're hurrying for the phone, in case someone's died. Now there was nothing to look at, so I tracked the viewfinder across John Gant's fields towards the village, taking in several cows and the odd chicken, until something else caught my eye. I lowered the camera, blinked, and looked again. There could be no doubt about it. It was a woman reclining, entirely naked. A nude in Wiltshire? In Sarum Magna? In full view of the church? In March? The apparition was in the garden of one of the cottages close to the river, and she was lying stretched out on what appeared to be a sofa, propped up one elbow with her head resting on her hand. Dark hair tumbled across her body, and her breasts did much the same.

As I was puzzling over this phenomenon a man appeared, waving what appeared to be a short stick. Was he about to beat her? I was riveted. He was bald, and looked quite elderly. Then I saw him walk up to her and, with his free hand, reach down and rearrange one of her breasts before stepping back to admire the effect. After a moment or two he stepped forward again and did the same with the other breast. It was as though they were pillows; I half-expected him to plump them up, or unzip them. The woman appeared quite unperturbed by all this manhandling. She yawned, scratched her thigh, and lay still. At that moment the postman appeared. I saw him doff his cap and offer the man a letter. Then he must have made some observation about the weather because all three of them looked up at the sky. This sudden movement caused the woman's breasts to fall sideways again, whereupon the man casually leaned forward to readjust them. The postman waited until all was in place once more, doffed his cap a second time, and departed.

At that point I understood. This must be the artist I'd heard about, of whom Mrs Teape disapproved so strongly. I even remembered his name – Winston Cash. And the woman was the one I'd seen a week ago crossing the fields barefoot. 'The best udders in Wiltshire,' John Gant had commented. Well, at least I could now see what he meant.

By this time I'd had enough of being a *voyeuse*, and made my way down the chalk slope towards the village. The path met the road exactly opposite the church, and as I passed the lich-gate I caught sight of Emelda Bustard: she was closing the church door behind her and carrying an empty basket on one arm. She must have been doing the flowers.

She saw me and, after untethering Lloyd George from his tombstone, began taking robust strides in my direction.

'Fourth Sunday in Lent,' she called out. 'My ordeal's nearly over. Passion Sunday and Wendy Normington takes over the flowers. Odd timing: not many passions in Wendy's life – except bridge. Hope you haven't got roped in, my dear.'

Emelda put down her basket and let out a deep breath as if the flowers had been exceptionally heavy. She was wearing her customary purple tweeds, though I noticed the cleaner's label had been removed, so possibly they were different tweeds. There was an egg-stain on her white blouse.

'An early walk with the camera, eh?' she went on.

I explained about the zoom-lens, and how you could use it like a telescope.

'Is that really so?' she said, looking surprised. 'And what did you zoom in Sarum Magna?'

'Tom reading a newspaper, and a woman naked,' I answered truthfully.

Emelda gave a boisterous laugh, and began to rub vigorously at the egg-stain which she'd just noticed, making it worse – a free-range egg-stain, I thought, trying not to smile.

'A naked lady!' she exclaimed. 'Well, there's only one naked lady in Sarum Magna, and that's Concha. She *has* started early. Must be the warm spell. Winston always paints her out of doors. Thinks he's Renoir, I suppose,' Emelda went on. 'I've always meant to ask him what he did in the winter, though that might be indiscreet. Certainly in summer she draws quite a crowd up there where you've been. Men with binoculars pretending to be bird-watchers. They even bring their lager and sandwiches. Ayrton thinks they *are* bird-watchers, and invites them to come and look at our reed warblers: can't understand why they say no and wish he'd go away.' She chuckled, and attacked the egg-stain again with her handkerchief. 'Oh, it's quite a local event on a warm afternoon, I can tell you. I've told the tourist people in Salisbury they should include it in our brochure. The Japanese never know what to do once they've photographed the cathedral, and they could so easily take in Concha on their way to Stonehenge, don't you think? There has to be something we Brits can teach the Japanese. After all, none of their women have breasts like that, do they? Flat as omelettes. No wonder they all worship the microchip.'

Emelda gave a conclusive nod, and picked up her empty basket.

'I must be off and find Ayrton some lunch,' she announced, yanking at Lloyd George, who was already finding his own among the roadside garbage.

Then suddenly she stopped.

'Oh, by the way, you mentioned Tom was reading some newspaper. Now, I saw something about him in the *Mail* this morning, didn't I?' Emelda gazed heavenwards as if her memory resided there. 'Some affair he had a while ago. Yes, that was it. Long before your time, of course, my dear. Sounded a load of nonsense, I must say, but it did make jolly good reading. All those things he used to do with mayonnaise in Los Angeles. Most ingenious: quite changed my view of the stuff. Much more interesting than Marlon Brando with his butter. What was the name of that film? *Last Tango in Paris*. Yes, that was the one.' She laughed delightedly. 'You know, I took Ayrton to see it, and he couldn't understand what was going on at all: merely said it looked more like margarine than butter to him, and how like the Americans not to be able to tell the difference. Must have been the last time I ever took him to the cinema. Left him to his dragonflies after that, the dear man.'

But I wasn't listening. I mumbled a goodbye to Emelda and hurried home in a state of panic.

So I'd been right about Tom's antics in the garden. I opened the front door to be met with a volley of blind fury directed at a newspaper which now lay spread across the kitchen table as if he had just murdered it. Tom was almost incoherent, his language reduced to the single word 'fuck', employed in every possible part of speech and delivered in clusters like grape-shot.

'What the fuck's the matter, Tom,' I said to keep him company.

With that his vocabulary dried up altogether, and he merely stabbed a finger at the offending page. I picked it up. It was the gossip column. The first thing that caught my eye was a photograph of a woman with a smile that ripped her face apart, and a body that was trying to explode from her dress. The caption read: 'Samantha – bursting for revenge.'

I read the piece in silence. It was still hot from Tom's eyes. The talk of California, it said, was the million-dollar palimony claim by 'beautiful actress-turned-chef Samantha Parsons against her former lover, English journalist Tom Brand. Curvaceous Ms Parsons', it went on, 'is insisting that the recipes in Mr Brand's best-selling seafood cookery-book *Prawnography* were created by her during the period when he was her live-in lover in Los Angeles.' The article then claimed that friends of Ms Parsons had recalled evenings at the Brand apartment when newly-invented dishes were sampled by guests as a prelude to what have been described as 'orgies'. There followed the reference to mayonnaise, and its unusual uses, to which Emelda had alluded. 'Mr Brand', the article concluded, 'had declined to comment.'

'Have you?' I asked, feeling somewhat stunned.

Tom was wearing his battered bear look, shoulders slumped, pacing up and down the room.

'No one's ever asked me. They don't know where I am, thank God. But the agency phone's been ringing non-stop, so Valerie says. She got through to me about half an hour ago. And d'you know, the bloody woman thinks it's *funny*? Particularly the mayonnaise bit. Says it'll boost sales no end. And she wanted to know if it was true.'

'And is it?' I asked.

The bear stopped pacing the room and looked at me almost pleadingly.

'No, not a word of it. I promise you. Not a single word. Samantha and I hardly ever gave parties, and if we did they were for *my* friends, not hers. And *I* did the cooking – always; Samantha would have given them salmonella poisoning, or worse. Anyway, she was usually drunk. As for mayonnaise, when I made that it was for fish, not fucking. It's . . . it's . . .' – Tom's hands were grasping at an imaginary neck – 'total crap. The woman's barking. She's certifiable.'

'But maybe she's also dangerous,' I said.

Tom was chewing his lip, hating to admit I might be right.

And then the phone rang. Tom put up his hands and backed away. I answered it cautiously. It was Scott Campbell in LA, not entirely sober and just back from a late party. Could he speak to Tom? It was important, he insisted.

I handed Tom the phone.

Tom listened with a blank expression on his face, saying very little. I made some coffee, and felt helpless and exasperated. Finally, I heard Tom say, 'Well, I'm coming over on Thursday. We'll talk about it then, and I'll see what Kollwitz has to say. Christ, he'd better have something to say.'

He replaced the receiver and was silent for a few moments while he sipped his coffee. Finally he managed to tell me what Scott had said. There were these people at the party he'd been to – media slobs who were rubbing their hands in glee over the whole Samantha business. It was wonderful copy; they couldn't get enough of it. No one could. Samantha was holding news conferences like other women give tupperware parties. Something for everyone every time. If you wanted tits, she gave you tits. If you wanted mayonnaise, she gave you mayonnaise. The latest offering was bananas: the story was that Tom used to enjoy watching her peel them. And there was something else he liked doing with lobsters – Scott couldn't remember precisely what. Of course everyone knew the bitch was making the whole thing up. But that didn't matter; it was terrific stuff. Scott's view was that she'd been looking at my less-than-demure illustrations for *Prawnography*, and was pretending that was the way it really had been – 'poetic injustice', as he put it.

But it was more serious than that, Scott explained. At least six people Samantha knew were now prepared to swear in court that everything in his book Tom owed to her – that he'd nicked the lot. Probably they all thought the case was a pushover, and they'd already agreed to a percentage of the blood-money. That was California for you. Tom had better get moving fast if everything he'd earned wasn't going to get drowned in a sea of mayonnaise.

There was one piece of good news. Scott had managed to locate Samantha's ex-husband.

The bad news was that the man had fled to a monastery. What was more, it was a silent order.

Tom groaned.

There was a heavy silence in the house all that day, as though we too had become a silent order.

As a gesture of normality I walked up to the village shop late in the afternoon to buy a few things I didn't need. The shopkeeper's wife looked up from the *Daily Mail* as I entered.

'Good evening Mrs Brand,' she said sharply. 'It's Hellman's you'll be wanting, I imagine.'

6

AIRPORT farewells are a kind of dying. I loathe them. Even 'darling, it's only for a few days' seemed a rash promise as Tom disappeared waving a boarding-card and a weathered passport. I felt bereft: too much that mattered passionately to me was being entrusted to those fresh-faced youths, dressed as pilots, who 'fly the friendly skies' as though there were no such things as electric storms, computer misinformation, semtex or – heaven help us – pilot error.

We are neither of us good at parting. We retreat into opposite extremes.

'Lady Caroline Lamb sent Byron a lock of her pubic hair when he was away,' was Tom's contribution to our fond last moments. 'Please don't feel you need do the same: she cut herself.'

Terrific!

For my part, I just tried hard not to burst into tears, and then did.

As I drove out of Heathrow on to the M4 I had an impulse to turn right towards London instead of westward for the rolling shires and 'home'. London knew me so well – comfortingly well. It had witnessed my good days and my bad days; it was where I'd been nourished, torn apart and healed; it had been my cradle and my bed. London had been a mirror I could always trust to tell me who I was. It was all my memories, all my past. But now the past had a 'For Sale' sign outside, just like the little house in Chiswick where I'd lived and fought with Harry, where I'd decorated Clive's bedroom in Tottenham Hotspurs' colours, where I'd played with Spindle the cat until the day she got run over, where I'd come home after sleeping with Tom for the first time, knowing he was the man I wanted to sleep with for ever.

I felt an urge to hurry back and tear the 'For Sale' sign down. Why should I bury my own past when the only reward was to be plunged deeper and deeper into Tom's?

Even at this moment he was leaving me at the rate of six hundred miles per hour in order to stir up a bit more of it.

Samantha, the fucking bitch! With her mayonnaise! I wished I could stick the stuff where it hurts, all fifty-seven varieties of it.

Just after the Basingstoke exit I caught sight of a roadside billboard which displayed a woman locked in a prison cell with a pack of nightmare monsters. They were supposed to represent the horrors of indigestion. I didn't suffer from indigestion, but I did understand about nightmare monsters. Mine were female: they were from Tom's private zoo, and someone had left the cage door open. I was reminded of our conversation early that morning. Tom always brings me tea in bed, then comes up with some off-the-wall comment I'm too sleepy to respond to. Today's offering was: 'You know, Jan, I don't think I have so much in common with Lord Byron after all. Except in one respect: we both woke up one day to find ourselves famous – the difference being that Byron was twenty-four and had written a romantic poem. I was fifty-four and had written a cookery book.'

He sighed as if the comparison did him scant justice.

'And both of you were plagued by women as a result,' I said grumpily and half-awake.

'Ah,' Tom said, slurping at his tea, 'but there's another difference. Byron's women all wanted to marry him; mine are women I've already married – in the eyes of God at least.'

'I hope for your sake God turns a blind eye,' I muttered. 'I wish I could.'

It hadn't been the best way to begin the day. And driving home alone past Basingstoke wasn't making it much better. I thought about the days ahead while Tom was away, and what I'd be doing. Christ, the builders would be turning up at sparrow's fart tomorrow to start work on the mill house. And the mysterious Mr Minton was arriving for lunch to sign me up for a children's book to illustrate. I suppose I should have felt flattered to have this publishing hotshot pursuing my talents. You *are* flattered. Don't be so snooty, I told myself, even if he does turn out to be a bloodless old wimp reeking of the Groucho Club. I was perfectly happy for him to notice that I'm pretty and wear no wedding-ring, if that improves his offer.

Between Andover and Amesbury I planned what to give Mr Minton for lunch, and wondered whether inside this sweet little blonde which the world saw I had the heart of a real bitch. Then I thought of Tom and convinced myself it wasn't true.

South of Amesbury the road climbed among the ploughed prairies that were once Salisbury Plain, where Ayrton's namesake the Great Bustard used to flock, until his own ancestors – no doubt – shot them to extinction leaving only their image on the family crest. The road dipped and wound among fields that were emerald green with winter wheat, straddled by pylons whose cables wired up the sky. And over the last hill suddenly I could gaze down on our village, compact and dormant down there, asleep by the river. And there was our mill, as from tomorrow to be transformed into a home fit for our new life, assuming we were ever going to have a chance to live it.

At the sight of it I forgot about Minton and my polite dreams of seduction. I wanted Tom back. I wanted him back *now*. And I laughed as I remembered how we'd made love by the fire until it died down and we shivered, and Tom, still poking me, poked *it*.

My thoughts being invariably a chain of *non sequiturs*, the idea suddenly came to me that I wanted to give Tom a surprise. I would make his new study a place of wonder and delight. Ruth, when she'd come over last summer, had talked ecstatically about a shit-hot interior designer she'd met. If only she had a home of her own to let him loose on, she declared. Very beautiful and very young, she said, but a pure genius – 'a Raphael of the bedchamber'. I was sceptical, as ever, about Ruth's assessment of beautiful young men – 'genius' tends to be a synonym for 'prowess' – none the less I'd taken down his name and telephone number and promptly forgotten all about him.

But tomorrow I would phone him, send him photos of the room that was to become Tom's study overlooking the river, then wait and see what astonishing scheme he might come up with. I even remembered the man's name – Ashley de Vere. He sounded extremely aristocratic, and was no doubt extremely expensive. Never mind, I would do it. If Tom was to be Lord Byron, or Lord Byron's biographer – even if he settled for a Lord Byron cookery-book – then he'd better have a lordly environment in which to cultivate those fancies.

There was a familiar squelch of mud under the tyres as the car lurched through the potholes of our track which not even an estate agent would dare to describe as a drive. It was almost one o'clock. In a few moments I would help myself to a drink. I was alone. I realised I'd never been here alone.

I wasn't.

Three cars were parked side by side on the small area we'd gravelled to stifle the mud in front of the cottage. Before I had time to wonder what this visitation could possibly be about, six men converged on my car from behind walls and bushes. Three of them wielded note-books, while the others swooped on me with cameras as I opened the car door.

Instinctively I raised one hand in front of my face, and in that split-second I understood why so many press photographs show people doing exactly that, as if they were murderers caught red-handed. I was half in the car and half out, paralysed, eyes lowered in self-protection, and mumbling something, I had no idea what. Questions were being fired at me. I managed to stand up – did I smile? More photographs. I was aware of having a very short skirt, rucked up even shorter by the long drive. I tried to smooth it down, dropped the bag I was carrying, bent down to pick it up and realised they could probably see my breasts. More photographs. More questions. Had I said anything at all? Perhaps I had and I didn't know what.

I needed to pull myself together somehow. I could hear questions bouncing off me.

'Gentlemen,' I said (why on earth did I went to flatter them?), 'Yes, I *am* Janice Blakemore.'

My answers came out in a volley.

'Yes, I do live with Tom Brand.'

'No, we're not married.'

'No, he's not here.'

'No, he's not hiding anywhere; he's in California seeing lawyers.'

'What d'you mean, "Is it true about the orgies?" I wasn't there; you must ask him.'

'No, I won't tell you where he's staying.'

'No, he's not still having an affair with Mrs Parsons.'

'Yes, I *am* quite sure.'

'The mayonnaise? How would I know if it's true? I doubt it very much.'

'No, we only use it as salad dressing.'

'Bananas? Everyone peels them, don't they? How else are you supposed to eat them, for Christ's sake?'

'Lobster! I've no idea what Tom used to do with lobsters! Boil them, presumably.'

'No, you certainly can't photograph our bedroom, and even if you could you wouldn't find any lobsters there. Nor anything else to excite your dirty little minds. Now why don't you just fuck off?'

'Yes, I know you have a job to do; try getting a better one.'

'No! Goodbye, gentlemen!'

There were more photographs as they scurried backwards to get between me and the front door. I realised that they must have caught me crying. There was nothing I could do. I couldn't help it. I just sobbed – for the second time that day.

Then they'd gone.

I was still crying as I poured myself a large vodka and tonic. Then I remembered Ruth saying once, 'If you ever get doorstopped, darling, make sure you smile deliciously and say absolutely nothing except, "Good morning".' Well, at least I'd called them gentlemen, even if I had told them to fuck off.

Oh God, I thought, what photographs would they use – the legs, the breasts, or the tears?

And who *were* they, anyway? If they said, I never listened.

It was then I caught sight of a note Mrs Teape had left. At this moment it was something I could have done without. Mrs Teape once told me she had great trouble understanding the principle of capital letters, and it had taken many years before she'd got it right. As a result she'd now settled into the steady rhythm of writing the first letter of every word in capitals. Sometimes she'd vary this procedure by making the last letter a capital as well. To add to the confusion, where capital letters were actually necessary she tended to omit them altogether. There was never a hint of punctuation to spoil the flow. Mrs Teape's bizarre messages were an art form, and decoding them was like trying to understand someone talking non-stop with chronic hiccups. Fortunately the note was brief.

'Dear mrs brand,' it began, 'i Hope i Did Right Three Young Gentlemen From londoN Called While i Was Dusting AskinG For mr brand And YourselF Seeing As They Had Driven All This Way i Made Them Tea i Hope You Dont MinD But i Thought It Must Be About You Becoming A Minister In mr majors GovernmenT they Swore They Didnt Know AnythinG About That And It Was SomethinG Else They Wanted To Know perhaps You Have Another Little SecreT mrs brand But As ive Always Said i Wont Be A nosey parker we Need More persil And mr muscle Please KindlY Yours Nora Teape.'

By some mistake she'd got the capitals right in the end. It was the first time I knew her first name was Nora.

Banishing from my thoughts all the other possible things Mrs Teape may have said to the 'Three Young Gentlemen', I decided I was in need of a very quiet afternoon.

I should have known by now that decisions like that are fatal. Around two-thirty there was a knock at the door. Concerned that it might be more reporters, I peered cautiously through the bathroom window. But there was no car. I could see no one. A little fearfully I opened the front door an inch or two. The figure standing before me could have walked straight out of an early *Punch* cartoon. Two large feet were planted a yard apart on the gravel. Above them, a pair of slender legs disappeared into plus-fours, which in turn vanished under a Norfolk jacket whose pockets bulged sideways like donkey panniers. A tongue flickered to and fro across a moist slit of a mouth, each traverse narrowly missing an eagle's beak of a nose on whose bridge rested the brim of a tweed hat. I could detect no eyes. The man was carrying a large wicker basket in one hand, while the other grasped what looked at first sight to be a sheaf of thin saplings.

I had no need to ask. Ayrton Bustard had come fishing.

'Good afternoon, madam,' he said, offering a little bob of the head. The tongue flickered more vigorously. 'Mr Brand, is he at home, I wonder?'

I explained that he wasn't.

'But do please come in,' I said.

He shook his head almost fiercely. Several dewdrops were sprayed to the left and right.

'No, no. You're most kind. But no,' he exclaimed. 'I was just hoping I might enjoy a little sport with your husband.'

I felt like commenting that all the people who'd done that up to now had been women. Emelda would have enjoyed that, but not, I imagined, Ayrton. So I explained that Tom was in California, and wouldn't be back for several days.

Ayrton nodded sadly, and this time a dewdrop fell vertically.

'A pity. I never seem to be in luck,' he said, half-turning to leave.

Again I invited him in, and offered him tea.

'You're very kind, but no,' he insisted. Then he paused. 'But would you mind, I wonder,' he added, 'if I had a little inspection of your water?' He made it sound like a urine test, and I fought back a smile. 'So clever of your husband to have acquired the best stretch of fishing for miles. He must be very skilled with the rod.'

Indeed, I thought. And look at the trouble we're in as a result.

It was impossible not to be fond of Ayrton. Emelda, while being frightful about him, always referred to him so affectionately as 'the dear man'. And he was a dear man. I decided to put on my coat and accompany him. He led the way eagerly towards the river, his stooped shoulders projecting the long nose towards the water as if he were sniffing for trout.

After peering for a while, Ayrton appeared satisfied.

'Yes, they're rising nicely,' he said. 'As soon as your husband's back . . .'

Then he turned to me almost buoyantly.

'Emelda tells me his name was most prominent in the papers. How very interesting. I never read them myself, but may I enquire as to the subject? Fishing, perhaps? Does he write about fishing? I should most like to read it.'

'Not exactly fishing,' I said. 'He's in California seeing lawyers.'

Aryton nodded approvingly, carefully trapping a dewdrop on Mr Toad's handkerchief.

'As a fisherman he must know California well, of course, your husband.' And he gave another nod, dispersing another dewdrop. 'Clever people, the Americans. Remarkably knowledgeable about dragon-flies, you know.'

'Really!' I said.

'Oh yes! Especially the *Zygopterae*, which you wouldn't expect, would you?'

I shook my head hopefully.

'No, I suppose not.'

He gave a satisfied grunt, and then picked up his rods and wicker basket.

'Well, I've been keeping you too long with my chatter. I'll await your husband's return.' And he touched the brim of his hat politely with his hand. Then, as he turned to leave he tilted his head, and his eyes gave a quick scan of the trees along the river-bank. There was another grunt. 'Heard the chiff-chaff yet, have you, I wonder?' he added.

I looked bewildered: what the hell was a chiff-chaff? But Ayrton didn't seem to notice.

'Earliest of all the migrants. Once he's here, then I know spring has come. Brave little fellow, the chiff-chaff, I always think. Wouldn't you agree?'

I murmured something, but Ayrton was already loping across the grass, rod over his shoulder, still glancing at the trees from time to time.

'Good day, madam,' he called out. 'And thank you for your excellent company. My deep respects to your husband. I look forward to sharing his water.'

I turned away so as not to laugh.

The afternoon continued the way it had begun, except that now the interruptions were more sinister. Approximately every ten minutes the phone rang. The first time there was silence – not even heavy breathing, just silence. Exactly the same happened the second time, and I replaced the receiver more rapidly. When it rang again and there was silence, I slammed the phone down. By now I was thoroughly rattled. I was alone in the house. Tom was x-thousands miles away at 35,000 feet. I'd been doorstopped by tabloid gossip-hounds all morning. Now I was being haunted by a phantom caller. For the first time in my life I felt paranoid.

Then it rang a fourth time. I pumped myself up, seized the phone, and without waiting for the silence, yelled 'Go and fuck yourself!' I gazed down at the receiver triumphantly for a second or two – just long enough to detect a faltering woman's voice enquire 'Is that Mrs Brand?'

I swallowed.

'It is,' I said as calmly as I could. 'Who is that?'

'Wendy. Wendy Normington,' came the answer, the voice beginning to recover itself.

Oh God!

'Well, hello!' I said shakily. 'I'm sorry, we got some sort of crossed line.'

'Yes. indeed.' I could tell she didn't believe it, and felt awful. What on earth could I do?

'I'm just trying to arrange another evening when you and your husband can come to dinner,' she continued.

The only thing I could do was what I did.

'Of course,' I said weakly. 'How very nice. We'd like that.'

Through a fog of misery I heard myself agree to an evening the following week. I seemed to hear some mention of a former governor of Bermuda, and the chairman of something fizzy.

'Charming people,' Wendy assured me. 'You probably know the Mogg-Barlows.'

You bet I didn't.

'It won't be dressy; just informal,' she added. 'That's the way we like it.'

Fancy dress or stark naked, I couldn't imagine any way I was going to like it. As for Tom, even now getting pissed Club Class over the Arctic Circle, I dreaded what he would have to say.

Oh London; please let me get back to London, I thought as I put the phone down. This was the worst thing about the country: you were forever being collected by people who in London you wouldn't even know existed, and who certainly wouldn't notice your existence. Here it was: the oasis mentality – share my date-palm!

I slumped down in a chair, still wondering who the phantom caller might have been. A wave of anxiety struck me. Perhaps it was the airline trying to tell me Tom's plane was missing over the Atlantic. Or Clive's school informing me he'd been expelled again. Or my mother, unable to tell me she'd suffered a stroke.

Then the phone went once more. This time it was my estate agent in Chiswick. He had a serious buyer for my house, he announced. The price I'd asked was agreed, and the survey was fine. They were cash buyers, what was more; no chain of other purchasers down the line and out of sight, not even any mortgage requirement. The perfect situation, the agent assured me: all most unusual in the middle of a recession; it really couldn't be better. There were just a number of small details to be cleared up before contracts could be exchanged. So, could I possibly come up and meet the clients? They were about to go skiing, but would be back within a couple of weeks. Might that be convenient?

It felt as though my life-line was about to be cut. Goodbye London!

'All right,' I said. 'Why don't you ring me when they're back?'

I couldn't help hoping he never would; that the buyers might conveniently fall down a glacier; that he'd meet someone like Ruth on the ski-slopes and then be caught in mid-*après-ski*; that she'd develop an incurable passion to live in Hawaii; that they'd both have simultaneous brain tumours. Anything. Anything at all.

I made myself some tea. I had half a mind to make it a double Scotch, but feared I might become maudlin. I blew at the steam rising from the cup, and gazed out of the window in a listless way.

Then the phone went yet again. I picked it up, thinking it might just possibly be a friend this time. There was a crackle and a few distant bleeps, then snatches of far-off conversations in various foreign languages; perhaps I'd been connected to the United Nations. I said 'Hello' several times, and was about to replace the receiver when a male voice shouted at me through the ear-piece in French.

'*Allo! Monsieur Brand?*'

My French is not up to conversing with someone who thinks I'm a man. I got as far as '*Non!*', then broke into English.

'Who is it?'

There followed a further confusion of sounds, and a prolonged clearing of the throat.

'Ee is not there, *Monsieur Brand?*'

'No, ee is not there or here,' I said. 'Who is it speaking?'

'This is Professor Montblanc from the *Université de Montpellier*,' the voice continued. 'I telephone on the suggestion of Mrs Brand. Who are you, please?'

I was already seeing red. Today was getting worse and worse.

'This *is* Mrs Brand,' I said firmly.

'*C'est impossible, madame.* Mrs Brand is 'ere in Montpellier.'

'There are a great many Mrs Brands, *monsieur*,' I explained, wondering how I was going to get out of this. 'Of varying ages and states of sanity.'

'Ah, *maintenant je comprends.*' There was a note of relief in the man's voice. 'So, you are his mother – naturally.'

I don't know whether Professor Montblanc heard me laughing or not, but now he'd established that I was Tom's mother he proceeded to deliver a lengthy message for me to pass on to my son who – I explained – was away on business. He was, he assured me, an embryologist – an eminent embryologist, he made quite clear. His special interest was animals, *les animaux mis en danger*, which was how he had come into contact with

Mrs Brand – *une très grande conversatrice, bien sûr*. We were well aware, he understood, of the plight of the Madagascan vampire bat. The *crise* for these unfortunate creatures was the severe depletion in the number of male bats. Accordingly he was planning to set up a project for a *banque de sperme* for these creatures – a difficult and costly enterprise due not only to the deadly nature of the *chauve-souris* in question, but also to the miniscule size of its sexuals organs. The professor was certain I would be able to explain to my son the exceptional value of this project, and the vital need for funds to support it. He himself would shortly be in England for meetings with the World Wildlife Fund – who had so far been sadly unforthcoming on the matter – and would be pleased to visit *Monsieur Brand* at his home to discuss his contribution. Would I kindly convey Mrs Brand's greetings and respects to her husband, and his own trust that *Monsieur Brand* would very shortly become the *grand sauveur de la chauve-souris vampire de Madagascar*.

Before ringing off I requested that Professor Montblanc should extend to Mrs Brand the most cordial wishes from her mother-in-law, knowing that even someone as stupid as Anne-Marie was likely to remember that Tom's mother had died when he was three.

I desperately needed to get out of the house. It was early evening, and the mist was beginning to rise from the river, spreading like buttermilk across the damp fields. I pulled on my gumboots and an anorak, and suddenly wished I had a dog to accompany me. Perhaps we should get one: a dog that had a special loathing of retired naval commanders and their wives; a dog that would savage all endangered species; a dog that would cock its leg against palimony lawyers and their over-endowed clients. A dog that would love and protect me from the lot of them.

It was soft and lush along the river-bank. Water-voles were doing a ferry service this way and that, leaving V-shaped ripples in the water. There were squawks from the reed-beds that no doubt would have excited Ayrton. A swan glided silently through the mist. It was lovely here. How could I make life match it?

I wished Tom were here. He'd be landing in LA about now. Tonight he'd ring. That would be the one phone call of the day I would welcome. I should miss him in my bed tonight.

It was dusk by the time I returned. I would have a large drink – several large drinks; then make myself an omelette and try to forget everything about today except saying goodbye to Tom at the airport and hearing him say 'darling, it's only for a few days'.

And tomorrow I'd be meeting Howard Minton. Serious talk. Work. I'd bend my mind to that – to keep it sane.

As I turned the key in the lock I glanced towards the river. I could just make out a figure on the bridge. I gave a start, then realised it was Mooncalf. She was there again. What *did* she want? I felt a spurt of anger and on impulse ran down the path towards her, waving my arms for her to stay. But seeing me, she slipped away into the woods.

It seemed a fitting end to the shittiest of days.

*

I woke early, eyes glazed with too little sleep. Tom's phone-call from LA never came through until two in the morning, due of all things to an earthquake which had thrown local services into confusion. He sounded cheerful, had already convinced himself that the quake symbolised his arrival, and made some crude remark about Samantha's San Andreas Fault and the tremors to be felt along the whole length of it by the local press corps and anyone else who cared to explore. He then became more serious and assured me he was seeing Abram Kollwitz first thing in the morning.

I told him about the press doorstopping me, and he swore.

'Why the hell are they pestering you? I'm the one who's supposed to be in trouble.'

'Because I've got better legs,' I suggested.

I could hear him chuckle. But he didn't think that was a particularly good reason.

'I miss you,' I said.

'What do you miss?'

'Your arms around me.'

'Nothing else?'

'Yes, but I'm not letting on in case it throws the local services into even greater confusion.'

Tom laughed and sounded sexy. I didn't tell him about the Normington dinner-party, nor about the mad professor from Montpellier who thought I was Tom's mother. They could wait. I explained that the builders were coming in the morning, and that we'd soon have the house of our dreams.

'I only have one dream,' he said.

I'd melted into sleep after that.

The memory of Tom's phonecall was overcast by thoughts of what the morning tabloids might bring. I didn't dare go and buy them from the village shop, so I decided to drive into Salisbury. It wasn't even eight o'clock yet, I'd be back well before the builders turned up around nine, and well in time to hide anything embarrassing in the papers from Mrs Teape.

The first shop I found was close to the station. Ahead of me – and very soon a long way behind me – was a queue of unsmiling commuters in dark suits waiting to purchase their *Daily Telegraph* and *Financial Times*. The shopkeeper, an expressionless Indian, was handing them out almost without asking. When it came to my turn I realised I didn't know which papers to buy, and there seemed a vast number of tabloids spread across the counter. Clearly I had to get the lot. Conscious of shuffling feet behind me, and watches being consulted, I snatched one from each pile as quickly as I could. A puffy-faced young man behind me in the queue reached over my shoulder for his *F.T.* and, with a patronising glance, said, 'Having a serious read today, are we?' There was a snigger behind him.

I now had an armful of about a dozen tabloids. I could scarcely hold them. And how could I reach for my purse? More people were pushing past me for the *F.T.* or the *Telegraph*, looking at me with some amusement. The Indian shopkeeper registered no amusement at all. I was still struggling to get at my purse.

Then I realised I hadn't brought it. I didn't have a penny on me. I moved hastily to one side to let the queue advance, and walked straight into a postcard rack. Snoopy cards split over the floor. As I tried to pick them up, newspapers began to slither from my grasp page by page, like autumn leaves, all over the floor.

I'd had more than enough. I abandoned the Snoopy cards, dumped the mess of newspapers on the counter and hurried out of the shop. A man with a belly and a bow-tie smirked as he opened the door for me with exaggerated courtesy.

'Had a rough night, then, dear?' There was a strong stench of after-shave as the man turned to his companion with a laugh: 'Lover-boy obviously didn't pay up before he left, did he?' he added loudly.

Everyone laughed. I managed a sweet smile and crunched the door on his fingers as I left.

By the time I was back at Sarum Magna I was feeling calmer. It even seemed quite funny. But not for long. It was a quarter to nine. The builders' truck was already parked outside on the gravel, and my front-door was open. Mrs Teape saw me coming and hurried out with a beatific smile.

'Oh, Mrs Brand,' she announced, 'I saw the builders arrive and you weren't there, so I came over quickly and let them in as it was raining: I hope you don't mind. And I'm making them some tea.' She was looking unusually pleased with herself. 'And I've left them with the papers. The gentlemen yesterday told me who they wrote for, so I went out and bought all three papers specially, knowing you'd be mentioned. I wanted them to know what an important person you were, so you'd get good service. I used to say just the same to Mrs Normington. It never does any harm to tell people who you are. Class is class, I always say.'

And she made an emphatic jab at her hair with her comb, as if to thrust home the point.

I hurried into the house.

Half a dozen builders were sprawled round the table in the living-room. None of them looked up. They seemed unaware of my existence. And then I saw why. Spread among a great many tattooed arms were three tabloids, each of them opened to reveal photographs of myself. Yesterday I'd wondered which photos they might use – my legs, my breasts, or my tears.

There was one of each.

As I stood there they began passing the papers round. Still they didn't notice me. I watched them. There was a silence of horrible concentration. Then one of them made a growling noise in his throat.

'Cor! Look at that, Fred!'

And he thumped a forefinger on the table. I winced. It was the shot of me struggling to get out of the car feet first.

'Got good legs, 'asn't she?'

There was a general murmur of approval.

'Yeah!' the others echoed. 'Great!'

Another of the men removed a pencil from behind his ear and peered closer at the paper in front of him. Then he glanced up at the others and grinned.

'Pretty good all over, I'd say.'

It was the photo of me bending over and revealing all.

'Yeah!' said the first one. 'Wouldn't mind getting me 'ands on those tits.'

There was a snigger all round. Mrs Teape appeared at the door with mugs of tea on a tray. I took it from her and walked over to the table with a smile.

'Perhaps you'd also like to get your hands round these.'

The men looked up, recognised me, and froze. I handed round the mugs. The 'tit' man mumbled something that sounded like an apology.

'That's quite all right,' I said, and with a jerk of the wrist tipped the mug of hot tea cleanly over his crotch.

He leapt up with a gasp.

'Oh dear!' I exclaimed. 'What a cock-up! Never mind! I expect you always wanted to be called "Hot-rod".'

The others hid their embarrassment in laughter, glancing at me with looks of amazement and grinning delightedly at the stricken Hot-rod. Then they gulped their tea and shambled awkwardly after him into the rain. I noticed the foreman's car was just pulling up next to their truck.

'Thanks for the tea,' several of them called out.

Mrs Teape was busy folding the papers neatly into a pile, and clearing away the mugs.

'A bit rough round here, some of them,' she said sharply. 'Country folk.'

And she bustled away into the kitchen.

Howard Minton was due at midday. I didn't feel in much of a state to receive anybody – even less so with Teapot chattering away while I prepared lunch. I told her I'd be happy for her to leave early, anxious to avoid any further indiscretions.

'Are you quite sure, Mrs Brand? I'd be perfectly happy to stay and serve lunch.'

I shuddered at the thought of Mrs Teape telling Minton I was about to be a cabinet minister in Mr Major's government. I also prayed that so superior a publisher didn't stoop to reading the tabloids.

'Absolutely sure, Mrs Teape. Thank you.'

She looked disappointed.

It was eleven-thirty. So, what should I wear? Minton was sure to have a concave chest and dandruff: none the less I needed to make an impression. After all, this was my new life – successful freelance artist courted by serious publisher. The disreputable illustrator of *Prawnography* was a creature of the past.

I settled for tight jeans and a gorgeous Joseph jumper I'd treated myself to on the day my divorce came through – pink and baggy, with huge embroidered roses. I love it. Heads turn at a hundred yards. Sexy, but not openly so; and calculated to look casual. And at the last minute of course – a touch of Giorgio.

I laughed. I was about to give my first business lunch.

A bottle of white Mâcon Villages was in the fridge. Lunch was under clingfilm on the kitchen table. The builders were busy next door – I could hear the sound of a transistor radio. Mrs Teape had gone. Tom was tens of thousands of miles away. It was midday.

It was ten past twelve.

It was twenty past twelve.

No Minton.

Another hurried touch of Giorgio.

Then the phone went. It was the builders' office in Salisbury. Was everything to my satisfaction?

'Yes!'

Would I mind giving a message to the foreman?

'Can it wait till this afternoon?' – Oh Jesus, hurry up! – 'All right, if it's brief.'

It wasn't brief. A white Alfa Romeo drew up as I was still writing the message down. The man on the phone was droning on, saying the same thing three times. Finally, I said 'Sorry, I have to go.'

The doorbell rang while I was still explaining that I *really* did have to go. It rang a second time.

At the door, bearing a smile and a large bunch of flowers, stood the young Harrison Ford.

7

LATER, the telephone was hot with Ruth's curiosity. I should never have mentioned Howard Minton's visit.

'How old did you say he was?'

'Thirtyish; perhaps even less,' I said. 'Alarmingly young, anyway.'

'And alarmingly attractive. High-flyer. Unmarried. Well, my darling, what are you going to do about it?'

I said I intended to do absolutely nothing. I had Tom, and I wanted Tom.

'Yes, yes, of course.' Ruth's voice was becoming brisk. 'But wants can be plural, don't you think? It's nice to have a change of menu, even if you decide not to order anything from it. Did Mr Minton fancy you?'

I said I thought he did, and Ruth sounded pleased.

'So he likes older women. That's always good news at our age. And he offered you a job as well?'

'Several, it would seem,' I said. 'Starting with Hilaire Belloc: you know – "Matilda who told such dreadful lies".'

'And how many dreadful lies are you prepared to tell Tom, I wonder?'

'None,' I said. 'Well, only white ones.'

Ruth laughed.

'Does that include off-white ones?'

Ruth, who has a husband she loves dearly, swears none the less that to be truly happy in marriage one must be truly happy outside marriage. Lovers are a way of life for Ruth, and fidelity a way of death: her marriage would die of it, she insists. The Aids scare, far from curbing her lifestyle, has merely made her safaris more selective and her precautions more thorough. God knows what gets popped into the diplomatic bag bound for Liechtenstein.

'I've never wanted to sleep with a publisher,' she went on pensively. I tried to explain that I didn't want to either, but Ruth was already launched on her own train of thought. 'A curious profession, publishing; always dealing in other people's passions, never their own. Makes you wonder if they have any. It must be like being fucked by proxy – D. H. Lawrence tonight, Tolstoy tomorrow. I suppose it makes for variety, though. Perhaps I should try. Why don't you send your Mr Minton out here? I could write him a very small guide-book on Liechtenstein as a return favour – or even a large guide-book if his favours are large enough. Perhaps you'd find out for me.'

By the time she rang off I'd told her almost nothing about Howard Minton, and felt relieved. I had no particular plans to seduce my new publisher.

But – Jesus! – it would have been easy. And I had to admit that he was extraordinarily handsome. A mop of dark hair. Striking cheekbones. Sensuous mouth. Dangerous eyes – I thought of Tom's 'Greek olives' and smiled; at which point Howard looked at me, obviously wondering what I was smiling at, and whether it might perhaps be some sort of invitation. Then he went on looking, no doubt hoping he'd find out.

It was one of those powerful moments when one stands at a crossroads with absolute freedom of choice. I could go any way I wished. With Howard's eyes boring into me I realised I'd been here on countless occasions before and, at different times in my life, must have taken all the paths available to me. When I was at art school and hysterically virginal, each of those paths had seemed deliciously dangerous, so much so that I'd panic and hurry back the way I'd come – which usually meant a swift visit to the loo – after which I'd curse myself for being such a coward.

Meeting Harry had been rather different. I wasn't offered a choice at all. He just frogmarched me up the path which led straight to his bedroom and, not long after that, to the registry office, swiftly followed by the maternity ward.

After that came the years of being a model wife, when all eye-meets were instantly cut short by a demure lowering of the lids; and the only path to be taken was the straight and narrow one back to the marital bed, even though Harry was quite likely to be usurping some other man's marital bed at the time.

Then the post-Harry fiesta. And suddenly none of the paths was in the least straight or narrow, and on the principle that all roads led to Rome there invariably seemed to be some other woman's marital bed waiting for me at the end of them – which was perfectly all right as far as I was concerned, provided she wasn't actually in it at the time.

And now? I was perplexed to realise that the situation was an entirely new one for me. Here in front of me was a gorgeously attractive man. I fancied him a lot – of course I did. It would be wonderful to have an affair: I would only have to hold the eye-meet until it scorched. The house was empty. The afternoon was long. The path to my bed was short and beckoning; the only sign-posting it required was the mere raising of an eyebrow. Ruth wouldn't even have given it a second thought.

I scarcely gave it a first. I lowered my gaze.

'Have you ever met Tom?' I asked with a smile, as he touched my hand as though by accident.

'I believe not,' he said, removing it.

'You must come down next time when he's here.'

'I'd like that.'

So, Howard Minton was a man who understood the rules of the game very well, and clearly knew them by heart, as I was sure most of the female staff of his prestigious publishing house would be able to attest.

But he was very, very attractive.

I told Ruth as little of this as I could get away with, and I certainly had no intention of telling Tom. Absence permits its own discrete license, and I was happy to guard a flirtatious secret between myself and my new young publisher, which could sit quietly on the back-burner. I had no intention of turning up the heat. Those days were over, and I was relieved that they were. I wanted Tom back. Tonight he would ring me and tell me when that would be.

If I'd asked Tom to nominate his least favourite way of spending a first evening back from California he might well have said 'dinner with the Normingtons'.

'Guess what!' I said, trying to sound breezy.

Then I told him.

Jet-lag didn't do much for his sense of humour. It didn't help reminding him that he'd returned two days later than he intended; he put on his Frankie Howerd face and moaned gently. At first he said he wouldn't go to the dinner-party at all.

'Tell them I'm knackered. Tell them I've got Llasa Fever. Tell them I'm a violent dypsomaniac. Tell them having dinner with the navy makes me seasick. Tell them anything.'

It's never any use reasoning with Tom in this mood. I've learnt to agree.

'All right. I'll tell them all that, and go alone. You can field the phone calls tomorrow – including the invitation for me to spend next weekend on a luxury yacht.'

Tom looked sour. 'I suppose it's DJ, is it? Medals. I'll wear my old nuclear disarmament badge.'

I told him it was informal.

'Well, that's one relief.'

Tom's interpretation of 'informal' was to put on jeans and a T-shirt I'd bought him in Italy decorated with a photomontage of Prince Charles placing his hand on Princess Di's naked tit – which I thought was an unlikely scenario, but Tom was delighted with it.

'I'm not sure it's *that* informal,' I said.

'Sod it.'

Tom compromised by adding a loose cardigan which hid the offending tit and showed a patriotic double portrait of our heir apparent and smiling queen-to-be.

'All right?'

I said it was all right so long as he didn't stretch, or unbutton it.

Tom then looked on with curiosity to see what I considered appropriate to wear for an evening with the navy. He offered the occasional helpful suggestion.

'You could match me by going topless, of course, then I could place my hand on your breast just like Prince Charles. That would show our solidarity with the royals, wouldn't it? The Royal Navy would approve of that.'

'Thank you, Tom.'

I settled for black satiny leggings – very tight – and a yellow silk blouse with a black leather laced belt.

'Christ, you've got a tiny waist, Jan.'

'Get your hands off me,' I said, pushing him away.

I piled my hair up and put on dangly black earrings. Finally, black heeled shoes.

Tom was making bedroom noises.

'No, we can't just "have it off before we go", as you delicately put it. We're late as it is, Tom,' I insisted. 'You know perfectly well you'll enjoy it.'

'I'd enjoy making love to you much more. It's been nearly a week.'

'That's your fault for pissing off to California. Then this morning you went straight to sleep saying you were too tired and couldn't possibly get it up. Makes me wonder what exactly you *were* doing in Los Angeles.' I looked at him questioningly. 'You've still hardly told me anything, you know.'

It was raining, so we took the car.

'There's very little to tell,' Tom said in a resigned voice, pulling out into the pitch-black village street – not a soul around. 'Kollwitz is absolutely clear. Samantha has the case nicely stitched up unless we can somehow get that "ex" of hers to talk. There's no one else: I spent three days searching.'

'Can't we get the man subpoenaed? Prime witness and all that?' I suggested.

'Kollwitz has been through all that. The answer's no! This is not a criminal action. Now, if Samantha were accusing me of physical violence it'd be different.'

'Is it too late?' I asked. 'How about a sharp kick in the groin. Maybe she'd change her plea.'

Tom didn't answer. We were turning into the Normingtons' drive. Two other cars were already parked crisply on the gravel – a Rover and a vintage Bentley, both glistening darkly in the rain under the light of twin lanterns from the pseudo-Georgian porch.

Tom held the umbrella over us as we made for the front door, shivering.

'Think of it,' he said in that I-am-going-to-the-gas-chamber voice of his. 'Here I am about to sip sherry with the wife of the retired Governor of Bermondsey, or wherever it was. ('*Bermuda*, Tom,' I reminded him.) And only yesterday I was sweltering in the Mojave Desert trying to persuade a community of fruitcakes in togas to

144

let me talk to "Brother Michael" – that's what Samantha's "ex" calls himself now. The Brotherhood of Divine Witnesses: would you believe it? Finally I asked the Father Superior or whatever he calls himself – "How about being an *earthly* witness for once? Sod your flying saucers." It was probably the wrong thing to have said. Anyway he motioned me to leave at once, and flicked incense around where I'd stood.'

Tom paused while he pressed the doorbell.

'Perhaps if I'm lucky they'll motion me to leave here too,' he added with a laugh.

Oh God, I thought, it's going to be one of those evenings.

We got through the introductions all right. Apart from Commander Normington and his wife – our hosts – there were just two other couples. The retired Governor of Bermuda was grey all over with a mouth that scarcely moved while he spoke, as if more accustomed to speaking with his nose. He was called Fludde – Sir Hector Fludde – which came out as a nasal echo. Lady Fludde, in matching grey, stood a little behind and to one side of her husband with hands softly folded, a habit formed I imagined from attending countless ceremonial parades. Tom surprised me by being charming to them both, even if he did persist in referring to Bermuda as Bermondsey, which didn't go down particularly well. He even managed to sip his thimble of sherry as though it was his favourite tipple, though I saw his eyes roving to the drinks tray several times to see whether anything more bracing might be on offer.

It wasn't.

The other couple were the Mogg-Barlows. He was a crisp little man with a watery and wandering eye which surveyed my breasts a great deal but never his wife's, which was just as well since she had none as far as I could tell. She was dressed in a discreet little black number with a skirt which ended nicely at mid-knee. Mrs Mogg-Barlow was a plaster-cast of a company chairman's wife. I could tell from the fixed sadness of her smile that every rung of her husband's promotion to the top had been engraved with the initials of ladies who did *not* wear discreet little black numbers with skirts which ended nicely at mid-knee. The air of quiet resignation about her suggested that her one consolation was that before long she would be Lady Mogg-Barlow, and all those other little ladies would not.

Tom was already bored and wishing we could at least get on with the food and – more to the point – the wine. He had a hunted look on his face, and occasionally gave me a desperate wink. Conversation was wearing so thin I resorted to commenting on the nibbles that Wendy Normington was busily passing round.

'Good nuts,' I announced loudly.

Tom looked surprised and said 'Thank you!' equally loudly.

I corpsed.

Sir Hector drew on his experience of the colonial service to offer a distraction by drawing attention to Tom's T-shirt. He affected a sudden bonhomie.

'I must say I rather like this new casual wear,' he was saying between razor lips. 'Good likeness of their royal

146

highnesses, what's more, wouldn't you say, Normington? Where d'you get it from, Mr Brand, if I may ask?'

Tom explained that I'd bought it for him in Italy.

'Italy! well, well!' The eyebrows rose in surprise. 'Don't think of the Eyeties as monarchists exactly, do you? I suppose they must admire our ancient institutions, not having too many of their own.' He peered a little closer. 'Yes, most respectful.'

By now everyone was admiring Tom's T-shirt.

But Sir Hector's curiosity wasn't entirely satisfied, and he stretched out a hand to touch the fabric.

'How the devil have they done it, then? Taken from a photograph, I suppose. Darned clever!'

And he moved Tom's cardigan aside to appreciate the complete image. The naked breast with the royal hand placed upon it met the gaze of seven people.

There was a rumble around the drawing-room as of a distant thunderstorm, punctuated by much coughing. Lady Fludde said 'Aoh!'

Wendy Normington did her best to recover the evening, announcing dinner and scurrying round her guests like a sheepdog. There were place-names. I noticed that Sir Hector's surname was spelt 'Ffludde'. Tom noticed it too, and I saw him rehearsing how a four-letter word would sound beginning with two f's.

After polite manoeuvring we sat down to some murky soup which Tom and I gratefully tucked into until the silence round the table told us Commander Normington was waiting to say grace. We wiped our mouths and exchanged appalled glances, mumbling the half-forgotten words. After another ocean of silence, small glasses of claret were poured. Tom fell on his like a man who has just crossed the Empty Quarter. I saw Wendy looking at him icily.

'Mr Brand, surely you'd like to save some for the main course?'

But Tom's glass was empty, and remained so.

And so did the evening. The sound of knives and forks was deafening.

Towards the merciful end of dinner there was a temporary revival which did little to improve Tom's spirits. The Normington's dog, no doubt enflamed by the sight of Tom's T-shirt, developed a sudden passion for his left leg and decided to rape it. For a while Tom ignored the thrustings going on down below, every so often throwing me glances of dismay and horror which I took to be comments on the company or the goulash we had just been subjected to; until finally he decided he'd had enough. He rose and lifted the besieged leg aloft for all to see, the dog dangling and still thrusting away in mid-air.

The situation brought out the best in Wendy Normington. She flung herself at the dog with an embarrassed shriek and inflicted *coitus interruptus* on the poor creature by plucking it from Tom's leg and hurling it, still rampant, out of the door.

'I'm terribly, terribly sorry, Mr Brand. What can I say? What can I do?'

Tom is not stupid.

'Perhaps I could have another glass of wine.'

I was tempted to explain to Wendy that Tom's was not the only leg being embraced at that very moment; I might have got an extra glass of wine too. Instead I gave Mr Mogg-Barlow a sharp whack on the shin with my shoe, and spared him his blushes.

Tom's misfortune had the spirited effect of uniting the party. Conversation began to trickle around us almost as if nothing had happened. Not that it was exactly jolly; the asphyxiating sobriety of the company made it sound like a Methodist convention, and from time to time Tom and I tilted our empty glasses in the hope of a divine miracle. None came.

Eventually the talk round the table limped on to the subject of royal marriages and the public disasters that were attending them almost daily. Three different solutions were confidently offered. Our host took a naval line. In his view, he said, marriages – royal or otherwise – invariably worked best when the husband was away on active service for lengthy periods and at home only for short ones. This meant – though he didn't put it quite like this – that there could be a maximum concentration of lust with only the minimum opportunity for boredom or discord. The royals, in other words, should have remained in the armed services and all would have been well.

I suggested that neither Princess Di nor Princess Anne might have been entirely happy firing howitzers or piloting Tornadoes as a way of life, but the commander didn't seem to think this affected the strength of his argument.

Sir Hector took a sterner line. The younger royals had simply lost all sense of public duty; getting on with one's partner was a matter of training and self-discipline. I looked at Lady Ffludde and saw what he meant.

Mogg-Barlow held a different view: he put it all down to the press. Without the attentions of prying journalists all would be well in the House of Windsor. It was disgraceful that one's every small indiscretion should be plastered across the front pages of the wretched tabloids. I put on my sweetest smile and agreed that if, for example, every time a man felt a woman up under the dinner-table it hit the headlines in *The Sun*, that would certainly be most unfortunate. Mogg-Barlow looked the other way. His wife looked down at her plate.

Eyes then turned to Tom, who had said nothing since the episode with the dog, for which I was very grateful.

'What is your view, Mr Brand?' asked the commander.

It was my turn to look down at my plate.

Tom put on his most dedicated expression, which always means trouble.

'I have a perfectly simple view,' he said quietly. 'Since it's all about sex, and none of the royals seem to enjoy doing it with each other, why not harness the wonders of modern gynaecological research? This would ensure the necessary heir to the throne without the messy business of anyone actually having to *do* it; then the princes and princesses would be free to have their lovers and mistresses just as they always have.'

Tom gazed at the faces around the table with a look of mild curiosity.

'After all,' he added, 'a test-tube prince is no less royal than any other – genetically speaking.'

Wendy Normington hurried in with the cheese as if she were on famine relief.

'I managed to get some Blue Vinny,' she announced breathlessly. 'Or there's Double Gloucester if you wish. And those little round ones are French *crottins*.'

Lady Ffludde then made her one contribution to the evening.

'How very delightful, Wendy,' she said. 'But no one has ever managed to explain to me what *crottin* actually means.'

Tom looked at her impassively.

'It means "goat droppings", madam.'

The evening was saved by the front doorbell. As we were sipping coffee from tiny floral cups, and all further attempts at conversation had been abandoned, Wendy Normington rose with undisguised relief.

'That'll be my son Gerald. He was supposed to be fetching a distant cousin of ours from the station. But he phoned to say the train was two hours late. A bomb scare at Paddington.' She flapped her hands around dramatically. 'So I suggested they both call in for coffee. She's an actress – a charming gal, though we've hardly ever seen anything of her. She just rang up and invited herself, out of the blue.'

Any fresh blood, I thought, would be a welcome transfusion; then in ten minutes or so we could release ourselves and forget this entire evening had ever happened. Tom was by now looking as though he was under a deep anaesthetic.

The late guests appeared smiling at the door. Gerald was willowy and fortyish, with a collar a little too loose and hair that made the most of covering lost ground. His companion was a large, handsome woman of about the same age whose designer clothes were skilfully tailored to disguise an enormous bum.

Tom came to with something of a start.

'This is my son Gerald,' Wendy Normington was saying. 'And this is our distant cousin Harriet.'

By now Tom was on his feet.

'We must go,' he muttered sharply.

And suddenly he was nodding hurried thank-yous and good-byes all round. I noticed he never looked at the woman who'd just arrived. I also noticed that she was looking very hard at him.

'Well, well!' I heard her say as he passed her. 'The famous and rich Mr Brand.'

Wendy Normington was trying to steer her towards the other guests, and took her firmly by the arm. Suddenly our hostess looked perplexed.

'It's an awful thing to say, my dear, but I'm afraid I don't even know your married name.'

The Harriet woman turned to look at me, instead of Wendy or the other guests. The face was granite.

'I'm Harriet Brand,' she said.

8

I SAT wondering whether nightmares might perhaps be better, because at least nightmares hit you one at a time; whereas ours were becoming multiple. First Samantha. Then Anne-Marie. And now Harriet. I began to think of them as the three witches in *Macbeth*.

'I'm getting to know your women quite well, Tom,' I said rather sourly. 'We could have a party. A reunion.'

It was four days after the unspeakable dinner-party, and I still felt bruised.

'Harriet loathed me,' I added. 'That look she gave me. Utter loathing!'

Tom nodded.

'She would,' he said. 'Hatred is the fuel she runs on. Always has. I tell you, after vampire bats – now we've got the real thing.' He was gazing suspiciously out of the window. 'Doorstopping reporters are nothing compared to Harriet. That woman's got fangs. Next to her, Samantha's just a fat tart.'

'None the less, a fat tart who's giving us a heap of trouble,' I reminded him.

It was the first morning for several days that the press hadn't been lying in wait for us the moment we chose to step outside. Once they'd realised Tom was back they'd all wanted statements, interviews, gobbits of news, titbits of gossip, anything that could be smeared across the printed page.

'How are you going to fight the palimony case, Mr Brand?'

'Who are your defence witnesses, Mr Brand?'

'When did you and Samantha stop being lovers, Mr Brand?'

'What went wrong, Mr Brand?'

'Did you make love while she was cooking, Mr Brand?'

'Did she cook for other lovers too, Mr Brand?'

And sometimes, just for good measure! 'How's the mayonnaise these days, Tom?'

It was invariably a salacious question when they addressed him as 'Tom'.

Then they'd look at me as though I was his latest bit of fluff. I was the little blonde before breakfast. ('Get your clothes on, darling. The press are here.') I felt dirty.

Mercifully, I was no longer the one who had to deal with them. My chief worry was Mrs Teape, who wanted to deal with them all the time. ('Here come those kind men from London again, Mrs Brand. You *are* famous.') And if it wasn't Mrs Teape it was the builders, who'd scarcely ever met Tom, yet found the opportunity to address the nation on his behalf irresistible. At least they were loyal – 'A real gentleman, Mr Brand.' 'Oh yes, always courteous.' 'No, I can't say I've ever noticed orgies

– as you put it.' 'Mrs Brand? Oh, a lovely lady.' 'Well, if they're not married that's none of my business. A free country: folks can do as they like, I reckon.'

(To my amusement, my little act of retribution with the scalding tea had engendered grovelling respect among the workforce.)

One of the doorstoppers had been a cub reporter who'd worked for Tom several years back. Tom took him aside and promised him the exclusive story of his life with Samantha Parsons if he lost the case. It seemed to me a huge sum of money to be paid for nothing. Tom loathed the idea, but said at least it would cover the lawyers' bills, and go a small way towards compensating for what he might have to pay Samantha from the book royalties.

But this morning they'd all gone. They really had gone.

Suddenly the phone went. It was a measure of recent events that we immediately froze and looked fearfully at one another. After about eight rings Tom roused himself to answer it.

'Who is it?' he bellowed aggressively.

I saw his face soften. He turned away from me and began talking quietly. Christ, what now? I wondered.

Eventually the conversation ended. Tom replaced the receiver. He gazed at me with a blank expression, then burst out laughing.

'Your son!' he said. 'Your beloved son in whom you are well pleased! And d'you know what? Clive's opened a book on the size of Samantha's tits – taking bets from the entire school. He wanted to know the exact measurements so he can clean up.'

I tried to look appalled, and failed. We were both sobbing with laughter.

'But that's not everything,' Tom went on. 'He'd guessed absolutely right, even down to the cup size. Anyway, he says he'll make a fortune and buy me a drink as my cut. How old's the little bugger? Thirteen?'

Tom laughed even more loudly, a huge rollicking sound that bounced off the walls. Then he threw his arms round me.

Something about Clive taking a mental tape-measure to Samantha's boobs made me suddenly convinced that everything would be all right. I gazed out over John Gant's fields, and it was spring. A heron was standing sentinel on our river-bank. I even thought I could hear Ayrton's chiff-chaff. The Normington dinner-party was already fading from my mind. Even the shock of meeting Harriet. Even Tom's prophecy that we might not have seen the last of the poisonous creature.

'Screw the lot of them,' I said to Tom. 'You have, so why shouldn't I?'

Tom laughed.

'You're right. Why should we worry?'

The sun was pouring through the window. The garden was a carpet of crocuses, blue and yellow and white. There was bird-song. We weren't even dressed, but sitting lazily over late coffee and toast. We'd been making love in the night, hungrily, banishing the bad days. We'd even talked of possibly having a child. It felt like a rebirth of our life.

At that perfectly-timed moment the letter came.

Tom opened it automatically, along with a pile of other mail. Then I watched his face age several years. After a while he just handed it to me across the breakfast table.

The no-nonsense letterhead announced that it was from Messrs Crouch and Crouch, Solicitors, with an address somewhere important in London WC2. They were writing on behalf of 'our client' – 'our client' being none other than Mrs Harriet Brand. The substance of a long and pompous spiel was a claim by Mrs Brand for substantially increased maintenance. Under the 'one third of income' rule applied by the London magistrate's court at the time of the divorce, Mrs Brand was now demanding a monthly amount proportionate to what Messrs Crouch and Crouch understood to be 'the greatly improved state of Mr Brand's finances as a result of the publication of a cookery book which we have reason to believe has been what is termed a "best-seller"'.

A great deal of bullshit about 'our client's restricted circumstances' followed, which I skimmed over. The last paragraph contained the threat. Failure to agree to these proposals would necessitate an immediate appeal by 'our client' to the original magistrate's court for a change in the maintenance order. Alternatively, continued Messrs Crouch and Crouch, Mr Brand might prefer to avail himself of advantages offered by the law 'subsequent to our client's divorce' – namely those laid down in the 1984 Matrimonial and Family Proceedings Act. This, as Mr Brand was doubtless aware, encouraged divorced couples to agree on a 'clean break' as a way of settling their money and property problems. 'Our client', the letter ended, 'would be prepared to agree to such a settlement provided that the sum in question was both fair and acceptable to herself.'

The sum suggested made me choke on my coffee. It was half a million pounds.

Tom was on the phone to Kyra Vansittart within two minutes while my stomach churned. The conversation was brief.

'Well, here we go again,' he said in a resigned voice after replacing the receiver. 'It's back to solicitors. She wants me to go and see her. She needs the full story.'

I remembered what Ruth had said on the phone yesterday.

'For Christ's sake, darling, get him to tell you the entire saga. Old marriages are great theatre: you can enjoy the performance and walk out at the end.'

All right, I thought.

'If Kyra Vansittart needs the full story, then so do I, Tom,' I said. 'I'd like to know exactly what kind of beast we're dealing with.'

Full stories are never full of what one really wants to know. Perhaps with Tom this was because, in telling me about his wives, he was telling me things about himself which he'd much rather I didn't know. To have been married five times seemed, when I first lived with Tom, to be an eccentricity not to be taken entirely seriously. It was just a series of endearing mistakes, like failing one's driving test five times. I rather liked the idea of having a man who always did more of everything than other people – a man who was never frightened of excess. Tom was *more* romantic than other men, *more* glamorous, *more* canny, *more* kind, *more* sexy. I would never starve for lack of incident with Tom. Or lack of loving. And in any case, those absurb mistakes all belonged to the past, where they added a sort of glow to the man I loved. Here was no ordinary man. And being with him, *I* would never be ordinary; life would never be ordinary.

It wasn't quite like that any more. Tom was no longer the delightful roué who played at being Byron. I began to see a man who had stumbled through a great deal of pain, and now – just when it should have been all over – was being made to carry that pain with him. This made me want to hold him closer. Or rather, sometimes it did. At other times it seemed as though it was I who was carrying the pain. And I resented this. It gnawed at something within me. I remembered the pain Harry had caused me, and how it had felt to be spontaneous and free without Harry; to hold my life in my own hands at last.

There were times now when I yearned for that again. I longed for the taste of honey.

As it was, I was getting precious little honey, and a great number of bee-stings.

'You want the whole story! All right, I'll try,' he said.

He began with the prelude, because between Anne-Marie and Harriet there'd been Jo.

I don't think I'd ever registered Jo's existence. She was a wife who'd come and gone unnoticed.

'So, how did *she* manage to enter your life?' I asked.

'By mistake,' Tom assured me. Anne-Marie had been a long mistake, but Jo was a short one. 'At least she'll be no trouble,' he insisted. 'I promise you. Jo never wanted a thing from me once the twins were born. A self-sufficient woman, Jo, and determined to keep it that way.'

It had been a shotgun wedding. She was a BBC producer in her mid-thirties when he met her. Earnest. A teetotaller. Hard-line socialist. Do-gooder. Short on humour.

'More or less everything I least desired in a woman,' Tom said wistfully. 'And I was more or less everything she least desired in a man. Amazing, isn't it? How incompatibility can bring two people together under the right circumstances.'

The circumstances were that they made a film together about illegal abortions in Ireland.

'And when she became pregnant she refused to have one herself – on principle,' he went on.

'Hang on a minute, Tom,' I said. 'Jo was everything you least wanted in a woman. How come you ended up in bed with her?'

Tom was looking thoughtful.

'A challenge. I think we both felt it. Dislike can be extremely erotic.'

And for their sins, she had twins. Out of loyalty to the party, Jo insisted on naming them after two Labour prime ministers – Clement and Harold.

'Names that didn't go down too well at Brent Comprehensive School, the poor little buggers. Now she's determined they go to Neasden Polytechnic. With their education I doubt if they'll even get in. You'll meet them one day. They're great kids. Well, hardly kids – they're nearly eighteen now.'

The marriage, Tom explained succinctly, limped as far as Kilburn Registry Office, and expired.

'And she's never accepted a penny from me since,' he said. 'Refused point-blank. Not even for the twins. An unyielding *nyet!* I'm determined to change that now they're almost of age. God, they could do with some help – even if they decide to blow it all buying an Arab racehorse. In fact I'd rather like that; Jo would be so horrified.'

I tried to imagine not knowing Tom at all, and creating a character profile based on the kinds of women he'd fallen for. The profile would be incomplete because there were still two wives to come – and then me! But so far, what did we have? A romantic passion for a long-legged student with eyes like Greek olives. An erotic loathing for a dour BBC producer. And a drunken dalliance with an American nutcase who had nothing going for her except enormous tits.

The profile was neither clear nor very appealing. And sandwiched between the dour producer and the nutcase with tits was Harriet. She sounded the worst of them all.

'She was – and is,' Tom agreed.

At least I could understand why he'd fallen for Harriet. Tom painted the scene so vividly for me I began to feel quite jealous.

This is how it went: Tom is by now an extremely successful journalist who has managed to shed two extremely unsuccessful marriages. He is thirty-eight years old and desperately available. Enter – at some party or other – Harriet. Age: twenty-six. Profession: actress. Appearance: voluptuous. Marital status: wobbly.

All eyes turn towards her as she enters. The reason? However little she is wearing for this party it is still ninety-nine per cent more than she has been wearing in a current drama series on television. Tom, who has been glued to the set for weeks, feels he knows her already – and very soon he does. Harriet makes a pitch for this raffish, youngish journalist, and that night awards him the same delicious pleasures she has been awarding several actors on the screen for weeks. Over the next few weeks Tom is permanently in heaven, and almost as permanently in bed. He is the envy of every rampant male in England, including the lady's husband who promptly sues for divorce.

Harriet, kicked out of the marital home, moves in with Tom.

Meanwhile, the critics have been more appreciative of her body than they have her acting abilities. Some have gone so far as to suggest that she might never have got the part – or indeed *any* part at all – were it not for her appealing contours.

Tom, not primarily interested in her skills as an actress, remains unperturbed by these harsh judgments, until it becomes clear after some six months that Harriet is never going to get another part, except in films that no critic would be invited to see unless he happened to have a private interest in videos made in Amsterdam.

Harriet is therefore out of work, and remains so.

This in no way deters her from buying designer clothes and drinking Dom Perignon. Nor does it stop her spending evenings at Tramp when Tom is away on assignments. The male clients at Tramp are not immune to her charms, and are even prepared to escort her home.

Tom suspects his voluptuous wife is now sharing out her favours, but is not entirely sure until one night he returns from abroad unexpectedly early to discover her *in flagrante delicto* with a rock star, whose face would have been familiar had he not hidden it under a blanket before leaping from the window.

Tom decides that one rapid exit is not enough and pushes Harriet naked into the street, locking the front door and ignoring her cries.

Harriet, though accustomed to being naked, prefers not to be so in the street at six in the morning. But she is a resourceful lady. Dustbins have black plastic liners. Once the garbage is removed and two holes torn at the base, a bin-liner can serve as a dress, even if the scent of kippers and Camembert is scarcely Jean Patou.

As it happens, the dustmen choose this particular morning to arrive somewhat earlier than usual. Hardened to disposing of unexpected objects, they content themselves with passing ribald comments about the unusual contents of the bin-liner before courteously agreeing to drive Harriet to a taxi rank, after which her precise movements remain undocumented.

That was Tom's story of Marriage Number Three.

The postcript was that Harriet's hatred of Tom grew incandescent from the moment of the dustbin episode. It was further enflamed by the fact that the celebrated rock star, on whom she had pinned a great many hopes, injured himself in a delicate place when jumping from the window, and became impotent thereafter.

'She's a monster,' Tom assured me. 'A total monster.'

'And how long were you married to her?' I asked.

Tom did a rapid count on his fingers.

'Five years, of which more than half was taken up with endless wrangles over the divorce terms.'

But even after the divorce it didn't stop. There were abusive phone calls day and night. Tom was trailed in the street, harangued in restaurants. She broke into his house to remove pictures and books she claimed were hers. She even turned up at his next wedding and screamed obscenities in the middle of the ceremony.

Tom was shaking his head as if it was only yesterday.

'Harriet was the main reason I got the paper to give me a transfer to California,' he explained. 'Then, the moment I returned, it started all over again. Screaming phone calls. Poisonous letters. Lies recycled to make more lies. It was ten years before things quietened down, and that was only because she finally lost track of me.'

'And now she's at it again, you think?' I said gloomily.

Tom didn't answer, but his face said yes.

'Just our luck to move to a sleepy village and find she has a relation living down the road,' I said. 'But now, please tell me, Tom,' I asked, 'why *did* you marry her in the first place?'

He pulled his shoulders up round his ears and looked mystified. Then he laughed.

'Because I'm an old-fashioned man.'

And that was all he would say.

*

164

The first clue that Harriet was prowling came from the builders. Tom had left for his appointment in London with Kyra Vansittart. I spent the morning in Salisbury, nosing around antique shops for furniture we might acquire for the mill-house. By the time I returned, Bob, the foreman, was going off to the village pub for lunch. He had a grin on his face.

'Morning, ma'am,' he said. You always knew what time of day it was with Bob. In the mornings I was always 'ma'am'. In the afternoons, after a few beers, he'd address me as 'Janice', or if he'd had a particularly thirsty lunch, it was 'Hello Mrs Brand darling'. In the evening he'd sign off with 'Goodnight, sweetheart!'

'Strange friends you've got, ma'am,' he went on, winding down the car window and giving me a sideways look. 'Lady Phelps, she said she was. Saw her poking around the place, so I asked her who she was looking for. "Nobody in particular," she said. Told me she'd known Mr Brand for years. Just wanted to see what sort of new place he'd got. I saw her casting a quick eye around it. "Must have cost him quite a bit," she said. Did I know how much? And how much was all this building work setting him back? Right nosy she was, if you don't mind my saying.'

I didn't mind at all.

'Tell me what she looked like,' I asked.

Bob described a woman who could only have been Harriet. It was the big bum that did it.

I felt a horrible chill. The fucking bitch – how dare she?

Bob drove off to the pub, and I went indoors. Mrs Teape was just about to leave, clamping her man-trap combs firmly into her hair and re-lacquering the cupid's bow of her upper lip. Her face radiated good news.

'Oh, Mrs Brand, such a charming lady was here,' she announced, hands fluttering. 'A real lady, too – *Lady* Phelps.' Mrs Teape's voice purred with pride. 'So I invited her in and made her a cup of tea, I hope that was all right. But I felt I had to; she was showing so much interest in the house, and explained how she was such a very old friend of Mr Brand. She was most interested to hear all about you. She'd only met you once, she said, and thought you seemed a rather shy person. So naturally I told her you were about to be in Mr Major's cabinet, and she seemed quite surprised. "Well, well! Who would have thought it?" she said. She'd already looked round the mill-house, she told me, and how wonderful it was going to be when it was finished. It must be costing an awful lot, she thought, and I said, "Yes, I expect so, but Mr Brand's so terribly successful and I'm sure there's no shortage of a bob or two as far as he's concerned. He's always off on business somewhere or other," I said. "California was the last place. I expect it'll be Monte Carlo next. Today it's just London – he has to see his solicitor, I believe. But I expect he'll bring back some caviar," I said laughing. We had a real giggle about that, I can tell you. Not at all stuffy was Lady Phelps. You'll like her ladyship when you get to know her, Mrs Brand. I told her so.'

Christ Almighty!

I needed some fresh air after that. I threw on a coat and walked down the lane towards the village. John Gant stopped his tractor as I was passing the gate to one of his fields.

'How's my lovely filly, then?' he called out. 'Met a friend of yours this morning. Lady something-or-other. Staying in Salisbury, she said. Came over to see your new place. Quite a heifer, isn't she? What a rump, eh? You'd want to give it a good thwack, wouldn't you?'

'What did she say, John?' I asked nervously.

'Nothing much. Wanted to know what you'd paid for the place. I thought that was a bit cheeky. Then she asked if you gave wild parties – champagne, venison and stuff. I felt like saying "From the look of your arse you must have put away quite a bit of the red meat and bubbly in your time." But I'm a polite bugger, so I didn't.'

He laughed, and started up the tractor again.

'Bye bye, my lovely.'

He drove off.

Oh, the peace of the English countryside, where no one disturbs your tranquil days and the only fear is that everyone will forget you exist.

Right now it was my fondest wish that they would.

I walked up the village street. It was a soft spring afternoon. There were violets tucked in under the hedgerow, and here and there a patch of primroses and, in the sheltered places, fragile wood anemones. I passed the village store, which I'd avoided ever since the shopkeeper's wife made that remark about Hellman's mayonnaise. Nowadays I chose to shop in the next village, even though I was lucky to find anything with a 'Sell by' date more recent than last year.

Just then the shrew came out and saw me.

'Good morning, Mrs Brand,' she called out in a voice sharp with disapproval. 'A lady was asking where you lived earlier today. No doubt she found you.'

I explained that I'd been in Salisbury. She gazed at my loose blonde hair as if it made me the village whore.

'I see! Well! A largish lady she was. She said she knew Lady Bustard. I said Lady Bustard *often* came in here.'

The look of reproach was unmistakeable. I made a move to continue my walk, but the voice pursued me.

'Yes, she said you and Mr Brand must be about the richest folk in the village. I said "How would I know, since you neither of you spend any of it here?"'

I camouflaged my discomfort with a smile and called out 'Goodbye!'

The thought of Harriet knowing Emelda Bustard took my mind off my walk. I suddenly remembered the conversation we'd had several weeks ago, when Emelda explained how Harriet had paid them a visit one weekend, and how she'd got drunk and caught up in Ayrton's fishing-line while bathing naked. That made me feel a whole lot better. Now I'd actually set eyes on the woman the scene pleased me even more: I had a delightful vision of that huge arse bobbing in the water-weed all gift-wrapped in fishing-line and with the hook and fly lodged, I hoped, somewhere extremely painful.

I decided to call on Emelda. She was exactly the person to see on a day like this.

A purple shape was visible among the greenery. Emelda was gardening. So was Lloyd George. I went up to her.

'I hate gardening,' she announced, glancing up at me. 'Which is why I'm so good at it.' She threw down a pair of jumbo secateurs and heaved herself upright, supporting her back. 'I massacre everything, and they all love it.' Beside her stood the stump of a buddleia that didn't look at all as though it loved what Emelda had just done to it. She surveyed the carnage with a look of satisfaction. 'There we are! It's no good being gentle to plants, or talking to them like Prince Charles. They just die on you. Plants need to know who's boss.'

And she demonstrated her authority by stamping on the one remaining stem of buddleia that had survived the earlier onslaught.

'Now, that'll be wonderful in July,' she assured me.

'Butterflies. Dragonflies. Any bug you care to mention. Ayrton'll be in seventh heaven, and I shan't have to talk to him till the autumn. How's your garden, my dear?'

I explained that it was heavily trodden over by builders, and by unwanted visitors.

'Oh my God, you mean Ayrton. I keep telling him to leave you two alone.'

I said I didn't mean Ayrton at all – he was perfectly welcome and delightful. I meant one of Tom's ex-wives.

Emelda looked puzzled for a moment. Then, wiping the earth off her hands as if they were a pair of cymbals, she brightened.

'Ah, of course!' she exclaimed. 'So that's who it was. I knew I'd seen that bum before. Last time it was floating in the river. Of course!' she said again. 'Yes, she was here this morning. Introduced herself simply as Harriet, as if I was supposed to know who the hell she was. So she's Tom's "ex". Yes, I do remember now.' Emelda looked around pensively. 'She smelled rather, I thought, though that may have been because one of the cats sprayed on her leg. The wrong kind of Tom, eh?'

She laughed heartily and invited me in. We drank tea, and I told her the whole story, beginning with the rock star and bin-liner episode.

Emelda was enthralled.

'How simply wonderful!' she said, throwing back her head. 'I adore stories like that. Well, it certainly explains a lot.' And she leaned forward confidentially. 'Apropos of nothing, the woman told me she had an ex-husband who owed her half a million – he'd abandoned her, gone off with another woman, stolen her furniture, never paid her a penny, ruined her career, was an utter louse. It went on and on, my dear. She must have assumed I knew who she was talking about. But I had no idea – none at all.'

Emelda began to laugh again, smoothing her purple tweeds with grimy hands. Then she leaned forwards and tapped my knee, still laughing.

'The funny thing is, my dear,' she continued, 'I was so bored by this blistering tirade from someone I didn't know from Eve that I decided to humour her. I was really most unkind. I said the man sounded just like every husband I'd ever met, which was why I'd married Ayrton, who only cared about dragonflies and left me free to have affairs with Corsican fishermen, and why didn't she consider doing the same? Frightfully good in bed, I assured her. I could recommend several, I added; a bit long in the tooth by now perhaps, though at least they'd still be long where it really mattered, and she didn't look to me like a woman who gave up easily.'

Emelda was wiping tears from her eyes, leaving earthy marks like mascara gone berserk.

'Oh, my God!' she went on, almost speechless with laughing. 'The look on her face. Lips all stitched up. Little jerks of the head. It did get rid of her, at least. Said she had to get back to Salisbury. Apparently she's staying there for a while.'

The laughter suddenly dried up, and Emelda looked at me seriously.

'She did say as she left that she was determined to get her own back on her husband if it was the last thing she did. I hope this doesn't mean trouble for you, my dear.'

I said it *was* trouble already, and it wasn't the only trouble either. And with that I burst out crying. A large purple arm enveloped my shoulders.

'You need a drink. I don't care what time it is.'

I snivelled into a glass of white wine and told Emelda the rest of my troubles. She raised her eyes a little when I told her about the sperm bank for the Madagascan vampire bat, and clicked her tongue when I described how Harriet had been doing the rounds of the village pretending to be Lady Phelps.

When I'd finished, she sat back in her chair and nodded decisively.

'Well, my dear,' she said, 'I never give advice because I never know the answer to anything. But I would say one thing to you. Do you have a bolt-hole?'

I explained that I still had my little house in Chiswick which I was about to sell to pay for my share of the mill. Emelda raised a large hand as if about to give a blessing.

'Then don't! At least, not yet.' I'd never seen Emelda look quite so serious. 'You may need a place to breathe. Keep it. Remember! These are Tom's problems, not yours. Let him deal with them.' She paused to fill my glass, and her own. Then she chuckled. 'Goodness, I thought I had marriage problems enough with Ayrton's dragonflies. But then you're not married, are you? Sensible girl. Often wish I wasn't, except that Ayrton's such a lovely old fart. It's like being married to Caliban. Well, come and see me often, my dear. We'll sort it out between us.' And she raised her glass with an exaggerated swoop of the arm. 'The great house of Bustard hasn't been here since 1066 for nothing, you know. Cheers!'

Emelda's irrepressble high spirits were always a tonic, and I returned to the mill cottage with a lighter heart and a head swimming with wine.

It was also swimming with something else. My lighter heart wasn't only due to Emelda's wine and high spirits. The firmness with which she'd advised me not to sell my house had come as a shock at first. Until then I'd only flirted nostalgically with the idea. Tom and I had come here to bury our past and begin again. Selling the house was part of the agreement, and I'd never seriously considered breaking it. Why should I? But now, with Emelda's stern words ringing in my head, I began to wonder. I did more than wonder: I felt a deep longing, an unburdening, almost a sense of joy. It was like being offered a key to escape from a kind of prison. Self-preservation meant freedom, and freedom meant keeping something of my own which Tom's women couldn't touch. A place where they would have nothing to do with my life – where I wouldn't even have to think about them. Why the hell should I bury my past when Tom's past was swarming all over us like the Valkyrie?

The thought of my 'bolt-hole', as Emelda had put it, was bliss. Air to breathe in. Room to move. A place to be myself. Oh yes!

It was four o'clock in the afternoon. With two hours of daylight left, I decided I must do something constructive; so I opened the copy of Hilaire Belloc's *Bad Verse for Worse Children* which Howard Minton had given me, and began to read, wondering how I might illustrate them.

I'd got no further than 'The chief defect of Henry King was chewing little bits of string', when the phone went. It sounded like a frog on the other end of the line.

'Who is it?' I said.

At least with a voice like that it couldn't be one of Tom's wives.

'Clive,' croaked the voice. 'I'm catching the five-thirty from Waterloo.'

My son! With a voice like a frog!

'What on earth's happened to you?' I asked.

He sounded put out.

'Nothing's happened,' he croaked. 'It's the end of term. Remember, Mum?'

Christ! I no longer had a little boy for a son. Wasn't thirteen rather young for the voice to break? Precocious little beast. What would it be next? Acne and wet dreams. It made me feel old.

I began to get Clive's room ready. Suddenly the Winnie the Pooh posters and the tattered volumes of Asterix seemed out of place. Any day now the walls would hang with thrusting pelvises and stupendous nubilia, and the air would be blue with heavy rock and a scent of the great unwashed.

The phone went again. My heart sank as I listened to the half-familiar voice.

'*C'est Madame Brand?*'

Oh, godfathers! It was Professor Montblanc, and he sounded dangerously close. I remembered I was supposed to be Tom's mother.

'I am in London, and very much wish to visit *Monsieur Brand*,' he went on.

I panicked.

'*Monsieur Brand* died yesterday,' I said.

There was a silence for a few seconds, and in that time I knew I was already in worse trouble. The news would hurtle straight to Anne-Marie, and she'd be here in a flash.

'Sorry! Excuse me?' the voice said.

With relief I realised he hadn't understood.

'A ride!' I exclaimed. '*Monsieur Brand* has gone for a ride. Since yesterday. On a horse.' This was becoming ridiculous. 'He likes that. Goes off for days. Riding. Jig-a-jig.'

There was another silence. I felt a total idiot.

'Oh, I see.'

Professor Montblanc sounded baffled, and I wasn't surprised.

'And when will he return?'

I was absolutely *not* going to see this bloody man.

'Maybe in June,' I said. 'It depends on the weather.'

'In June!' He sounded less surprised than I would have expected. 'But I will be here again in June. I shall visit you then.'

Oh no you won't, I thought.

'I mean June next year,' I said confidently.

An even longer silence.

'*O là là!* That is too late. We need money so very badly. The *banque de sperme* is urgent, you understand. His wife assured me *Monsieur Brand* would be most *généreux.*' Well, he wasn't bloody well going to be *généreux.* '*Alors,*' the voice continued, 'then I shall visit you instead. You will be speaking to *Monsieur Brand* of course – from his riding. You will make this possible, I am sure. You are his mother.'

I played a trump card. I told him I had terminal cancer.

This was altogether too much for the professor's English.

'*Madame, je suis toute à fait désolé.*'

But the desolation didn't last very long.

'Then I shall come quickly, *madame*. You are near Salisbury, I think.'

I closed my eyes in horror. I was too deep in this to go back.

'No! Not Salisbury,' I said firmly. South Uist. In Scotland. The Outer Hebrides.'

He seemed mystified.

'Oh, really! And how do I find you?'

'Very easy,' I said confidently. 'Get off the boat and ask. Everybody knows us.'

I made an excuse to ring off, and tried to take stock of what I'd said. I never knew I could lie like that: it was disgraceful – I must do it more often. I decided after a moment or two that if the professor did turn up, I'd say that *Monsieur Brand*'s mother had died, her brain having been sadly affected during the last weeks of her illness. At least with any luck I'd bought myself a week or so while the eminent professor vomited his way across the northern seas.

I dared the telephone to ring again. It did. In fact it went three times within the next half-hour. I took the hand-phone into the garden so that I could remind myself that the world around me still looked normal.

The first call was a sweet and gentle voice in broken English. Was that Janice? she asked. She gave it a French pronunciation – *Janees* – which I liked. Who was this warm, soft-spoken creature?

'I am Solange,' she said. 'I am so happy to talk to you.'

I realised. Solange – Tom's daughter. The fat, spotty one.

'I am coming to stay with you. You are so kind. I desire to meet England.'

I wanted to say that this particular bit of England had no desire whatsoever to meet her. Where would she sleep? The mill-house was far from ready, and we had no spare room. What on earth would a spotty French teenager do in Sarum Magna? And how long was it for?

Shit! I wanted to scream at Tom: 'Will you please hire a zoo for all these women? Just get rid of them. Get them out of my hair. Tell them all to go to hell!'

'How delightful,' I said to the sweet girl. 'I've been so looking forward to meeting you. When will you be arriving?'

My hypocrisy was painful.

She asked if early May would be all right. And would two months be too long? I swallowed. I wanted to spit. Two months! Two whole months cooped up with a fat, spotty teenager!

'*Ma chérie!*' (Ye gods! Just listen to me.) 'Of course! It will be our pleasure. We could do with some youth about the place.'

The last thing I could do with was some youth about the place. What with Solange's acne and Clive's acne – I'd be having spots before the eyes before long. Perhaps Tom and I could persuade a posse of French lorry drivers to mount a blockade for the entire summer.

We chatted for a few minutes longer. It felt like a Berlitz course in how to relate to a step-daughter. All those magazine articles I'd read, never imagining it might one day be me. I heard myself being desperately welcoming, while wanting to say, 'Of course, do come! Do stay as long as you like! But I shan't be here!'

Solange rang off with a '*Je t'embrasse*'.

Spotty or not, she sounded delightful, and I felt mean.

The second phone call was from the estate agent in London. The would-be buyers of my house were back from their skiing holiday and 'terribly anxious' to exchange contracts as soon as possible. Might I be able to come up to London early next week? They would so enjoy meeting me and be taken round the house personally. There were only a few minor questions they wished to ask — nothing at all serious: they loved the place. So quiet and exclusive. So close to the shops. And that charming little garden.

Again my mind grabbed at what Emelda had said. 'Don't. At least not yet.'

What on earth was I going to do? With the phone held to my ear I felt the acute loneliness of indecision; the loneliness too of realising that the one person I couldn't bring myself to discuss it with was Tom. This horrified me. The decision wasn't just about the house: it was about us. I was being strangled here, and Tom couldn't help me; perhaps couldn't even understand what was happening.

'I could come up to London on Tuesday,' I said.

We arranged for eleven o'clock. I still had no idea what I was going to say or do. I would have to trust my instincts. God, I hoped they wouldn't betray me.

The third phone call was from Howard Minton. He'd like to talk over the Belloc project with me in greater detail, he said. He'd had a few ideas, and perhaps I had too. Might I be free to have lunch with him in town one day soon?

I felt ashamed at how much pleasure the thought gave me.

'How about Tuesday of next week?' I suggested.

He sounded pleased and named an expensive restaurant in Soho.

'I'll look forward to that,' he said, and after a slight pause, added – his voice a little more resonant – 'very much.'

There were prickles in my stomach that oughtn't to have been there. But I was pleased.

He rang off. It felt suddenly cold in the garden and I went indoors. I replaced the hand-phone and looked at my watch. It was half past five. Tom would be back any time now. But thinking of Tom brought the Valkyrie back into my mind, and my heart sank. I went to the window, and everything looked so tranquil – the place of peace we'd always wanted. The sun was low, the willows along the river were fresh-laundered and green, swathes of bright daffodils spilt down to the water's edge. Water-voles were criss-crossing from bank to bank. The kingfisher flashed past.

How lovely it all was. How lovely it should have been. And it didn't seem to belong to me any more.

I stiffened. There she was on the bridge. For a second I wished it *was* Harriet: then I could have comfronted her, told her what I thought of her; told her I knew all about her behaviour with the rock-star, knew all about the bin-liner and the dustmen; about her pretending to be Lady Phelps, about Emelda Bustard laughing at the size of her arse; told her she was sick, vicious, mendacious, deformed; told her to fuck off out of our life for ever.

But of course it wasn't Harriet, and all that anger went to waste. By the time I'd rushed outside, Mooncalf had gone. Only the water-voles were there to receive the volley of abuse I directed at the silent trees.

Tom's car was bumping along the track towards the house.

It was the first time I'd ever felt ambivalent about seeing him. I didn't want to know what kind of day he'd had, where he'd taken Kyra Vansittart for lunch, what advice she'd given him about how to deal with Harriet. I wanted him to ask me what sort of day *I'd* had, so I could have said 'shitty!'

He didn't. He reached for a drink.

'They've set the date for the palimony case,' he said in a flat voice. 'July the seventeenth. Abram Kollwitz phoned Kyra yesterday evening. He doesn't believe we'll win.'

There was something else we weren't winning.

If we'd had a separate room, I believe I'd have slept in it that night.

9

Two events rescued me from despondency.

The first was the arrival of Mrs Teape on a Monday morning in a state of high indignation. It was the first of April, and had it been anyone other than Mrs Teape I would have reminded myself that it was April Fool's Day.

She had been watching breakfast television.

'Dreadful what's going on in Surbiton,' she announced fiercely.

'What *is* going on in Surbiton, Mrs Teape?' I asked.

She removed a hat-pin that could have taken a large kebab, clamping it between her teeth like a cutlass while she adjusted her hair-combs.

'The killings,' she said, removing the cutlass. 'They're no better than animals, those people. I'm so glad you moved to Wiltshire, Mrs Brand.' She pursed her lips angrily. 'Wicked men they must be in Surbiton. Don't mind who they murder, do they? Women. Children. Just because they want to steal a piece of Croydon for themselves. I don't know why Mr Major doesn't do something.'

I hadn't heard the news or read the papers, so I was mystified. Surbiton at war with Croydon sounded odd, to say the least. And I said as much, trying not to reveal my ignorance. Perhaps living in the country had isolated me from the real world.

'Wicked!' Mrs Teape repeated vehemently. 'And to think they're Christians on both sides – Serbs and Croats. I can't imagine what the world's coming to.'

The day already felt a lot better.

I made some coffee and retired to my studio. Out of the window I could hear Tom joking with the builders. Through the wall came the jungle beat of Clive's music.

It was like having someone I didn't know around the house. I kept telling myself it was less than three months since I'd seen Clive. In that case, I decided, one of us is lost in a time-warp. It wasn't just the sound of him – that his voice was strangled into a monotonous croak. Nor the look of him – that his limbs no longer seemed to belong naturally to the rest of his body. Or even the smell of him – Clive's aftershave was splashed on like the holy waters of the Ganges in the hope that the gods would cause the three hairs on his chin to multiply. It was the whole package I found hard to recognise. Where was the bright-eyed urchin who used to smile and laugh? Where was the little boy I could cuddle? What had happened to the wickedness and the wicked charm? Now it was as though all his senses were turned inwards, engaged in a gloomy contemplation of some chrysalis of the soul, from which – with enough aftershave perhaps – the gorgeous butterfly of manhood would soon emerge.

Heaven help Sarum Magna when it did. Lock up your virgins!

Clive's presence around the house was scarcely the tonic my spirits needed at this moment. Even the prospect of Solange seemed brighter by comparison, until I realised I might have to sacrifice my studio to accommodate her. Oh, shit!

Then the phone went. I'd grown twitchy about the telephone these past weeks, and said hello cautiously, half-disguising my voice out of habit. But it was Ruth.

She became my second samaritan of the morning.

'What's the matter?' she asked. I'd scarcely said a word, but Ruth must have picked up something in the silence. 'Are you bored? I did warn you about the country, didn't I? Take a holiday and come out here. I'd love that, and so would Piers. The snow's melted, and there are spring flowers everywhere.'

I told her I wasn't at all bored. That I rather wished I was. It was quite the opposite. I was plagued. Haunted. Suffocated. All these women. And if it wasn't women it was loony professors. And if it wasn't loony professors it was the press – or lawyers – or Tom's spotty daughter turning up any day now. Even Clive was a pain in the arse with his rock music throbbing night and day. The bloody child, why couldn't he sit quietly and read a book sometimes?

'I bet *you* didn't at thirteen,' Ruth said.

'True,' I agreed. 'I was too busy admiring myself in the mirror. But at least I was quiet about it.'

'Is that all that's wrong?' she said unhelpfully.

I felt exasperated.

'No, it isn't. There's the water.'

Ruth laughed.

'Water? Try gin and tonic instead.'

I didn't feel amused.

'It's the mill. The river. It's like living next to a loo that won't stop flushing. It's driving me mad.'

Ruth said she didn't believe me. What was *really* was the matter? she asked.

I hesitated. I didn't know. Then suddenly I did know.

'It's Tom, I suppose,' I said, surprising myself for saying it. 'It's just that the whole thing's mostly his fault, and all he does is bleat. He goes off to see lawyers with a long face, and comes back with an even longer face. But he doesn't *do* anything. I want to scream.'

I hadn't realised how much I did want to scream.

'It's all too much,' I added. 'Far too much.'

Ruth has her practical moments. And this was one of them.

'Right!' she said firmly. 'Give me a Disasters List. Then let's see which ones are actually going to affect your life, and which are just storms in a teacup. OK, shoot! And don't worry about the phone call, by the way. The boss of the telephone service fancies me and tells me to send him my bills. That's what they call "seduction" in this part of the world. Even sex is tax-deductible in Liechtenstein. So, fire away. Disasters List.'

'Well,' I said, 'there's Anne-Marie and the vampire bats.'

Ruth just laughed.

'Ridiculous! Forget it. She's barking.'

'Then there's this French professor turning up to get funds for his sperm-bank.'

184

She laughed even louder.

'Tell him you hate vampires, and that you're already funding a project to vasectomise the little buggers.'

'He also thinks I'm Tom's mother.'

There was a sigh down the phone.

'I'm not even going to comment on that one. Next please.'

'There's the palimony case in California,' I said. 'That's really serious.'

This time there was a snort.

'Listen, darling. I had an affair with a brigadier once. He used to practise battle strategy while we made love. Very erotic, I can tell you. He told me about the risk factor involved in storming an enemy position uphill – using my left nipple to illustrate. First you decide what you want to do, then work out what's the worst that can possibly happen achieving it. And if the very worst means you still survive, you do it. So, what's your worst?'

I thought about this for a moment. Storming Ruth's left nipple would indeed have been uphill: the brigadier must have been a powerful climber.

'We lose half the royalties on *Prawnography*,' I said.

Ruth came straight back at me.

'So what? You've still got the other half. Christ, a year ago you didn't have a bean and you were perfectly happy. Next.'

I was beginning to feel a lot better. It was like being scrubbed with a stiff brush.

'Well, then there's Harriet. She's sniffing about like a tracker-dog, and her solicitor's asking for half a million.'

Ruth came straight back on that one.

'Ignore the bitch. And her solicitor. She's just trying it on; she'll settle out of court for a tenth of that. Anyway, if Tom loses the palimony case you won't have half a million to give her; and if he wins, fifty grand isn't going to hurt. End of problem. Any more?'

'Solange,' I said. 'Tom's daughter from France. A spotty teenager. She's coming to live with us. Wants to get to know *papa*. And we don't even have a spare room for her.'

Ruth was chuckling.

'Oh, that'll sort itself out quick enough, you wait. Spotty or not, no French teenager wants to live in an English marsh inhabited by retired naval officers and pot-bellied stockbrokers. She'll take one look at *le high-life* in Wiltshire and decide it's not worth the sacrifice just to get to know *papa*. And if you put her up on an uncomfortable sofa in the sitting-room she'll be gone even quicker.'

To my surprise I found I'd come to the end of my list. Suddenly it didn't sound too bad at all.

'That's about it,' I said sheepishly.

'Really?' Ruth's voice sounded sceptical. 'How come you've managed to leave out the only two things that matter?'

I blustered something incoherent. 'What d'you mean?' I managed to say.

'That you can't stand the bloody countryside, and you're suddenly not sure about spending the rest of your life with Tom.'

I realised that both thoughts were actually buried in my mind, and I hated to admit either of them. After only a month – a little month! How could everything change so quickly?

'What would *you* do?' I asked, knowing perfectly well what Ruth would do.

'Well,' she said rather slowly, as if it had been in her mind all the time. 'You've still got your little house in Chiswick, haven't you? So, take a break. See what it feels like. Be a town-mouse for a while. And enjoy yourself. Remember the old Janice. I'm sure your beautiful young publisher friend would oblige. And if he doesn't he's not the man you described to me so breathlessly the other week.' She gave another laugh. 'After all, Tom's plaguing you with all his women; what about a bit of quid pro quo?'

I tried to explain it wasn't the same.

'My darling Janice,' said Ruth, 'it's *always* the same. Go for it.'

The sight of Tom lounging around reading his wretched Byron biography made me angry. A few weeks ago it had seemed charmingly absurd, and I'd loved him for it. That was before the Valkyrie descended. We hadn't made love for what felt like ages. I told him my period kept stopping and starting, which was untrue. And when that excuse was exhausted I found others: the walls were so thin that Clive could hear us; I had a touch of cystitis; something in those scallops must have upset me. I even played the 'headache' game. The worst of it was that it took me back to life with Harry; and I'd been so certain it would never be like that with Tom. It had all seemed so easy at the beginning, so natural. The wheels oiled by sex and laughter – the way it ought to be.

And it wasn't like that any more. At night I had dark dreams which I could never remember when I woke, but they left me troubled, tense. My body felt an inanimate thing. Even my fantasies bored me: I'd conjure up scenes of wild love on moonlit beaches, and they'd fade away as if someone had turned the video off; and I'd be left lying there in the grey dawn, thinking about shopping.

I was thirty-seven. Was I having a mid-life crisis? Should I see a psychiatrist?

Questions like these merely bounced back at me off the trees. This was the trouble about living in the country: there was no one to talk to; no friends round the corner I could ring up, or call round for coffee and dump my troubles on. There was only Emelda, and delightful and raunchy though Emelda was, she was an old woman living in her eccentric memories with a *Wind in the Willows* husband.

What worried me most was that I couldn't talk to Tom. I knew I ought to – he was what my troubles were about, after all. But somehow I couldn't. I told myself *he* didn't want to; that he had enough problems on his plate, and no room for mine too. Then I told myself this was nonsense; that if he loved me he would make room, he would care. But he didn't appear to care. He could make jokes with the builders, but he couldn't make love with me.

That was a lie, and it hurt to admit it. *I* couldn't make love with *him*. I was the one who kept my distance, because I wanted to – or needed to. I wanted to cry with the confusion of it all. Oh Tom, where has our life gone? Your past chased it away.

Having Clive about the place didn't help either. He went around the cottage croaking moodily and bumping into things because he was growing too fast to know how tall he was.

'What is there to do in this place, mum?'

'Go and explore,' I said testily.

He did. I should have known my son better. He returned at lunchtime with eyes twice as large as before.

'Cor, mum. There's a woman out there with nothing on.'

It had taken him ten minutes flat to discover Concha. I noticed Tom's video camera went missing that afternoon. Well, at least home movies seemed likely to take care of Clive's boredom for the rest of the holidays. His rock music was even louder now, orchestrating his pubescent dreams.

Then Monday came, and everything felt quite different. I found it hard to recognise myself. I knew exactly why. I was going to London. I was going to spend a couple of nights in my little house all on my own. Tomorrow morning I'd be seeing the estate agent and the couple who were apparently keen to buy the place. Then there was my 'business lunch' with Howard Minton: I was looking forward to that. Meanwhile I'd be alone – my first nights alone for months. And in London! It was like playing truant. I was being 'bad'. Not that I was going to *do* anything – at least not the sort of thing Ruth had in mind for me. I didn't want that.

Or, rather, I thought I didn't until the second post came about mid-afternoon. I'd just put my overnight bag in the car and was saying goodbye to Tom. Clive was off 'bird-watching' with his video camera.

There was just one letter – for Tom. His face suggested he recognised the handwriting on the envelope. He opened it in silence. Inside was an entirely blank sheet of paper, except that attached to it – spiked right through the middle – was an enormous safety-pin. Only a safety-pin, yet hanging there, clinging to the paper. It looked obscene and menacing. A threat. And with no words.

'Is it her?' I said. I felt quite sick.

Tom nodded, and replaced the offensive thing in its envelope. Then he looked at me wearily.

'That's Harriet all right.'

My stomach was churning. I didn't even ask what it meant.

I could hear the phone ringing. I knew the answerphone was on, so I ignored it. Then, just as I was about to step into the car I wondered if it might perhaps be a message for me – the buyers had backed out, or Minton was cancelling our lunch. So I went back into the house and pressed the playback button. I didn't recognise the voice, and didn't need to. It couldn't have been anybody else.

'I know you're both there because I'm watching you,' Harriet began. There was a slight pause, presumably while she was still watching. 'I hope you understand the message, Tom. And you, you little tart – drive carefully.'

That was all. There was a click.

I stood shaking. And then I screamed. Tom put his arms round me. I didn't want them round me.

'I'll get the police,' he was saying.

I rushed to the front door, but there was no sign of a car anywhere except our own. I felt soiled: it was like a burglary. She must have been watching from the end of our lane, waiting for the postman, knowing what he was going to deliver. But how did she know it would be in the *second* post? Maybe she didn't. Maybe she'd been there since early morning – just waiting.

I managed to calm down a bit. Tom was already on the phone to the police.

'They're sending someone round,' he said, and his voice was expressionless. 'They need to hear the phone message and see the letter. I explained that it wasn't exactly a letter, just a safety-pin,' Tom went on, 'and the bastard just laughed. "Oh, that's unusual," he said. "Never 'eard of that one before. A safety-pin! Might come in useful, I suppose." . . . Fucking bumpkins.'

I didn't give a toss what the police had said.

'Tom, was Harriet always like this?'

He breathed in deeply and pursed his lips.

'Yeah! Always. Except that the safety-pins have grown bigger.'

'In proportion to her bum,' I suggested. 'And what did you do about them before?'

'Got a restraint order put on her.'

'And what does it mean – the safety-pin?' I asked.

'It means: "I've got you, and if you try to get away I can draw blood."'

I really couldn't believe all this.

'And what about the "drive carefully" bit?'

'Oh, that's just to scare you,' Tom tried to assure me. 'She won't do anything. She wouldn't dare.'

I didn't feel in the least convinced. Anyone fuelled on hatred as much as Harriet might be prepared to do anything, it seemed to me. I wanted Tom to go out and strangle the bitch. Even better, I wanted him to bring her back here so that *I* could strangle her. Or perhaps I'd be satisfied with just sticking the safety-pin into her fat arse.

One thing was quite certain: I had no intention of meeting the police. This was Tom's problem, let him deal with it – just as Emelda had said. What I needed most of all was to get away. Two days in London. Two whole days! Freedom. No Valkyrie. No lawyers. No Teapot. Just an empty house that was all mine to be selfish in. I didn't even feel guilty about leaving Clive. He'd be in seventh heaven with his rock music and his video camera. And Tom would enjoy indulging him with amazing pasta sauces and tons of Mars ice-cream, and at last my son would have the chance to discuss 'men's matters' – in other words, what had *really* gone on between Tom and Samantha in California, and what was it *really* like to have had five wives? Tom had become Clive's role model; my only obvious virtue in his eyes was to have had the good fortune to shack up with such a paragon.

I drove off. By the end of the lane I felt better already. I gave a cautious glance left and right to see if a strange car might be lurking. But there was nothing. Only an empty village street – empty, that is, except for a hunched figure in brown plus-fours who, the moment he saw me, began waving a fishing rod vigorously to attract my attention.

After the events of the past hour Ayrton Bustard seemed to me like the purest normality, and I was smiling broadly as he hurried towards the car a little breathlessly.

'I was wondering if your husband might possibly be at home,' he panted, giving his hat a polite bob and planting his fishing rod upright on the road as if it were a Roman centurion's spear. 'I was hoping I might at last have a chance to inspect his tackle.'

I explained that Tom was about to tackle the police at any moment. Ayrton looked alarmed.

'Oh dear! Nothing serious, I trust.'

'It's actually about a safety-pin,' I said, not wishing to explain any further.

Ayrton looked shocked.

'A safety-pin! You mean some bounder's been fixing his bait with safety-pins to catch your husband's carp? Well, I've heard tales of skullduggery in my time, but that takes the biscuit.' Ayrton's eyes blinked ferociously, and the dewdrop on his nose quivered with indignation. 'Then I certainly won't disturb him. He has important work to do. I'll bid you adieu, madam. And I trust you will drive carefully.'

Hearing Ayrton echo Harriet's words so precisely took all the menace out of them, and I dismissed the fat cow from my mind.

By now it was a bright April evening. The young poplars along the river-bank gleamed bright emerald. I put on a tape of Delius and drove off into the spring-time.

*

To wake up in a bare house where I'd lived and loved and worked not so long ago – it was like meeting an old friend who could no longer speak to me. The house was cold. Water ran brown from the tap. The telephone was disconnected. Everything looked a little smaller and shabbier. But the view from the window was the same: the neighbours' cars kept their usual orderly places; and in the tiny garden the crocuses were splashed across the overgrown flower-beds as if they'd been celebrating my absense.

I'd brought a few basics with me – coffee, bread, marmalade, and a bottle of wine for the evening. I could have returned to Otters Mill later today, but I wanted a second night here. Who knows, by then I might have sold it (or not, as the case may be). The agent was bringing the prospective buyers round at eleven, he had said.

The thought gave me another jolt of fear. My house – sold! My old life – sold! My independence – sold! From my bedroom window I could see the estate agents' board raised like a flag above the gate: 'Under Offer' it announced in a bold diagonal swathe across the words 'Charming Victorian Detached Residence – Freehold'.

'Under Offer'. By tomorrow morning it could say 'Sold'. Christ, I thought, half the middle-classes in England are praying desperately that their expensive pile, expensively mortgaged, might say 'Sold' outside it before their early-retirement pensions get swallowed up in the cost of keeping the place going. And here was I panicking at the prospect, hoping against hope that the couple this morning wouldn't want it, that no one else would want it, that I could confront Tom with the tearful news that because of the recession my house was totally unsellable and I was terribly sorry but there was nothing whatever I could do about it; I'd repay him just as soon as I could.

It was more than just the house, of course. I realised that. In these sad and empty rooms I began to relive the days I'd once spent in them, the person I'd been, the life I'd led. Yes, there'd been the tears and the miseries – the nights alone knowing Harry was screwing someone else, the reconciliations that never reconciled anything, the final break-up, the money worries, and most of all the terror of being terminally alone. But then there were the other things which lingered in my mind so much more brightly. The joy of knowing that I *could* be alone, that it was wonderfully easy not to be alone if I wished, that I could pick and choose my lovers like a menu – or not, if I chose not to. My choice.

And Tom had been my choice. I hadn't needed him. I wanted him. And I loved the life we'd led. The *frisson* of night phonecalls, unexpected visits, unplanned seductions. All impulse and adrenalin. We trod paths scented with lust and flowers.

Oh, how I wanted it all back! And yet a dead, dark voice inside me was warning me it had gone for ever. In the midst of this present nightmare how was I to know what was true?

I saw the agent pull up in his car – five minutes early. I remembered the name: Mr Comely. He looked like it, too – youngish, of the puffy school, pinkish, fair hair curling behind the ears, grey suit with chalk-white stripe, signet ring. He was carrying a sheaf of documents – the health report on my house, no doubt.

He coughed as I opened the front door.

'Good morning, Mrs Blakemore. Good of you to make the journey.'

It pleased me that he called me Blakemore. In Sarum Magna I'd all but forgotten this was my real name. Between riffling through his documents he was glancing at me appreciatively, no doubt calculating my age, what had happened to my husband, why I was selling the place, and might there perhaps be a little private perk for him in this deal if I happened to be free this evening or tomorrow – a little restaurant he knew? I found myself hiding a smile. ('Oh Mr Comely, how you make me come!')

Mr and Mrs Pitt would be here any minute, he assured me, as if I didn't already know.

And even as he spoke I saw a BMW drive up. I wondered about Mr Pitt – would it be the Elder or the Younger?

He was half way between the two. And he smelled strongly of money and aftershave (so Clive hadn't quite used up the nation's supply).

I realised I had no plan for the next hour, but suddenly I knew what I wanted. It was not what Mr Comely wanted. It was not what Mr Comely thought *I* wanted. And it was certainly not what Mr and Mrs Pitt thought I wanted.

This was going to be an interesting encounter.

They began with a list of small questions they felt they needed to ask me. The whereabouts of this and that. Then came what Mrs Pitt confessed was perhaps an indiscreet question. There was a note of careful gentility in her voice.

'The neighbours, if I may ask,' she said. 'Are they . . . agreeable?'

Now, here was an invitation to strike my first blow.

'Well, I don't know all of them,' I said, which was a half-truth: there were one or two of them I hadn't been to bed with in my roaring days after Harry departed. 'But our immediate neighbour is a film director,' I went on. 'Kevin Vance: you may have heard of him. He makes porno films.'

I glanced at Mr Pitt's face out of the corner of my eye, and was pleased with what I saw. He was nervously easing his collar. But Mrs Pitt, to my surprise, brightened visibly.

'Oh, what fun!' she exclaimed. 'Porno films. I've always wanted to meet someone who made those. Perhaps he has private viewings. Save us the trouble of hiring them from the video shop as we usually do. Won't it, Horace?'

The gentility in her voice had slipped quite a bit. Mr Comely was beginning to look uncomfortable, turning away from us and folding his hands behind his back like the Duke of Edinburgh.

I wasn't prepared for Mrs Pitt's reaction. So I tried again.

'Yes, he does have private viewings, though they tend to be rather public, I'm afraid,' I said. 'Kevin rather enjoys exhibiting his prowess. You'll have noticed he doesn't have curtains.'

Mr Comely cracked his knuckles. Mr Pitt coughed. But Mrs Pitt clapped her hands delightedly. She dug her husband firmly in the ribs, and a cockney accent crept into her voice.

'Well, think of that, Horace!' she exclaimed. 'We might learn a thing or two, mightn't we, darling? Make a change from those magazines you like to look at.'

Mr Pitt looked mortified, and promptly changed the subject to the roof. The surveyor, he explained, had noticed one or two structural weakness in that area.

I decided I had a better chance with Mr Pitt than with his wife.

'More than one or two structural weakness, I'm afraid,' I assured him, turning my back on Mrs Pitt. 'We had the roof repaired after the hurricane, of course. But there's only so much you can do. You see, we *are* right under the flightpath to Heathrow, and the vibration always takes it toll. Bound to, when the jumbos go over about every thirty seconds in the summer, day and night. In the end we just didn't use the top floor at all. You can't go on shifting the bed around to avoid the drips, can you? Besides, the wiring gets in the way, and frankly I was always worried it would short and burn the whole place down. That's one of the reasons we're moving.'

Well, that should do it, I thought.

Mr Comely was struggling to interrupt, assuring Mr Pitt there was nothing about any of this in the surveyor's report, and Mrs Blakemore was really going too far in being honest: he was sure it wasn't like that at all. Perfectly sound – the roof. He knew a lot about roofs, he explained.

Mr Pitt was about to say something, but got no further than opening his mouth.

'Oh, I don't think that matters, Horace, does it?' declared Mrs Pitt. 'There's only the two of us and we always prefer to sleep on the ground floor; so if we get pissed there are no stairs to fall down.' She gave out a shriek of laughter. Then she looked at me very seriously. 'The point is, Mrs . . .' – she forgot my name. Mr Comely supplied it in a quavering voice. 'The point is, Mrs Blackamoor, it's such a charming place, isn't it? And a Conservation Area too, I understand.'

Mr Comely leapt in with the huge benefits of living in a Conservation Area. Mr Pitt, looking thoroughly battered, was nodding miserably in agreement.

'Of course,' he said glumly.

'Yes,' I chipped in. 'Of course, it does mean you can't change anything, or repaint the house without permission from the local authorities. Double-glazing's not allowed, I'm afraid. Or satellite dishes. And any plants you want to put in have to be approved by the parks department – and they're a pack of bastards, frankly. Weeds, too, they can be a bit of problem: they're not allowed. You get fined quite heavily; evicted, I'm told, if you don't comply.'

I smiled sweetly at Mr Comely, who was speechless. Mrs Pitt wasn't. She placed a hand confidentially on my arm.

'I have to tell you, Mrs Blackwood, we happen to know His Worship the Mayor rather well. Very well, in fact.' She gave a little shudder of the shoulders, and a coy glance at her husband. 'There was a time, you see, when the mayor and I were . . . how shall I put it? Very close. That was before Horace's time, of course. But it wasn't before the Lady Mayoress's time, I assure you. Oh, no! So, you see we share a little secret, the mayor and me. Very helpful when it comes to getting things done, we find. Don't we, darling?'

Mr Pitt blushed, and nodded meekly.

'Besides, my husband's big in the construction business,' she assured me, tilting her head loftily. 'Well, we've got no further questions, Mrs Blackman. I think it's all perfectly lovely.' The genteel voice had suddenly resurfaced. She turned imperiously to Mr Comely who was still looking shell-shocked. 'Perhaps we could exchange contracts straight away. How about this afternoon?'

I panicked.

'Not till tomorrow,' I said helplessly. 'I have a very important meeting this afternoon, I'm afraid.' It was the only entirely truthful thing I'd uttered for the past hour.

Mr Comely awarded me a ferocious glare as he led his clients away. Nothing could have been further from his mind than the surreptitious perk he'd been hoping for an hour earlier.

I shut the front door and looked at my watch. In half an hour I would have to leave to meet Howard Minton.

Then I closed my eyes. What the hell was I going to do? The darkness behind my eyelids offered no more clues than a black screen. I looked for messages, and there were none. I opened my eyes, and there were still none. I tried spelling out the issues to myself, but these grew so complicated that I lost the thread. Each wish seemed to have its own built-in contradiction, as though I were two people arguing with one another.

'I love Tom, and want to spend the rest of my life with him.'

('I'm not sure that I do love Tom all that much; he was just someone it was lovely to have an affair with.')

'Our life in the country is the dream I've always wanted.'

('Our life in the country is a ridiculous fantasy I should never have tried to live out.')

'This present nightmare will pass. Tom's women will just fade away. And we'll always have enough money to live exactly as we please.'

('This nightmare is our life. Women like Harriet never fade away. And we'll be left penniless.')

'I've always wanted to commit myself sexually to one man, and now I've found him.'

('I'm quite incapable of commitment to anyone for any length of time; by nature I'm emotionally promiscuous.')

'It was hell leaping from bed to bed after my marriage broke up, and I never want to go back to that.'

('What I can't bear is the thought that I may never again experience a new relationship; I'm burning to have an affair.')

Oh God, this was getting me nowhere. I had barely fifteen minutes to get ready for my 'business lunch'. Well, at least there was no dilemma about what I should wear. I'd only brought one change of outfit.

I dressed hurriedly, wondering what I'd been thinking about when I chose it. Dove-grey Lanvin suit – that was the 'business' part of it. The skirt was short and straight – not much 'business' about that, I decided, nor about the tightly-fitted waist or the black seamed stockings with the little bows where they touched the shoes. The sky-blue T-shirt was probably neutral, though it certainly wouldn't be if I unbuttoned the jacket; and that would be up to me, depending on how the lunch went. I wound my hair up and put on a pair of chunky silver earrings. Finally, I made sure there was a tiny bottle of Giorgio in the jacket pocket.

'Well, Howard Minton,' I said to myself as I locked the front door behind me, 'let's see what you make of this.' Contract? Or proposition? Or both?

My evening, after all, was free.

The taxi dropped me at the corner of Soho Square, and I walked across to the restaurant. The *maître d'* consulted his list and guided me to a far table where Howard was already waiting. He rose and kissed me half-politely on one cheek. He identified the Giorgio, and I enquired how many of his girlfriends wore it. That was a promising start: hit the right note straight away. He laughed, and summoned the drinks waiter.

'Shall we go straight on to wine?' he said, gazing at me with a slight smile.

Pretty smooth, I thought. He ordered a bottle of Meursault. I was fairly sure I'd never told him it was my favourite.

He knew about the things that weren't on the menu, too (he would, wouldn't he? I thought). The head waiter nodded impassively: 'Of course, Mr Minton. Fresh today.' There was nothing in the man's face to tell me how regularly Howard brought attractive women to his restaurant, or how I measured up.

'May I make some suggestions?' Howard said. I got the feeling he was going to make quite a few suggestions before lunch was over. 'Pierre's vichyssoise is a bit special, I have to say. Just a touch of the piquant.'

At each word his eyes touched a different part of my face.

'Then, perhaps scallops? Lightly poached in white wine. Wonderfully delicate. A Venus symbol, I believe.'

I began to imagine Tom's derisive snort at this caricature of a seduction. But never mind. I was loving every minute of it.

'Only the shell is a Venus symbol,' I said, smiling. 'For rather obvious reasons.'

He blinked. I could see him hurriedly rearranging his thoughts, cutting out even more preliminaries.

We cleared 'business' away rather quickly. There didn't seem to be very much of it. This lunch was clearly about lunch, or – more specifically – about lunch with me.

He had attractive eyes, slightly mocking.

'I like your earrings,' he said.

He didn't mean earrings.

'And that's a beautiful jacket.'

He didn't mean jacket.

Well, I thought, let's play this for all it's worth. I unbuttoned the jacket. His eyes did a rapid dive. I took a quick bet with myself on the next question.

I won.

'I suppose you're not free this evening, by any chance? Perhaps we could go to the new *Coriolanus* at the National.'

Or, more likely, something quite different, I imagined. There wouldn't be a hope of getting tickets anyway.

'I'd love that,' I said.

'And me!'

He refilled my glass. A little more wine and he'd suggest where to meet me for a drink first. Meanwhile there was a brief silence while our eyes acknowledged that perhaps *Coriolanus* wasn't quite the right mood for two people who were going to spend the night together.

This, I decided, was entirely ludicrous, and I intended to enjoy every single minute of it. I didn't give a damn about Howard Minton, but I wanted to be outrageously sexy. This was my self-indulgence, my little rebellion. I wanted him to undress me; I wanted him to screw me; I wanted to indulge in every erotic cliché in the book. I was going to out-Ruth Ruth; and to hell with everything – including tomorrow.

I gave Howard a look of undisguised complicity, and his fingers brushed mine. Oh Jesus, I thought, why do we have to wait for this evening?

Then suddenly he turned his head away. I followed his glance. An extremely elegant woman – tall, Scandinavian-looking – was being shown to a table not far from ours. I recognised her as an actress who'd been playing the young heroine in a recent Dennis Potter play I'd seen on television. Then I recognised the extraordinarily handsome man who was with her.

I gave a jolt. It was Harry.

I was about to tell Howard that my ex-husband had just walked into the restaurant when I heard Harry's voice.

'Janice!' he called out. 'How wonderful! I thought you'd moved out into the sticks. How are you?'

He was gorgeously suntanned and dressed in a light-fawn linen suit as if he'd arrived hot from Miami. The entire restaurant watched him as he came over to our table and kissed me on the cheek as if we were the oldest and dearest of long-lost friends. I introduced him to Howard – my 'publisher'.

Harry took both my hands in his.

'Marvellous to see you. Truly!' He glanced over to his own table. 'Forgive me, but . . .' He nodded in the direction of the beautiful actress waiting patiently, pretending not to notice. (Poor Harry. Duty calls again, I thought.) 'But you must give me your new phone number. Please! I'd love to talk to you. So much has happened. Let's have dinner. I'm over from the States for a couple of weeks – at the Savoy. Do jot the number down for me. You're looking absolutely lovely.' His eyes wandered over my body as though I was tomorrow's mistress rather than the ex-wife he'd betrayed for twelve years.

Then he glanced dismissively at Howard.

'Nice to have met you, Mr Minton.'

It all came back to me. I'd almost forgotten what it was like. Harry the charmer. Harry laying out his sexual stall. Harry who'd be perfectly capable of screwing that actress the entire afternoon, then phoning me in the evening as if I'd been the only thing on his mind ever since we'd met. Harry just like he always was: the louse you couldn't say no to. The delightful and irresistible shit, yet for all that – it infuriated me to have to admit it – worth ten of Howard Minton. At least Harry's clichés were real.

I glanced at Howard. Suddenly he looked different. The self-confidence was knocked out of him. He seemed almost to have shrivelled.

'Sorry about that,' I said unconvincingly as Harry returned to his table. 'My "ex".'

Howard looked thoroughly disconcerted. There was a silence. After a while he muttered something and looked at his watch. I found myself looking at mine. Still, neither of us said anything. His face looked grumpy and dull. He no longer came across like the young Harrison Ford: more like an understudy, an extra.

So Harry had done it again. But not at all like it used to be, when his charm would weave a spell round me. This time the effect was repulsion. I didn't want it. I didn't want to be any man's flavour of the month – today's flower, tonight's fuck, tomorrow's 'Thank you, darling'. The indecisiveness of the morning had simply faded away: all those fruitless debates within myself. And with it the anger and resentment had faded away too. I wanted to fight. I wanted to drive my nightmares away. I wanted – it came as a shock of pleasure – to be with Tom; to be by his side; to laugh with him, cry with him, be committed to him. How corny it sounded. But it was true.

I don't know how consciously I reached that decision at the time. Maybe it was yet one more incidence of my fortunes being dictated by the accident of chance – 'your rule of iron whim', as Ruth once described it.

In any case I found myself saying to Howard that there was a phone call I urgently needed to make, if he'd excuse me for a moment.

He smiled weakly, and I saw him signal to the waiter for the bill as the *maître d'* directed me to the phone. Thank God it was somewhere Howard couldn't hear me. I telephoned Mr Comely. I *could* exchange contracts on the house this afternoon, I explained, if Mr and Mrs Pitt wished to. My appointment had been cancelled. I tried to appear unconcerned. Mr Comely still sounded cross; his voice was flat. But he would ring Mr Pitt at his office. Why didn't I call round at four-thirty? He'd try to have everything ready.

So that was it. I was going to do it. I was going to burn my boats. And I was happy. Harry you bastard, I thought, you don't deserve to have done what you've just done for me, but perhaps that was your final overdue gift. As I put down the receiver, the idea of being seduced by Howard Minton seemed entirely absurd. Why should I want it? Why on earth should I need one more adventure, one more prick, one more dawn on a strange pillow? Tom was the best lover I'd ever had. Remember that, Janice!

I decided simply to turn up on him unannounced. I'd sign the contract first, then drive home. *Home* was no longer Chiswick: it was where Tom was, and Clive.

I made my excuses to Howard. My son was ill, I said. He was perfectly polite about it. He'd get in touch with my agent this afternoon, he assured me. He was just my publisher again. I thanked him for lunch, and decided I'd treated him rather badly. But – oh, what the hell?

In the taxi I raised an imaginary toast to Harry. He may have been a lousy husband, but he'd saved me from a lousy lover.

To my relief, the Pitts were waiting. Mr Comely had the contract open on his desk. A pen was resting on it.

'Sorry to have messed you around,' I said a little nervously.

Mrs Pitt gave a little flick of the hand.

'Perfectly all right,' she said cheerfully. 'But there *is* one more question I need to ask, Mrs Blake.'

Suddenly I was terrified it might all fall through. I winced at the memory of the monstrous lies I'd told that morning.

'Those tennis courts opposite the house,' she asked, 'May one use them?'

She must have noticed the look of relief on my face.

'Oh yes!' I answered, thrilled to be able to tell the truth. 'I used to play there all the time.'

'Wonderful,' she exclaimed, and handed her husband the pen.

Mr Pitt signed as though it was his own blood.

Then we all shook hands. Mr Comely's were clammy. He muttered something about a cheque in the post, and a completion date within a month.

Half an hour later I was leaving my house for ever, and leaving a kind of life for ever.

*

Tom had the good grace to say nothing; with an erection like that he didn't need to. I let go of it and took my clothes off while he lay back on the bed, watching me. Then I brushed my breasts along the length of his body, and came down on him. His hands were all over me; my hair was all over him. Our lips were everywhere. As I collapsed over him, he rolled me over and it began again, more urgently. I was naked inside and out, and I thought it would never stop. I prayed it wouldn't: could one go on for ever? Just fuck me, fuck me, fuck me!

He came inside me with a deep sigh, and I held him while he seemed to sleep, his hand on my breast. There were occasional burbling sounds. I was aware of Clive's jungle music next door, and wondered what noises I'd been making.

Eventually I heard Tom mumble something.

'Glad your headache's better.'

He gave a low chuckle. Then we both slept.

God knows what world I was lost in when the phone rang. I was aware of growling sounds from Tom as he reached out to answer it. The 'Hello' was more a gasp. I could hear a man's voice. Whoever it was sounded excited. There was a lot of laughter. Tom didn't do much more than grunt, though after what seemed ages he said, 'Well, well!' and then, 'Great! Terrific! Thank you! Talk to you tomorrow.'

I heard him put the phone down.

'That was Scott,' he said. We were both wide awake by now. 'And I have news for you.' He ran his fingers gently through my hair in the darkness. 'Samantha's blown it. Half Los Angeles is dying of salmonella poisoning. It'll be all over the California papers tomorrow. He's going to fax them to me. So – exit Samantha! End of case!' I heard Tom let out a deep breath. 'Maybe our life can now begin to begin. And, by the way,' he whispered, his lips just brushing mine, 'I've thought of a new cookery book we might do. *Tart Art*. Nothing personal, of course . . . Good night, sweetheart!'

10

Tom was unrecognisable. He made breakfast for the three of us. He embraced Mrs Teape, who went entirely silly for the rest of the morning. He swapped sexist jokes with the builders. He even promised to take Clive to EuroDisney.

Finally I pleaded with him.

'For Christ's sake, Tom, slow down and tell me everything Scott said to you on the telephone last night.'

He ignored me. '*Tart Art*! I like that, don't you?' he kept saying. 'Daughter of *Prawnography*.'

Finally, with Mrs Teape well out of earshot, he came out with Scott's story.

It seemed that Samantha Parsons, with her new-found fame, had taken to throwing dinner-parties in her Mandeville Canyon apartment for the Los Angeles glitterati, though it was unclear which prominent gift she was more keen to display – her seafood cooking or her bosom. There was never any doubt which her guests preferred, although by the rules of etiquette they couldn't partake of one without the other, and this finally proved to be her undoing.

The evening before last, Samantha had prepared a special culinary feature of Pacific prawns. These she presented, according to Scott, in the style of one of my more inventive illustrations in *Prawnography* – to wit *Prawns Soixante-Neuf.* Being no strangers to irregular forms of sexual athletics, the Hollywood fraternity tucked in hungrily, doubtless anticipating the real thing afterwards. Unfortunately, fate thwarted their hopes. Within an hour several ambulances were to be heard screaming in the direction of Mandeville Canyon, and before midnight the Intensive Care Unit of the Beverly Hills Clinic was stretching its resources to accommodate the assistant mayor of Los Angeles, the president of a leading film studio, a Californian press baron, two Oscar-winning actresses, and the wife of the Venezuelan consul.

By dawn one of the actresses and the assistant mayor were pronounced dead. Surviving guests were being stomach-pumped, and forensic experts from the police department were making an emergency study of the prawns. Ms Parsons, who for some reason had given her own prawns a miss, was being held for questioning, reputedly in tears. The sole comment extracted from her by the press was. 'I only followed the recipe.' But since the cookery-book in question was *Prawnography*, to which she was claiming authorship in the Californian courts, this was not believed to be helpful to her defence. A favourite rumour currently circulating in LA, Scott claimed, was that the luscious Samantha had indeed followed the recipe-book but failed to appreciate the difference between basil and belladonna. Both, after all, began with the same letter, and Samantha's literacy had never stretched very far.

More seriously, it was discovered that she'd bought the prawns six days before cooking them, the dinner having twice been re-scheduled to accommodate the now-dead actress – a famously capricious lady, Scott explained, though even in Hollywood it was deemed a little excessive to poison her.

Tom recounted this story with shameful relish, and – I suspected – a few colourful elaborations of his own.

So, now there was nothing to do except sit back and await further developments; though, as Tom morbidly pointed out, it was hard to see what further developments there could be beyond a few more deaths. As far as the palimony case was concerned, presumably it was just a matter of waiting to hear from Abram Kollwitz in LA, or perhaps Kyra Vansittart in London, that the plaintiff had withdrawn her plea, or perhaps had shot herself in the wake of multiple law-suits heading her way.

Tom gave me a hug. We took the builders a bottle of champagne. Mrs Teape got it into her head that I must be pregnant, and offered tearful congratulations. Only Clive was dismayed. Now that the case had collapsed he was perturbed lest his schoolfriends should consider the bet over Samantha's bust measurements to be null and void. His spirits only revived when he returned from the village later in the day with Tom's video camera and what he claimed was some excellent footage of Concha reclining in the nude. He announced that he intended to give a filmshow to all his classmates, and gather in the money that way. Honour was therefore satisfied, though I dreaded the letter from the headmaster.

The feeling of relief at Otters Mill was as balmy as the spring weather. The village was beginning to look like the picture on the postcards. And from my own life the storm-clouds had miraculously blown away. I even seriously wondered if some telepathic message had winged its way across the ether, and that Harry had only accidentally been the bearer of it. The message was that we'd all of us got it entirely wrong, that we were allowing the Valkyrie to dominate and destroy us; whereas if we only had a little patience they would destroy themselves. And – hey presto! – this was already happening. Samantha was the first: a somewhat excessive piece of destruction, perhaps, but then Hollywood was never given to moderation – why be content with one death when several will do?

And who would be next? I hoped it wouldn't all end in the mortuary: I might start having a bad conscience about it, and I could do without that on top of everything else.

Meanwhile I scarcely gave a thought to the lurking horrors of Harriet, or the imminent arrival of Tom's daughter. It wasn't until after lunch that day, when we'd drunk a good deal of wine, that Tom got around to telling me of other events that had occurred during my absence in London.

'I wasn't exactly in the best of moods,' he explained. 'You were away being chatted up by your publisher, and I was convinced you were about to have an affair with him.'

That shook me.

'Did you, by the way?' he added coolly.

The bastard must have known the answer. I shook my head vigorously.

'Of course not,' I answered.

I might more truthfully have said. 'By the skin of my teeth, I didn't.' But it might not have been well received.

'In that case,' Tom went on, a quizzical smile beginning to spread across his face. 'Perhaps you'd like to tell me what you know about a certain Professor Montblanc.'

Oh Jesus, I thought. I realised I'd never got round to telling Tom about the lunatic Frenchman from Montpellier whom Anne-Marie had unloaded on us. The first time he'd phoned, Tom had been in California; and on the second occasion he'd been seeing his lawyer in London.

'Ah well, yes,' I said hesitantly, struggling to recall what I'd told the man. 'Professor Montblanc. An eminent embryologist. Your wife sent him – I remember. Anne-Marie, that is. He telephoned twice when you were away. I tried to put him off.'

'I see,' said Tom, gazing at me steadily. 'Well, you didn't. He turned up.'

Tom's fingers began to drum a little dance on the table. 'Yes,' he went on, not taking his eyes off me for a moment, 'it was most interesting. I learnt a lot. For instance, that you were actually my mother. That you were about to die. That we lived in the Outer Hebrides. That I normally spend most of my time careering round England on horseback. That I'm absolutely thrilled by the idea of donating vast sums of money to rescuing endangered species. And that in particular I'm most anxious to fund a sperm bank to help save the Madagascan vampire bat from extinction.' He stopped drumming his fingers. 'I'd say you did a pretty good job there, Jan. And thank you for landing me right in it.'

I put my head in my hands on the kitchen table, and moaned.

'Oh God, Tom, I'm sorry,' I pleaded. 'I did mean to tell you. What happened?'

'Well,' Tom went on, 'while I was sitting here thinking about you looking delicious in the Gavroche, or wherever, the doorbell rang. And there was this man on the doorstep who looked like Einstein.'

'Yes,' I said cautiously.

'Then we had this remarkable conversation. Shall I tell you how it went?'

I nodded. I knew Tom well enough by now to realise how much he was going to enjoy telling me all this.

So, he explained, the man who looked like Einstein introduced himself as *Professeur Montblanc*, and immediately expressed regrets that *Monsieur Brand*'s mother had *le cancer terminal*. He had found his voyage to *les Îles d'Ecosse* most interesting, he said, though obviously there had been some *erreur*, and how happy he was at last to meet *Monsieur Brand* after so long a journey, and to discover that he wasn't riding across the country *à cheval* as his mother had claimed. He was most of all *ravi* that *Monsieur Brand* was happy to finance the establishment of a *banque de sperme* for the unfortunate *chauve-souris vampire de Madagascar* which was so incredibly *mis en danger* due to the *rites de fertilité ignobles* prevalent among *les tribus indigènes sauvages* of that benighted island.

Tom was producing more French than I ever believed he knew. There were tears of laughter in my eyes.

'And you agreed, of course,' I said.

Tom didn't think he had, exactly. He'd begun quite gently, he explained, pointing out to the professor that, what with millions starving in Somalia, concentration camps in Bosnia, flood victims in Bangladesh, damage to the ozone layer and Maxwell pensioners on the dole, frankly there seemed to be higher charity priorities than the fate of vampire bats, and in any case perhaps the world might be better off without such murderous creatures.

Professor Montblanc hadn't enjoyed that, Tom thought. Nothing in the professor's view could be more urgent than saving defenceless animals from extinction. He wished to point out that the human race was *not* in danger of extinction; the Madagascan vampire bat definitely was.

And so with any luck, Tom had suggested, was the tsetse fly and the malarial mosquito.

This hadn't gone down too well either.

Growing exasperated, the professor had then appealed to Tom's natural generosity – always an unwise step.

'Think of Anne-Marie, your wife,' he suggested.

Tom explained that he preferred not to, having been divorced from Anne-Marie for twenty years. The professor looked startled. He tried again.

'Think of your poor mother.'

Tom pointed out that she'd been dead for fifty years.

This produced a look of shocked disbelief. The professor grew incensed.

'*Vous vous moquez de moi, monsieur,*' he spluttered.

Tom insisted he was telling the truth. Montblanc shook his head vigorously, and thrust his hand deep into his overcoat pocket. Tom wondered for a moment if he might produce a gun. Instead it was a large buff envelope, which he held out before him.

'*Alors, regardez ça!*'

And the professor explained how *ce paquet* had been posted to *Madame Brand* with an accompanying letter of explanation and a promise of generous financial support.

Tom was beginning to look at me rather strangely as he described this scene.

'The professor left it behind,' he went on. 'Perhaps you'd care to look at it. You may even recognise the handwriting.'

It all came back to me – that early morning on the hill above the village armed with my superzoom camera which Tom had given me. The vision of a white ocean of mist, with the roofs floating on it and the birds marooned on top.

My little joke about the Wiltshire Carved Pheasants had returned to roost.

I opened the envelope. There was my letter to Anne-Marie. And there were my photographs. Tom reached over and began to lay them out across the table. And masterpieces they were, too. Rooftop pheasants dramatically shipwrecked, wonderfully realistic, their plight more desperate even than that of the Madagascan vampire bat.

'You little minx,' was all Tom said.

Thank God he took it well. Rather better, he explained, than Professor Montblanc. And he pointed to a small gash on his left cheek, which I'd assumed to be a shaving cut.

'That's where he hit me,' Tom said. 'And then he left – promising I hadn't heard the last of this.'

It wasn't quite the end of Tom's story. A puzzled expression lingered on his face, and he kept making little affirmative noises while his eyes wandered over the kitchen as if in search of some vital clue.

I asked him what was on his mind. It had just occurred to him, he said: there was something familiar about that man. Tom was certain he'd seen him before, and he was racking his brain to remember where. It was the Einstein look, and the mad vanity.

The puzzle continued to trouble him all afternoon. We went for a walk along the river in the last of the afternoon sun. I felt light-headed, aware that we'd seen off two of the Valkyrie within twenty-four hours, and that all of a sudden life seemed altogether rosier. But Tom was only half with me: Professor Montblanc was still churning in his head. It was just the same at dinner. Clive asked Tom when they might be going to EuroDisney, and Tom didn't answer. He didn't even answer when Clive asked if *Soixante-Neuf* was the number of Samantha's apartment.

Then suddenly, in the middle of the BBC news, he leapt to his feet. They were showing an item about a drugs swoop in Marseille.

'I've got it,' Tom exclaimed. 'Marseille. 1980, or thereabouts.'

I couldn't get a lot out of him – at least not a lot that was coherent. All I did gather was that there'd been a scandal about some French embryologist. Tom had covered the story at the time. Tomorrow he intended to dig it out – he'd ring a friend on the paper and get the cuttings faxed over.

'And then we'll see,' he said.

There was still something on Tom's mind. He wouldn't tell me. Instead, he chose a romantic moment later that evening to whisper an urgent message in my ear.

'Jan, I'm going back to being a journalist. Fuck Byron.'

And I'd imagined it was me.

Ruth telephoned to say she'd read in the papers about Samantha's fatal dinner-party, and how remarkable it was that Ms Parsons' cooking should have so much in common with hers. There'd been a number of such deaths at her own dinner-table, she assured me, but unlike Samantha she had always been protected by diplomatic immunity. And whenever there had been embarrassing enquiries, the Foreign Office would issue a statement lamenting the suicide of a would-be defector. It was always done in the most civilised fashion, and nobody's feathers were ruffled; though Ruth did admit that her guest list had shrunk over the years, which suited her fine. She loathed entertaining on a grand scale; there was far too much of it in the diplomatic world.

I wasn't quite in the mood for these pleasantries, and explained that I had a great many things on my mind. There was Clive deafening us with his rock music all night. There were the builders' transistor radios all day. There was Harriet demanding half a million pounds and sending Tom safety-pins through the post. There was his spotty daughter threatening to descend on us any moment. There was this mad French professor haunting us with demands to fund a sperm bank for vampire bats. And there was Mrs Teape telling everybody in the village I was pregnant and about to become a cabinet minister in Mr Major's government.

'And this was supposed to be our idyllic rustic retreat!' I shouted.

Ruth agreed that my life certainly sounded interesting, and that nothing like this ever seemed to happen in Liechtenstein.

'And how is Tom standing up to it all?' she asked.

I explained that he'd announced he was returning to journalism, and that I'd enquired how a working journalist could possibly operate from Sarum Magna unless he fancied writing the weekly Nature Notes in the *Salisbury Gazette*. Or alternatively, perhaps the man in my life was intending to make a triumphant return to sleuth reporting, with just the occasional whistle-stop visit to Otters Mill for a quick snack and a leg-over while "'er indoors" filled her lonely days illustrating books for other people's children. What was more, I'd just sold my place in London, and no longer had anywhere to flee when the first symptoms of madness struck.

'And *is* Tom returning to journalism?' Ruth asked.

'Thank God, no, as it turns out,' I said. 'He announced that he was an investigative journalist and a bloody good one, and that he was determined to employ those skills to rid us of our plagues – vampire bats and the lot.'

Ruth laughed.

'And knowing Tom,' she said, 'that means dishing the dirt.'

I agreed, and promised to keep her fully informed.

'They've abolished dirt in Liechtenstein,' Ruth added plaintively before she rang off. 'I miss it.'

Meanwhile, there was certainly no lack of it round here. The builders had by now emptied most of the infrastructure of the old mill into the garden, burying the spring flowers and surprising the ducks. Only the kingfisher seemed unconcerned, continuing to delight us with a flash of lapis lazuli between the leaning alders, and occasionally perching with a bright eye on a branch above the mill-race. I photographed it with my super-zoom, and planned to frame the masterpiece and hang it in my studio when the building work was finally done.

'Promise me you won't send it to Anne-Marie, that's all,' was Tom's comment. 'Or we'll have the loony professor back again in no time.'

'After the way you received him last time, Tom, that's pretty unlikely,' I suggested. 'It sounds as though you saw him off.'

Tom just muttered.

'Harriet's the one I want to see off. I'm still trying to work out how.'

Indeed, the frightful Harriet. What to do about her?

The first clue was offered to us a couple of afternoons later. Tom and I had taken the car into Salisbury to look at an old refectory table we'd seen in an antique shop, as well as perform some errands for Emelda. Clive had gone off to explore the neighbourhood on his bicycle, taking the video camera with him in the firm belief that every village in Wiltshire must have its naked Concha. His film-show, he assured Tom, was going to be a knock-out.

'What about your school holiday project?' I asked feebly.

'This *is* my holiday project,' he replied smugly.

Well, at least he was more cheerful now he had some burning ambition to fulfil. We left him to it, and I ruefully put his next term's fees in the post on our way to Salisbury.

It was nearly five o'clock when we returned to Sarum Magna. As we were about to turn into our track something caught my eye. A sleek white Audi was parked on the verge a hundred yards or so down the road. In a village you soon get to know every car, and this was one I didn't recognise.

'Somebody's thirty grand's worth,' said Tom.

'But whose?' I asked. 'You don't suppose Mooncalf's decided to lash out, do you? Or John Gant's come into a huge EC subsidy?'

Tom shrugged. Then the same thought came to us both.

'I wonder,' he said. 'It just could be, couldn't it?'

We left our car where it was and approached the mill cautiously on foot, keeping to the verge under the protection of the hedge. As we drew closer we could hear the builders whistling in the mill-house, and the sound of saws and hammers. They were laying new floorboards.

Suddenly Tom put his hand on my arm and pulled me closer into the hedge. Then he pointed. A woman was standing on one of our dustbins and gazing through the kitchen window of our cottage. Even from this distance the size of her bum gave her away. It could only be Harriet.

'Ah well,' Tom murmured. 'That'll mean a new dustbin.'

I laughed, and he clapped a hand over my mouth.

'Get through the hedge – quickly!' he said.

We did. Peering through the young leaves I could just make out an arse being cautiously lowered to the ground. Harriet looked furtively about her, dusted her hands, and began to make her way towards us along the track.

I crouched down, motionless, and then realised Tom was no longer there. Turning my head, I saw him hurrying doubled up along the hedge towards the road. He straddled a wooden gate and disappeared.

Harriet passed heavily by without seeing me. I could hear her muttering darkly to herself, refuelling her anger.

Shortly afterwards there was the sound of a car driving away. I struggled back through the hedge and caught sight of Tom striding towards me, a smile on his face.

'I just thought I'd get the number,' he said. 'A1 DOL. What d'you reckon?'

I suggested that A1 BITCH might have been more appropriate, but Tom wasn't listening.

'A brand-new Audi Quattro,' he was saying. 'There's no way she could afford that on the maintenance I give her. And if she can, I'm halving it.' Tom had a knowing look in his eye. 'More to the point, Jan, personalised number-plates are for certain types of people, and they're nearly always men. We'll see.'

It was beginning to feel like living in a command post. Tom, as Director of Combined Operations, was a man on fire. He was scarcely ever off the phone, and when he wasn't on it, it rang us. Certain words and phrases kept filtering through to me in my studio, where I was getting down to the Hilaire Belloc illustrations. They included such things as 'Special Branch', 'High Security', 'Crime Desk' and on one occasion – which caused Henry King to stop chewing little bits of string – 'Sleepy Joe'. No wonder, I decided, journalists refuse to disclose their sources. Tom clearly had no intention of disclosing them even to me, though I detected more than a whiff of professional vanity in the way he paraded his secrets around him, inviting enquiries from me which he'd then decline to answer.

'And who's Sleepy Joe?' I ventured.

'A hood,' was all Tom would say. It sounded dangerous, and I could tell he loved that.

There was no doubt about it – Tom the sleuth was a great deal more exciting than Tom the would-be Byron. I was reminded of the Duke of Wellington returning from Waterloo and leaping into bed with Harriet Wilson without taking his boots off; though Tom at least did that, except once when the laces knotted.

Clive loved the new sense of urgency about the place, eavesdropping on Tom's telephone calls and from time to time glancing contemptuously at my Belloc illustrations. 'Women's work,' his eyes said.

Mrs Teape loved it too, though she was convinced that the phone calls were from 10 Downing Street, and that Tom was about to join me in Mr Major's cabinet. 'How nice for you to be able to work together,' she announced. I shuddered to think what she was telling the builders.

One of the phone calls was from Kyra Vansittart, announcing her intention to come down for the day. Her explanation was that it would be more peaceful to work on the Harriet case here rather than in her London office. Also, in view of Harriet's trespassing habits, it would be useful to her as a lawyer if she understood the lay of the land. Tom thought she just wanted a day in the country. My own explanation was more sceptical: 'the lay of the land' rang quite different bells in my ears, and I was pretty sure she wanted a good look at me before deciding whether or not to make a move on Tom. In that case, I decided, I would have a very good look at *her*. And I would look absolutely stunning.

So I did.

Distressingly, so did she.

Tom, of course, loved it.

I didn't. I eyed her with morose suspicion.

Fortunately she was on the fat side, though she'd done her practised best to draw attention to where fat can be a plus. Her blouse swooped, taking with it Tom's eyes.

'More soup?' I said firmly. 'Or perhaps you feel you shouldn't.'

I felt mean the moment I said it. But she exuded the kind of overripe self-confidence which brings out the bitch in me. To make it worse, she just smiled.

Tom was giving me an old-fashioned look. I wasn't enjoying this at all, and it was my own fault.

'How come you're blonde if you're Jewish?' I asked.

Oh God, I'm behaving badly, I thought.

She came straight back at me, still holding her smile.

'There've been a lot of rapes in my family.'

That broke the ice. It was impossible not to laugh. And so did she.

I brought in the quiche I'd made. Feeling a lot better, I sat myself down with my elbows on the table and my chin in my hands. And I looked at her.

'I'm sorry,' I said. 'Forgive me for being on edge. It's not been easy.'

Kyra gazed at me for a moment. Then she reached out and placed a hand on my arm.

'That's OK,' she said lightly. 'In your position I'd be screaming by now. You're a brave woman.'

Oh, what sweet music to my ears! I heard myself mutter 'Thank you'. I realised how much I'd needed someone to say that. To tell me I wasn't just being a neurotic idiot. That the whole situation was intolerable. That I was actually being courageous and wonderful, and Tom was bloody lucky to have somebody like me to stand by him.

All my defensiveness fell away. We talked. We even began to discuss past lovers – which drove Tom out of the room in search of documents. And of course we discussed Ruth, who'd had more past lovers than either of us – including, Kyra acknowledged admiringly, all of her own except her husband whom Ruth hadn't fancied. I laughed and said she hadn't fancied Tom either. So that was something we had in common, we agreed, and raised a glass to it. Having set her up as an enemy, I'd made a friend. I invited her to stay for a weekend 'when this nightmare is over'.

'Will it ever be?' I asked.

'If I have anything to do with it – yes!' she said. 'And I'd love to come down.'

At this point Tom returned with a pile of papers, and after making some coffee I left them to work, feeling safer than before, though perhaps still not completely so.

After Kyra Vansittart's departure I found Tom sitting over mountains of notes, and quoting Lord Scarman.

'"The law now encourages spouses to avoid bitterness after family breakdown and to settle their money and property problems." That's what he wrote. 1979. Minton versus Minton. Any relation to your admirer in publishing, I wonder? Anyway, it all led to the Matrimonial and Family Proceedings Act of 1984.'

'Why are you telling me all this, Tom?' I asked.

'Because if only I'd hung on with Harriet until after 1984 I'd have been able to settle with the bitch once and for all, and she wouldn't now be snooping about, standing on our dustbins and sending me safety-pins through the post.'

I said that didn't seem to me a very helpful piece of information; and what was Kyra's advice?

Tom looked serious.

'That I'll have to pay.' He took a deep breath. 'There's no doubt about it – harassment or not. Thanks to *Prawnography*, I'll either have to give her a hugely increased maintenance or an even huger settlement. The law's an absolute bastard. You know *your* income is taken into consideration too, because I'm living with you and we're a partnership. Let's get divorced.'

Then he seemed to remember we weren't married, and swore. I expected him to do more than that: hurl something, or scream. Instead he smiled.

'Unless, of course, I can find out about Sleepy Joe.'

So we were back to being secretive again. All Tom would say was that he needed a few days in London – next week, he thought – and he hinted at the various people he had to see, managing to make them sound shady and important. Journalists, I realised, don't have friends, they have contacts.

The following morning a heap of stuff arrived. The post brought a letter from Abram Kollwitz confirming that 'Ms Parsons' had indeed dropped her palimony suit, and advising Tom that any counter-charges he might consider bringing on the grounds of defamation of character would have to wait their turn in a lengthy queue headed by police charges of manslaughter. Abram added a footnote to the effect that Samantha's husband, the would-be monk, had broken his silence to confess that he'd only retreated to a desert monastery out of fear of being poisoned by his wife's cooking.

'Sensible fellow,' Abram added.

I was distracted from feeling rather sorry for Samantha after all by the arrival in the same post of another safety-pin, this time addressed to me.

'Things are hotting up, Tom,' I said, showing him Harriet's eloquent little gift.

'Not half as hot as they will be very soon, I assure you,' he snorted, dropping the safety-pin into a drawer which I noticed he'd labelled 'Love Letters'.

Then the fax started chattering. Tom strode across the room and leaned over it like a vulture waiting to pick its prey clean.

'Well, well!' he exclaimed after a few minutes. And he turned and handed me a sheaf of paper. 'It seems I was right.'

They were newspaper articles, some French, some English. My eye fell on one headed, 'Fertility Scientist – Sex Scandal'. The by-line read, 'A Tom Brand Exclusive'. Tom was looking smug.

'The French medical authorities', the piece began, 'admitted yesterday that leading French embryologist Dr Jean-Pierre Eiger has been relieved of his senior post in the celebrated Lefargue Clinic, Marseille. The reason given was "poor health". But I can reveal that Dr Eiger has in fact been sacked for gross medical malpractice as a result of complaints by numerous women who have been recipients of his fertility treatment in the clinic over the past five years.'

The article went on to explain that Dr Eiger was one of the pioneers of I.V.F. (In Vitro Fertilisation), by which women long distressed by their infertility were enabled to conceive and bear children successfully. Several forms of treatment were offered, but where the cause of infertility was the husband's low sperm-count, Dr Eiger's method was to supplement the man's sperm with that of a donor, whose identity would never be revealed to the wife. He would be quite unknown to her, and she to him, so avoiding any possible claims or accusations which might otherwise arise later in life. This was accepted as customary medical ethics, and was strictly observed at the Lefargue Clinic, a spokesman confirmed.

Dr Eiger was believed to have successfully treated some two hundred women by this method. Unfortunately the case of Françoise Didier, wife of a local socialist *député*, cast doubts on the brilliant doctor's practice. Mme Didier had written a perturbed letter to the director of the clinic pointing out that as a result of Dr Eiger's treatment she had given birth to quintuplets, all of them male, and all them bearing a striking resemblance to Dr Eiger.

This letter was dealt with discreetly by the clinic, and was never made public. Neither, so it seemed, were a number of similar revelations brought to the director's attention over a period of several years. But when on 14 July 1985 – Bastille Day – no fewer than seventeen letters reached the clinic from different parts of France, it was decided that Dr Eiger's dynasty was attaining unmanageable proportions and endangering the fine reputation of the Lefargue Clinic. Copious denials of improper behaviour were issued to the complainants, and official inquiries were successfully stifled. None the less it was clearly time for the Bastille to fall, and Dr

Eiger was encouraged to retire in order to nurse his poor health. And that, as far as the Lefargue Clinic was concerned, was that.

But not for our 'investigative reporter'. He had succeeded in tracking down thirty-five of Dr Eiger's former patients, all of whom had complained to the clinic only to receive patronising disclaimers of malpractice and an assurance that physical similarities between human beings represented a not-uncommon phenomenon. But the women had now shown our reporter photographs of their offspring – seventy three of them, aged between two and six – and (give or take a difference in hair colour) they all looked quite astonishingly alike.

I stopped reading. Tom was laughing.

'And not just astonishingly alike. They all looked exactly like Einstein – all seventy-three of them!'

He then pointed to the photograph of Dr Eiger which accompanied the article.

'Isn't that our man?'

It clearly was.

'So the famous wanker went into hiding, changed his name from one mountain to another – Eiger to Montblanc – and re-emerged squeaky-clean to begin a new life among vampire bats. Any more trouble from him', Tom went on, 'and the French police might become interested in his past. That should cook his goose with Anne-Marie – or whatever endangered species he prefers to cook instead.'

'Do you suppose, Tom,' I said, 'that even now there are orang-utans being born who look like Einstein?'

Tom chuckled. 'How could you tell? They all do anyway.'

It was nearly midday. We took a walk along the river. I'd grown quite familiar with Ayrton's chiff-chaff by now, belting out his two notes high in the poplar trees. Proud of my new country lore, I drew Tom's attention to the bird. He looked at me askance.

'If that's another endangered species, so let it be,' was all he said.

If Ayrton turned up right now with his fishing rods it would serve Tom right, I thought. I was more of a country person than he would ever be; and yet I was the one who'd been pining for London. Tom, I realised, would simply be himself anywhere, and that was one of the things I loved about him.

'It's been a good morning's work,' he said.

It wasn't quite over, as it turned out. We hadn't reckoned on Mrs Teape. We returned to the cottage just as she was fixing the man-traps in her hair and preparing to leave. The newspaper cuttings about Professor Montblanc and the fertility clinic lay strewn carefully across the kitchen table.

Mrs Teape was looking radiant.

'So the news is out, Mrs Brand,' she announced. 'I'm so pleased. You both deserve it. And to know that you've got the top man to look after you. I'm quite sure the whole village will be delighted at the news.'

11

THE sounds of hammering from the mill were echoed here in the cottage by Tom methodically nailing down Harriet's coffin.

The telephone was still ringing constantly, and with each phone call a look of sly pleasure would pass over Tom's face. This wasn't at all the man who'd sweet-talked me into his bed a year ago. Nor was it the 'Mr Tom' whom the *maître d'* used to usher to his special table, discretely not noticing whether I was the same woman he'd brought last time. And it certainly wasn't the Tom who talked of abandoning being a tabloid hack and devoting his riper years to writing a biography of Lord Byron. This was a dangerous animal, and I was grateful it wasn't me in the coffin.

'I've got quite a dossier on Sleepy Joe,' he said languidly after about the tenth phone call that morning. 'Though not quite as thick a dossier as the one at Scotland Yard, apparently.' Tom began to flick through a pile of scrawled notes and cuttings. 'It's his car all right, by the way – A1 DOL. They're rather his speciality, dolls, it seems. Hence the name Sleepy Joe. He does most of his business from bed – lucky man.'

I didn't think Tom had done too badly.

'His "business" being what?' I asked.

'Officially – property development. Unofficially – gangland stuff. He's a sort of up-market Kray. Lives terribly respectably in Barnes. Kids at St. Paul's. A modest little château in Périgord. Ski chalet in Zermatt. A catamaran somewhere. Not short of a penny is Sleepy Joe – and I doubt if the tax-man sees much of it. The big question is – does Harriet?'

I said I was worried about him messing with a man like that, and Tom looked at me contemptuously.

'What d'you think I've been doing all my life, sweetheart? Growing roses?'

I felt crushed, and rather in awe.

It was now Thursday. Tom was due to go to London on Monday – probably for most of the week. I wasn't looking forward to it. I had visions of the late-night ring on the door bell. 'Excuse me, Miss Er . . . um, I believe you were a friend of a Mr Thomas Brand. I'm sorry to have to inform you . . .'

Then I decided I was being wet.

Tom had three days to prepare his 'brief', as he pompously put it. Not a great deal of time, he said wearily, but he would use every minute of it. The portcullis was down. There were to be *no* distractions.

The gods had other ideas, as gods do.

Their way through the portcullis was the answerphone, Tom being too hardened a journalist to cut himself off entirely. About mid-morning the phone rang, was stifled, and then the machine's little light began winking at me, beckoning, daring me to ignore it: it might be a wonderful contract, or my mother had died.

I was working. But I couldn't take my eyes of that light.

'Oh shit! I'd better get it just in case,' I called out to Tom.

I pressed the playback button. It was a woman's voice I didn't recognise – thank God! – but she'd obviously begun to speak without waiting for the bleep, and I was immediately plunged into mid-torrent. I didn't even have time to call Tom.

'Wow! Oh wow,' I heard. 'You have to believe me. The greatest thing that ever happened. It's blowing my mind. Incredible!' I listened in astonishment. She sounded as though she was having an orgasm. Heavy panting followed. Perhaps that *was* the orgasm.

'Tom,' I yelled. 'Quickly! We've got one of those dial-a-fuck phone-ins on a crossed line.'

I was getting quite turned on. I placed my ear closer.

'Oooooh!' Such a long, passionate sigh. Well, it must have been terrific. But was that all – over so soon? How long do you get for your telephonic wank? But no! She was trying to say something else amid the gasps. 'You must believe me. You must!' (Well, why shouldn't I? Sounds real enough.) 'He comes every night.' (I know, I can hear it, darling.) 'It's the biggest thing of all.' (Well, aren't you lucky, doll!) 'I want everyone to know; you *must* help.' (Tom, don't you dare; she's doing very nicely as it is, thank you.) 'It's so hard doing it all alone.' (Hang about. You're not alone, and *he's* supposed to be the one who's hard.)

'Tom! Tom!' I called out. 'We should do this more often. Can't we subscribe, or something? I want to go and make love *now*. Mrs Teape's done the bedroom.'

I should have noticed Tom wasn't exactly sharing my mood. His eyes were fixed on the answerphone. The message hadn't quite finished. After a few more orgasmic sounds the voice continued, less hysterical this time.

'Please, Tom. Please! It's Byron. I know how much you love him. You see, he's dictating to me. New cantos of *Don Juan*. Every night. Please, please do something. We need to . . .'

There was a click. The tape had run out.

Well, if I'd wanted to make love a minute ago, I didn't any longer. I raised my eyes from the answerphone.

'Tom, what the hell?' I said. 'It was for you! She knows you?'

He gave a deep sigh, and then another.

'It's Georgina, that's all.'

'That's *all?*'

There was a pause while I struggled to gather my thoughts. Just a moment earlier I'd imagined I'd discovered a new aphrodisiac. Instead, I'd discovered a new wife. It had all but skipped my mind that Tom still had two more ghosts in his cupboard.

Georgina! I remembered now, she was Wife Number Four.

Distractions or not, I needed an explanation. Yet another bloody explanation!

'Tom, this is becoming a regular seminar. What are you going to find to talk to me about when you've run out of wives?'

He put on his Frankie Howerd look.

'Jan, she's a complete fruitcake. That's all you need to know,' he said. 'She's out to lunch. She's barking.'

'Tom,' I said, beginning to feel more composed. 'What is it about you, I wonder? Do you attract them, or do you turn them into nutcases? D'you think I'll go the same way? I'm beginning to get quite worried.'

'Georgina wasn't always like that,' he went on. Suddenly there was a sad note in his voice. 'It started when she had a miscarriage. It tipped her over the edge.'

It became clear as Tom talked that Georgina had never been all that far from the edge. She'd entered his life post-Samantha, he explained. She was the intellectual one, a lecturer in English Literature at London University, and tipped for high places.

'Like the clouds,' I suggested unkindly.

He grimaced. Then he went on.

Georgina was dark, sexy, passionate. She wrote erotic verse, lived an eccentric life, and drank heavily. But she was very clever; also very funny, Tom added.

'Which was why I married her.'

I said that seemed a poor reason for marrying someone: how can a man live on a diet of brains and jokes? But Tom disagreed. At least it was a better reason than he'd had for marrying all the others – which was still a pretty poor answer, I thought.

'Then after a couple of years she had the miscarriage, and that was when it all began.'

She started to have fantasies about psychic meetings with literary figures of the past, usually when she was drunk. Tom persuaded her to join Alcoholics Anonymous, but even in her new-found sobriety the fantasies continued. At first these encounters were purely social – rather as William Blake used to announce that the prophet Isaiah had appeared to him at breakfast. And they were harmless enough, almost cosy. She would slip them into the conversation. 'By the way, Dr Johnson assures me that half the things attributed to him were made up by Boswell', or, 'Dante swears he couldn't actually stand the sight of Beatrice.' Humdrum stuff. And Tom got used to it.

Until suddenly Georgina suffered a breakdown. She was given sabbatical leave from the university.

'For nearly a year I looked after her,' he went on. 'I used to dash up to Fleet Street, and dash back again wondering if she'd taken an overdose or thrown herself out of the window. I never took a job out of London.'

Gradually she recovered, and went back to work; she even wrote a highly-esteemed book on the Brontës. But the marriage was dead. And the drinking had begun again, and this time it was fearsome.

'She'd run naked down the street at midnight, or throw up in the middle of dinner-parties. In the end I couldn't stand it any longer, and left her . . . plus yet another house!' he added ruefully.

For several years he heard nothing more from her. The divorce went through. Tom met and married Sarah – 'my last mistake'. Then out of the blue he received a letter. This was about a year ago. Georgina was being visited regularly by Emily Brontë, she claimed excitedly. More than that, Ms Brontë was anxious to dictate to her the sequel to *Wuthering Heights*, which death had prevented the lady committing to paper herself. Would Tom please help in this historic task? After all, being a journalist he knew shorthand, which Georgina did not. Always on the lookout for a good story, Tom agreed to go round, but the ghost of Ms Brontë failed to appear, and he returned home. The phone went. The ghost had arrived: would Tom hurry round in order to capture the creative moment? The same thing happened.

'Clearly ghosts didn't like me.'

Back home, again the phone went. Further pleas from Georgina. This time Tom used a four-letter word and suggested where Ms Brontë could put her *Wuthering Heights, Part Two*. Georgina was enraged by such callous indifference to literary genius, and to Tom's intense relief vowed never to speak to him again.

A year later she broke her vow to explain that she'd now managed to transcribe a complete manuscript of Emily Brontë's novel, but had received no fewer than fifteen rejection slips from publishers. This was particularly galling, she added, since John Milton was almost ready with *Paradise Re-Lost*. Could Tom help?

'I didn't. Presumably Paradise was lost yet again.'

But it hadn't ended there. Georgina persuaded a well-endowed spiritualist society to underwrite the publication of *Wuthering Heights Rides Again* – or however it came to be titled – under the imprint of The Afterlife Press. The book was enthusiastically received in psychic circles, and gained something of a cult readership due –

in Tom's opinion – to passages of explicit erotica which would have given Emily Brontë the vapours but closely resembled Georgina's own writings in that vein.

'You have to remember', Tom explained, 'that Georgina may be nuts, but she is extremely clever.'

I gazed at Tom dolefully.

'So now it's Byron's turn. I see. And why does she need you this time?'

Tom looked puzzled.

'I can only assume', he said, 'that the spiritualist society disliked the smutty publicity given to the previous venture, and have withdrawn their support for The Afterlife Press.'

'So she expects you to be the new godfather.'

Tom nodded.

'That's about it.'

I was puzzled about this, and puzzled about Tom. Nothing would have been easier, it seemed to me, than simply to ignore Georgina's ravings – or to say, bluntly, 'No!' But when I suggested this, he frowned. There was something fishy about this whole business, he felt sure. Someone else was involved, in what way he didn't know, but his journalist's nose had caught a scent from that phone message. Georgina was being exploited, he was certain of it.

'Do you mind?' I asked, surprised.

He did mind. That was when I learnt something new about him. Tom, who was prepared to play it dirty in order to see off any number of ex-wives who were exploiting him, none the less couldn't bear the thought of anyone else exploiting *them*.

'Goodness, Tom,' I said, 'you're a knight in shining armour after all.'

He merely grimaced. It would give him yet another little task to perform while he was in London, he explained.

At least, I thought, it promised to be less dangerous than bearding Sleepy Joe.

'You will take care, won't you?' I said, 'because I do love you.'

He looked puzzled and pleased at the same time.

'I wonder why,' he answered. 'There aren't many women who'd put up with all the rubbish I inflict on you.'

I laughed.

'Which only goes to show what appalling taste in women you have – until now, that is.'

At that moment Mrs Teape arrived bearing a cup of coffee still bubbling from the saucepan.

'I know you like it strong, Mr Brand,' she announced, and retired with a flirtatious smile.

'Oh God,' Tom murmured. 'Is this my punishment?'

I stood on the platform at Salisbury and watched the train until it passed out of sight, then drove home feeling as chill and damp as the afternoon. It might be as much as a week, Tom had said. He'd phone every evening, he promised, but that was small comfort.

In London I'd never minded being alone; but here in the country it was like being abandoned. I found myself wondering what people meant when they talked about 'the companionship of nature'. Did they mean flowers?

Most of ours lay buried under builders' rubble, so they weren't much use to me. Trees? Well, they were certainly pretty enough, growing more green and lush each day, but not exactly balm to the soul; you couldn't talk to them, though I imagined Mooncalf did. And what about birds? All I could hear was Ayrton's chiff-chaff urgently belting out the same two notes from dawn to dusk – like a simplified version of Mrs Teape.

'Why do we have to live in the country, mum?' Clive had asked mournfully.

I found myself thinking the same.

That evening Ruth phoned, and was unsympathetic.

'What did you expect, darling? If you didn't want to grow mould, why did you leave London?'

She only wanted to tell me about a crisis concerning her ski-instructor. Piers was beginning to ask why she still went off on skiing trips even though the snow had melted. So far she'd taken the line that dry-skiing was the most wonderful practice for the real thing, hoping he wouldn't ask what the 'real thing' was. Piers had said nothing except to comment that the terrain must be extremely rocky judging by the bruises on her neck and breasts. Besides, he had a nasty habit of paying her back. He'd already acquired a secretary who was the only woman in Liechtenstein under thirty, and 'rather good-looking' – which in Piers-speak almost certainly meant that she was gorgeous and sat taking dictation from Her Majesty's Ambassador with her blouse and skirt split to the waist. Ruth thought she might have to trade one lover for another and give monogamy a try until the girl could be repatriated.

'And how's your beautiful publisher?' she asked eventually.

'Purely professional,' I said. 'We speak on the phone.'

I could hear Ruth groan. It was all the result of burying myself in the depths of the country, she assured me. I was a much more interesting person when I'd lived in London; any minute now I'd be taking up bridge.

'And how's Tom?' she went on, having dealt with me.

I explained that he was in town sorting out two ex-wives, and she thought that sounded more like it.

'Do you still make love?' she asked suddenly. 'How often?'

'Every day – if possible,' I said.

Ruth sounded quite shocked.

'That's indecent. But then you aren't married. D'you think you *will* marry him?'

I said I didn't know; at that moment too much of my life with Tom was spent wrestling with his previous marriages to want to add one more to the list.

'But you do love him?' she asked.

'Yes,' I said. Then, thinking that wasn't quite enough, 'passionately,' I added.

There was a pause.

'Passionately! Wow! Lucky woman. I think I love Piers, but then I sometimes think I don't know what love means – until I'm in danger of losing him, and then I know. But passion? That's something different. My passions fly in one window and out the other, often too quick for me to grab them on the way. I'm a gypsy of the heart, that's the trouble.'

After that little homily Ruth rang off, but not before vowing to spy on Piers' new secretary to see if she was worth sacrificing her ski-instructor for.

As always, Sarum Magna seemed more than a little dull after a phone call from Ruth: though not, as it happened, for very long.

On Wednesday evening, two days after Tom's departure, I was preparing a risotto for Clive and myself when the phone went. I answered it cheerfully, thinking it was probably Tom giving me an update on his sleuthing activities. But it was a woman's voice. Just a 'Hello!' Nothing more, but my heart sank. Not another one! There was a hesitancy in the voice, as if she hadn't expected me.

'Who is it?' I said cautiously.

She didn't answer. Then she read out our phone number.

'Is that right?' the woman asked.

I said it was, and who did she want?

There was another pause. And then a laugh.

'Perhaps it's both of you,' she said. 'That's all right.' The voice sounded Irish.

By now I was getting confused and irritated. But before I could say anything further, she went on, still with a hint of laughter in her voice.

'The evenings are best for me, cos I work, you see. Any time really, I don't mind.'

'Excuse me,' I began, my mind now totally out of focus.

'No, it's quite all right – honestly. You can watch, or join in, as you like. I don't mind.'

This was getting ridiculous.

'Excuse me,' I began again, more forcefully this time. 'Something seems to have gone very wrong.'

There was another light Irish laugh.

'Oh, I'm sure it has. But don't worry, it's often like that. Couples get tired of each other, physically speaking, don't they? Nothing to be shy about. Need a little help, that's all. A lift. I could bring another man along if you like; well-built, if you know what I mean. But that'll be fifty quid extra. Now, I have your address, darlin', but where exactly are you? I've got a car.'

'Get off the phone,' I shouted. 'And *goodbye*!'

I was shaking. I realised I'd sounded just like Wendy Normington. Who the hell was this woman? And how did she get our number? I was grateful that Clive was out of earshot.

I tried to make myself believe it was Georgina disguising her voice; perhaps she'd totally flipped after an overdose of Byron. Or Harriet just being nasty. Or Sarah — Wife Number Five; was she Irish? Tom hadn't told me much about her, except that she was too nice and therefore didn't last very long. I wished Tom would phone.

But when he did phone he was dismissive. He said things like that happened all the time — people at parties get pissed and start playing games, phone a number at random and then say, 'I bet you've got lovely tits,' and stuff like that, just to see how you'll react. At least she wasn't obscene, he added.

I was furious.

'What d'you mean, "she wasn't obscene"? Offering to bring me a man with a large cock — isn't that obscene?'

'Sweetheart, men with cocks of all shapes and sizes have been pursuing you half your life.'

I slammed the phone down. The patronising bastard.

Five minutes later Tom called back and apologised. He'd been an insensitive pig, he said – to which I agreed – but he'd had an appalling day: he'd tell me about it. But tomorrow was going to be a hell of a lot better. He'd just had a hunch, and he was right.

'It's going to be OK,' he added. 'I promise. And I miss you.'

I didn't miss him at that moment, but I did after I put the phone down. I slept badly, and Clive's jungle music didn't help. Why was it the more you paid for education the longer the holidays were? Perhaps if I cut the fees they'd have him back early.

In the morning I made coffee quickly before Mrs Teape had a chance to boil it. She came in unusually briskly, eyes bright with mascara and her lips pursed in surprise. I wondered if perhaps she'd received the same Irish phone call, and the offer of a 'well-built' man had been too much for her. He'd have to be more than well-built to overcome that armour-plating, I thought.

'Well, what do you think about our Lady Bustard then, Mrs Brand?' she asked.

I looked mystified.

'Didn't you know? It's in the paper,' she went on.

'The paper' always meant the local paper. London papers were identified by name.

'She climbed the spire – the cathedral spire.'

I must have looked even more mystified. Had Emelda joined the madhouse along with just about everyone else?

247

'For charity,' Mrs Teape explained. 'What a wonderful lady. God must be very proud of her.'

That seemed unanswerable, and I nodded in agreement.

'Glad it wasn't you in your condition, Mrs Brand,' she added. 'My niece lost twins just climbing over a fence.'

'Careless of her,' I said, and immediately wished I hadn't.

'Not half as careless as my cousin who tripped over a pitch-fork and lost his you-know-what,' she went on.

I decided she'd won that round, and retired to my studio. I needed to ring Howard Minton. But first of all I needed to check Mrs Teape's remarkable facts about Emelda Bustard.

Emelda's phone rang a long time. Then eventually I heard her voice.

'Yes, it's quite true, my dear,' she said as if she were shouting to me across the fields. 'I raised £200,000. The appeal was going rather slowly. I'm a betting woman – you know that. Local industry couldn't resist it. Come to lunch and I'll tell you. I ache a bit.'

So, at midday I left Mrs Teape defying any speck of dust to invade my kitchen, and walked up the village street. It was warm. The grass verge was splashed with primroses, and everywhere there was the moist scent of spring.

At the far end of Emelda's garden I caught sight of a familiar autumn-coloured figure in plus-fours and a Norfolk jacket. His back was towards me, legs firmly apart, his head bracketed by arms raised so that both elbows jutted outwards. Almost invisible beneath the brim of a tweed hat was what I took to be the familiar pair of ancient brass binoculars. As I approached I noticed his head give an occasional jerk up and down as if his chin were stapling something. Twenty feet in front of him was a bush.

Ayrton Bustard was bird watching.

'Good morning,' I said softly.

He gave a little jump of surprise, lowering his binoculars and raising his hat with the same jerky motion.

'Mrs Brand, good morning to you,' he replied with another jerk of the hat. Then he gave a grunt and pointed his binoculars in the direction of the bush.

'They've arrived.'

He didn't say what. The bush looked empty except for young leaves.

'Good,' I said. And he nodded in agreement, wiping his eyes with a red handkerchief that a matador could have used to good purpose.

'I was thinking of calling on your husband,' Ayrton went on. 'I have some new flies I'd like his opinion on.'

I tried not to look mystified, and explained that Tom was away.

'Ah well! Another time,' he exclaimed. 'Good to have another angler to talk to. We're a dying breed. None of these stockbrokers and naval chappies know a thing about fishing.'

I shook my head gravely and changed the subject to Emelda and the cathedral spire. Was it true, I asked?

'Yes, I believe so,' he answered casually, binoculars once again raised in the direction of the bush. 'Hope she didn't disturb the peregrine falcons. They nest up there, you know.'

I left Ayrton to his bush, and went to seek out Emelda.

I found her hobbling about the kitchen, humming to herself. She was wearing a flame-coloured track suit which bore the marks of the lunch she was preparing. When she saw me she wiped her hands on the cleaner parts, and embraced me, transferring portions of the lunch on to my sweater.

She apologised for the 'sporting appearance'. She'd left this sort of thing a bit late in her life, she thought; at sixty-six to pretend to be Tessa Sanderson was a trifle absurd perhaps, but her family had always been eccentrics, and it had made her feel good climbing all those ladders from scaffolding to scaffolding, knowing that each rung represented a thousand pounds or so towards saving the spire. She'd have shown me the newspaper article, she said, only Lloyd George had eaten it.

Emelda gave one her throaty laughs.

'You know what I was thinking when I was up there on the spire, my dear?' she said, slitting open a trout and wrenching its innards out with a bloodied hand. 'I was thinking this could be a marvellous way of recouping the family fortunes. If I got into training I could do it once a week, divide the spoils with the dean and chapter, and retire gracefully on Champagne and caviar. The trouble is, of course, Ayrton would promptly discover a rare dragonfly under threat in Honduras, and the whole lot would go into financing some whacky expedition led by

Gerald Durrell. But two hundred thousand for the cathedral wasn't bad, was it?'

I was relieved to hear that Emelda had used a ladder, and not shinned up the outside like a steeplejack.

She went on chatting amiably until lunch was ready. She'd made a Pernod sauce for the trout, and thumped a bottle of Chablis on the table, which she commanded me to open. I noticed there were only two fish, and two places laid.

'Just us, thank God!' she said. 'The old fart can't be bothered with lunch once his migrants arrive.'

I enquired which birds so excited him. Emelda spat out a bone and smeared her mouth with the back of her hand.

'Christ knows. They all look like sparrows to me. Too small to eat, that's all I care about. Though I suppose the Italians would. Ayrton gets very cross when I say things like that. Now, tell me, how's Tom and that dragon of an ex-wife with the bum?'

Over lunch I told Emelda everything that had taken place over the previous week or so: Harriet's phone call; the safety-pins; the solicitor's letter; the dustbin episode; the mysterious car; Sleepy Joe.

'Goodness, how wonderful!' she exclaimed. 'Nothing like this has happened in Sarum Magna since I returned from Corsica with an heir to the Bustard line.'

Then I told her about Samantha and the deadly dinner-party in Los Angeles; about Professor Montblanc and the sperm bank; about Georgina having it off with Lord Byron's ghost; finally about the Irish woman ringing to offer her services to stimulate our sex life. Emelda was wide-eyed.

'My dear,' she said, pouring out the last of the Chablis, 'do send her to Ayrton . . . But no! On second thoughts – don't! It might bring back the most awful memories.'

She looked thoughtful for a moment.

'Tell me,' she went on, piling our dishes into the sink and turning on the tap, 'is there anything else that can possibly happen to you? It seems to me you already qualify for the *Guinness Book of Records*. I must say you're bearing up extraordinarily well.'

If that were so, I said, I didn't understand how. It had been the most ghastly six weeks of my life. As for anything else that was likely to happen, I couldn't get my mind round such a possibility. There was only one wife unaccounted for, I added wearily.

'And what do you know about her?' Emelda asked. 'Does she sound dangerous?'

'No,' I said. 'She sounds nice.'

'Goodness! A lapse of taste on Tom's part, eh? Well, Well!'

And Emelda chuckled, hurling a pile of soapy cutlery on to the draining-board. Then suddenly she came over and wrapped a pair of large, wet arms around me.

'My dear,' she said. 'When Tom's back and this is all over, we shall have a party and get very drunk.'

At which point Ayrton's sharp face peered round the door.

'I've counted twenty-three!' he announced.

Emelda looked at him impassively, then turned to me.

'Well, my dear, at least that's more birds than your Tom has notched up. Take comfort.'

I glanced towards the door to see what expression was on Ayrton's face. But he'd already left. And shortly afterwards I did the same, pausing to acknowledge the attentions of Lloyd George, from whose mouth dangled a morsel of what I took to be the newspaper account of his mistress's heroic feat.

Along the street I stopped to gaze at a row of swallows perched on the telegraph wires. More new arrivals, I thought – Ayrton must be getting to me. Would I have noticed them if I'd been in London? Any day now and I'd start keeping a nature diary. I could hear Ruth groan.

Then a voice broke into my country musings.

'How's my beautiful filly today?'

I glanced round and saw John Gant leaning down towards me from his tractor. His face looked as though it had been shaved with barbed wire, and his eyes did a rapid check on my body.

'Lovely as usual,' he went on. 'But you've got a rival – did you know?'

I shook my head and began to walk away. The X-ray eyes made me uncomfortable.

'Yes, she was asking for your house,' he called after me.

I stopped. I was used to my heart sinking by now. All the fun and warmth of my lunch with Emelda evaporated. Who the hell could it possibly be now? Wife Number Five? At least she was the 'nice' one.

'Foreign. French, I'd say she was,' John Gant explained. I could see he was savouring each bit of information, tasting every morsel before passing it to me. 'Dressed like a model. Legs . . . you wouldn't believe.

Slim . . . except where it matters.' His hands did the rest; the naked woman tattooed on his arm seemed like a caricature of what he was describing. 'Hair you could swim in. And eyes! Huge and black – never seen anything like them.'

Something clicked in my brain. What was that phrase Tom had used about Anne-Marie? 'Eyes like Greek olives.' No, it wouldn't be her; but eyes are hereditary. Could it? . . . No, it couldn't be the spotty, fat teenage daughter who'd rung up a few weeks ago to announce she was coming to spend time with *cher papa*? Solange – that was the girl's name.

'Lovely filly!' John Gant was saying. 'If she sticks around here long you won't get much peace, I can tell you.'

Could it be anyone other than Solange? Spotty, fat teenagers have an irritating habit of growing up, after all. The ugly duckling syndrome.

Oh God, I thought, I could do without this.

John Gant was still nodding his head appreciatively.

'Know her, then, do you?'

I said I thought so, and started to move away.

'Staying with you, is she?' he called after me. 'I'd keep her penned in if I were you: they'll all be round like a herd of bulls.'

His laughter was still undressing her as I hurried off. I heard the tractor start up with a vigorous thrust, and my mind pictured large Mrs Gant in her bedroom slippers and floral apron pegging out the long-johns on the washing line. Tonight, I imagined, her bull might have an urgent surprise for her.

A bright yellow Renault 5 with a French number-plate was parked in front of the cottage. A tennis racquet lay on the back seat, and in the front a road map was open with a sheet of paper on which our address had been scrawled. So I was right: it was Solange. I braced myself for this siren of a step-daughter-to-be, and opened the front door.

There was no one. I looked around me. Then I noticed a straw shoulder-bag lying on a chair. It was a cheap and rather battered object, yet around one of the handles a red Hermes scarf had been tied with casual elegance. Yes, the girl had style, curse her, I thought. 'Like a model,' John Gant had said. Oh, bring back the spots and the puppy-fat.

Suddenly there was what sounded like a scuffle coming from Clive's bedroom. A chair had been tipped over. Then a woman's voice cried out, '*Non!*' Further sounds of scuffle followed, after which, '*Non!*' – more angrily this time – '*Ne me touchez pas! Dégoutant!*' There was the sound of someone being slapped hard.

I was about to burst through the door when it was flung open and a young woman with wild dark hair swept past me. She was clutching her blouse, which I could see was partly undone. Behind her, lying face downwards on the bed with his head buried in a pillow, was Clive.

I felt stunned. I closed the door.

'Solange?' I said. What the hell else could I say?

She nodded, hastily doing up the buttons of her blouse and defiantly tossing back her hair.

'*Oui!*' she said breathlessly. Then she blinked several times and began to look more composed. She was

255

strikingly beautiful: tall, pale-skinned, slim as an eel. I felt like a dwarf.

'*Vous êtes Janees?*' she added.

It was my turn to nod. She held out her hand politely.

My mind was in a turmoil. I found myself wondering if this might be the only occasion in history when a woman had met her future step-daughter for the first time, half-naked from an attempted rape by her own thirteen-year-old son. There wasn't really a great deal I could say.

I led Solange into the kitchen to get her a little further from the scene of the crime. And I made tea, there not being much else I could think of doing. I wanted to go and murder Clive first, but decided that could wait.

The truth – at least the raw part of it – came out over the next quarter of an hour. I poured out the tea with a shaking hand, and produced some rather disgusting biscuits. Solange sat down at the table, crossed one leg elegantly over the other and combed her fingers languorously through her hair. Then she gazed at me with those huge Greek-olive eyes.

'It was some mistake, I think,' she said with her very pretty French accent. 'I am sorry. I don't understand.' Well, neither did I; I was hoping she'd tell me. Instead she said, 'But I am so 'appy to meet you, *Janees*. You are very beaut-i-ful.'

At that point I decided I liked her.

She was earlier than she'd expected because she'd decided to take a job as an au pair, she explained. In Vin-con-torm – which I realised must be Wincanton. She wouldn't be staying after all – she was just passing by.

It was a shame her father was not at home, but could she perhaps return for the weekend – several weekends – once she had settled in?

I said naturally we'd be delighted. And by then my son would be back at school; she could have his room. I hoped that bringing up the subject of Clive might draw out of her what had actually happened.

Solange looked at me winsomely, and then laughed.

''Ee is *précoce*, your son,' she said.

I agreed, and said I was very sorry. He was at an awkward age. I felt like saying that he was an apprentice sex-maniac, but the thought of Clive lying there miserably on his bed softened my heart.

He had met her at the door, she said, and given her the strangest of looks. 'Are you really French?' Clive had asked, ushering her into the house. 'How amazing!' He hadn't expected a *real* French lady, only someone who knew about French things. Solange hadn't known what he meant.

Neither at that stage did I.

They were alone in the house, Clive had explained. Wasn't that fortunate? They could begin straight away. And he had led her into his bedroom. Solange was '*un peu mystifiée*', she said, but followed him. He seemed a charming boy, and she was interested to see '*la maison de mon père*'. They talked for a while; she explained that she had come to England to look for employment. This place had proved quite easy to find, and she hoped she'd be able to come back soon if she was welcome here. A home from home. Clive had nodded vigorously and said he certainly hoped so too. He was very lucky.

And please could they now begin, as he could only afford an hour.

I looked at Solange in some puzzlement. My stomach was doing a little dance. My head was full of pieces of a jigsaw, and suddenly I was putting a few of them together. Clive's disgraceful behaviour just now, and the mysterious phone call yesterday evening – the woman who insisted on coming round and offering her 'services'. Could there possibly be a connection between the two?

'*Soudain, il m'a attaqué*,' she said. 'He tried to undo *ma blouse – très, très vite*. I was *étonnée*.' Solange laughed again.

I didn't laugh. I wanted to throttle him. I put my head in my hands.

'Oh God!' I said. 'I'm deeply embarrassed. What can I do?'

'Perhaps find him a girlfriend very queek,' she said, still laughing. 'And now I must go – to Vin-con-torm. *Embrasse mon père pour moi. Je vais lui téléphoner.*'

And she departed in a summer breeze of Chanel and wild hair.

Clive was still lying on the bed. He was sobbing. I put my arms round him, but he shrugged me off. I sat quietly by him until gradually the crying stopped. Then I put my arms round him again, and this time he curled up like a puppy. I went through every permutation of maternal guilt, alternating with hurling blame at Harry for having screwed anything in skirts throughout our marriage; then I started blaming myself for having kicked him out, at which point I put my mind in neutral and said quietly: 'Clive, what exactly *did* you do?'

He seemed relieved to tell me. In London he'd seen advertisements in stationers' windows offering 'French lessons', he said, and he'd known perfectly well it wasn't French lessons that were being offered, but something much more essential to a boy's education. It was about *girls*, what you did with them, and how you did it. He needed to find out. 'French lessons' was just a way of putting it because the French were supposed to be the great lovers, weren't they? So he'd decided to put notices in shop windows round here. Not in Sarum Magna, he explained; people would have known who he was. But all the villages around, as many as he could find.

I might have felt more admiration for his ingenuity and dedication if the telephone hadn't gone at that moment. It was another female voice. I could see Clive cringe with embarrassment – why hadn't the boy realised other people were likely to answer the phone?

I told the eager lady as coolly as possible that nobody here needed interesting massage, or gymnastic variations, or the secrets of a Parisian convent; that it was all a mistake and clearly she'd got the wrong number. Goodbye!

Then I had to act.

'Clive, get into the car!' I called out.

We had about an hour and a half before the shops closed.

'Clive, which villages? Tell me.'

He couldn't remember. He'd done it all on a bicycle without a map, following signposts. So, all those soft spring afternoons when I'd been delighted that my son had got off his arse to explore the beauties of the countryside, and this was what he'd been doing.'

'Try! Try hard! Was it Great Yatford? Upper Avonbridge? Lower Avonbridge? Middle Avonbridge? . . . What d'you mean Little Wallop? That's the way we've just come! . . . No, nobody's turned the signpost round, Clive. Try again.'

It was a nightmare rally among the sleepiest, prettiest villages of Wiltshire. We met sheep. We met tractors. We met roadworks. We followed a funeral cortège. British Rail had even installed a level-crossing specially for our delight.

Outside each village shop I insisted that Clive retrieve the offending notices while I waited grim-faced in the car. By five-thirty we had a collection of eight. Clive seemed to think there might be two or three more. Tomorrow, he promised, he would set out on his bicycle and track them down.

'I'll say you will, you horror!'

By the time we reached the brow of the hill over-looking Sarum Magna the absurdity of it all began to overwhelm me. I wasn't sure if it was how a good parent should behave, but I began to laugh. Clive looked nervously at me from the passenger seat.

'I am sorry, mum,' he mumbled.

'Clive, you're dreadful, and I love you,' I said, still laughing. I realised to my surprise that I felt closer to him than at any time since he'd been here. My son was a human being after all. I stopped the car and put my arms round him.

Then he looked at me.

'Mum, how did *you* learn?'

I didn't know what to answer. How the hell did we all learn?

'Clive,' I said. 'Truthfully I can't remember. But it certainly wasn't by putting advertisements for French lessons in shop windows.'

He looked sheepish, and I drove on. I couldn't help feeling deeply inadequate. If we were really in France, I thought, I could have made one of those traditional arrangements with a comely divorcee to instruct my son in the finer arts of living; but Sarum Magna didn't strike me as a likely venue for such enterprises. Wendy Normington wasn't exactly a candidate, and Emelda was considerably too old.

'Maybe it just happens,' I added feebly.

Clive shrugged. His expression put me firmly in the category of parents who call all the shots and never deliver the goods.

Back home I cremated the eight handwritten notices we'd retrieved, not wishing to put them in the bin in case the dustman was careless and a sudden wind scattered them around the village. Then I took the little pile of ashes outside. It was almost dark by now. There was birdsong. Farm smells wafted across the garden. I loved this time of the evening.

Suddenly there she was, on the bridge; just standing there, looking at me. Mooncalf.

This was too much. I started to run towards her.

Then the phone went.

Oh God, I thought – yet another French mistress.

And I dashed indoors. This time I would go straight to the point.

'Yes!' I barked. 'Who is it?'

There was a pause. Then a slight cough.

'Darling, what's the matter? It's me!'

Tom's voice drove Mooncalf and French lessons from my mind. He had good news, he said. He'd be back tomorrow. He'd tell me all about it then.

'Oh, thank God!' I yelled. 'Tom, you have no idea how much I need you.'

He sounded pleased, and laughed. I put the phone down and took a deep breath. Then I poured myself a very large drink, and called out to Clive.

'Darling, what would you like for supper? I'll cook you anything you like. Just say.'

My grinning son poked his head round the kitchen door and handed me a copy of *Prawnography*.

'You choose, mum,' he said.

12

SUDDENLY the old mill no longer looked like the victim of Serbian mortar-fire. The stone flags were re-laid, the roof tiled and lagged, the massive ships' timbers oiled and treated. From every surface electric wires still waved at me like sea-anemones, and a paint-spattered transistor radio occupied the armorial fireplace we'd discovered in a Salisbury antique shop. None the less my imagination could now complete the job perfectly and I gazed about, feeling her like a queen in her castle.

The foreman accompanied me proudly, from time to time offering unexpected gobbets of information.

'The Romans introduced the geared watermill to England, of course, madam. 5,624 of them are listed in the Domesday Book, you know.'

I looked at him appreciatively.

'I like a bit of history,' he added confidentially. 'I expect your husband knows all about that sort of thing.'

But not of course me, being a woman and a blonde. I was the one who knew about babies and flower arrangement.

I looked at him less appreciatively after that.

The builders didn't like the foreman much. I caught one of them mouthing 'fucking prick' behind his back. But they did like me. Ever since the hot tea episode they'd decided to act as my personal bodyguard. Certainly it was my body they seemed most concerned to guard, not surprisingly perhaps considering how much of it had been revealed in those tabloid photographs. One of them would gallantly assist me up ladders from above, while another remained below in case I fell; so between the two of them I imagine they acquired an almost complete picture of what it was they were guarding. Then I spoilt their game by wearing jeans and a high-necked sweater, whereupon I noticed they suddenly found ladders to be not at all dangerous, and let me climb them unaided.

'It's like being on a ship here, madam,' said the one who'd been fitting the long picture-window just above the mill-race. 'I imagine you'll be breaking a bottle of champagne when she's finished.'

I stood by the window, entranced. The river curled away beneath me among the leaning alders, and fifty yards or so downstream the current was braced by a flotilla of swans, as if they were towing my royal barge. I felt spoilt, and very happy.

I felt happy, too, that with any luck I'd had the last of the phone calls offering 'French lessons'. There'd been only one of them this morning, just after Clive had scooted off on his bicycle to retrieve the remaining two or three notices; and in retrospect I suppose I got what I deserved. A well-spoken voice enquired what exactly the young gentleman needed. It was important to know what stage he was at, she said, so she could bring the right material. I saw red and replied that we didn't want any of her vibrators, French ticklers, whips or rubberwear thank you, and why didn't she go and screw herself with a banana? A haughty silence followed; then the woman announced she'd never been spoken to like that in her life, and perhaps I'd care to know she was the principal of the Salisbury School of Modern Languages.

I tried miserably to explain, but by then she'd rung off.

That was when I decided to see how the builders were getting on at the mill. On my way out Mrs Teape saw I was flustered and offered helpful advice about morning sickness, which at least restored my sense of humour. I reminded myself that it was a beautiful morning, and put the Salisbury School of Modern Languages firmly out of my mind. The mill – *that* was my tomorrow. And at midday Tom would be back – 'with good news', he'd said.

The train was punctual for once. Tom hugged me as if we'd been apart for a year. On the platform he insisted I put on the Butler and Wilson necklace he'd bought me; so, to the surprise of the ticket collector and several upright citizens of Salisbury, I made my exit from the station clanking with gigantic artificial pearls set amidst a stampede of golden salamanders, crocodiles and diamond-studded armadillos, all presided over by the gilded figure of Botticelli's Venus with a flamboyant ruby in her navel.

'Thank you, darling,' I said as we drove off. 'And what would you like me to wear it with?'

'Giorgio,' Tom answered, producing a bottle of it from his pocket. 'And nothing else. Promise?'

I smiled at him in the driving mirror.

'Certainly. How about the Normingtons' next dinner-party?'

'Great idea. I'll invite Harriet.'

'Talking of whom, my darling,' I said, 'what news?'

Tom was looking smug.

'I'll tell you about it when we're home,' he answered. 'When you're just wearing your necklace.'

The champagne hadn't benefited from the train journey, and the kitchen floor got rather more of it than we did. Mrs Teape insisted on clearing up the mess before she left, enquiring as she did so whether the little celebration meant I was having twins. When I said no she looked disappointed, adding that she was sure it would be a beautiful baby all the same.

Then she speared her hat with her kebab skewer, freshened the lipstick, and departed.

'At last!' I said. 'Now for Christ's sake tell me.'

Tom likes to tease. I thought if he did so this time I'd hit him with the bottle. But he didn't: he may have seen the look in my eye. Instead, he raised one hand in front of him with the thumb and forefinger a fraction apart.

'We're just that much away from seeing off Harriet,' he assured me. 'One phone call – which should come through this afternoon.'

Then he began at the beginning.

It had started badly, he explained. The lugubrious offices of Kyra Vansittart were enough to convince anyone that in dealings with lawyers you always lose. But he needed to see her: he wanted to know precisely where he stood in the eyes of the law, and precisely what he needed to do.

'Christ, she can be a hard-nosed bitch,' he said, from which I deduced that she still didn't fancy him.

Kyra had listened, then without comment laid before him a wad of letters from Harriet's solicitors.

'I riffled through them like a flick-book,' Tom explained. The letterhead 'Messrs Crouch and Crouch' had danced before his eyes, only the date changing, the heading invariably the same: 'Mrs Harriet Brand – Maintenance Plea,' underlined. There must have been twenty of them. Phrases jumped out from the dense foliage of words – 'due to our client's restricted circumstances', 'a just and fair settlement', 'your client's responsibility', 'a magistrate would look most sympathetically'; and always the same final sentence, beginning, 'Awaiting your favourable response . . .'

'And what has been your favourable response?' Tom had enquired.

Kyra had explained that she'd perfected two responses to such letters. If they were of modest length, her reply would be, 'Dear sir, I think not.' But if they were unduly long-winded it was, 'Dear sir, No!' She was working on a briefer response still, but had yet to fine-tune it.

Tom had felt better after that, and pushed the wad of letters aside.

'It's all a matter of strategy,' Kyra had continued. 'Trying to wear your opponent out. You have to imagine yourself to be a boxer. You duck and weave, make your opponent miss, hope he'll fall flat on his face.'

Tom suggested that with a name like Crouch and Crouch they were already half way there. Kyra ignored the remark.

'But sooner or later you'll have to pay up. I can't duck and weave for ever,' she'd added curtly.

He asked what might be the advantage of 'sooner' rather than 'later'.

'Your legal bills will be less,' she replied.

Tom observed the Lanvin suit, and took the point.

'Supposing we stop ducking and weaving, and try a right uppercut?' Tom enquired.

Kyra looked sceptical.

Tom proceeded to lay out before her everything he'd found out about Harriet's activities. He described the incident of the dustbin and the Audi Quattro, A1 DOL; how he'd traced the real owner, a gangland millionaire by the name of Joseph Cutler, known in the trade as Sleepy Joe, with a file at Scotland Yard as thick as your fist and a powerful appetite for women.

Kyra began to look slightly more interested. Perhaps, she suggested, this might be a case of what lawyers like to call 'the phantom lover'.

'On the other hand,' she went on languidly, 'Sleepy Joe may be fucking Harriet five times a night – in the shower, hanging from the chandelier, among the garden gnomes, toe-jobs or blow-jobs – but if you can't prove money changes hands, then no magistrate in the country will listen to you. They'll just think you're jealous. So, what are you going to do – hire a private detective agency?'

Tom's response was: 'Sod that!'

He had left Kyra's office feeling he'd been challenged. It was like being back on the familiar tabloid trail, he said. He'd tried to think of himself as an old gunfighter returning for one final showdown; but somehow being the Clint Eastwood of Sarum Magna didn't have too convincing a ring about it.

I'm afraid I agreed.

'Tom,' I added unsympathetically, 'could you cut the Fleet Street heroics, do you think? We know how the Expressman cometh. What did you *do*?'

Tom looked bruised for a moment. His champagne glass was empty.

'All right,' he said. 'But I need to give you the anti-heroics first, or nothing will make sense.'

I sat back and let him spin it out.

The next couple of days were a dead loss, he admitted. Locating Sleepy Joe's house proved the least of his problems; a few local enquiries in Barnes led him to a rambling Edwardian mansion, not far from the pond, and cocooned by a high wall with wrought-iron gates set between snarling stone lions. But nobody ever seemed to enter or leave the place, and the garage remained firmly locked. There was no sign of A1 DOL, or of Harriet. Several shopkeepers in Barnes High Street knew 'Mr Cutler' as well as his two 'charming boys'; and yes there had been a Mrs Cutler – 'a very quiet lady' – but nobody had seen her for a number of years. Friends? 'No, I can't

say I do know who his friends might be. He's away a lot.'
Ladies? 'Oh, I wouldn't like to say. But I expect so, a man
that wealthy.'

Perhaps Sleepy Joe was spending his time in Harriet's
house. So Tom took to lurking at small hours outside the
house that had once been his own; but his only rewards
were the suspicious twitchings of neighbours' curtains,
and a warning from a policeman to 'move on if I were
you, sir'.

Enquiries about Sleepy Joe's various properties also
drew a blank. The house in Barnes, the château in
France, the ski-chalet – they all proved to be in the name
of Cutler, or of companies registered in his name.

Tom was getting nowhere.

'Then one lunchtime I took myself back to Barnes. It
wasn't even a hunch,' he said, 'more a professional
instinct to be near the scene of the crime.'

He had sat for a while, sipping a beer on the pub
terrace overlooking the pond and watching the girls
go by. Suddenly a white Rolls Royce drove past, a dark-
haired man at the wheel. Tom leapt up in time to see the
car draw up outside the house with the stone lions. A
burly man in a camel-hair coat got out, carrying a
briefcase.

'It had to be Sleepy Joe. Besides, I caught a glimpse of
the number-plate. It was A10 DOL. The man certainly
advertises his interests, I thought. The question was –
how much does he pay for them?'

Tom had waited until he saw the front door close,
then strolled along the pavement as far as the car.
The old Humphrey Bogart trick of pausing to light a

cigarette gave him a rapid survey of the interior. There seemed to be nothing of much interest: an umbrella, a pair of kid gloves, a road map, a packet of Monte Cristo cigars. Tom wasn't sure what he'd expected. Deeds to a villa in Mustique in the name of Harriet Brand? Steamy love letters lying open on the seat promising a further ten grand if she'd do it again like last night?

'I realised', Tom explained, 'that I was working under a severe handicap. If I'd been covering this story for a newspaper I'd have rung the doorbell and asked him straight: "What's your relationship with Harriet Brand, Mr Cutler?"'

'I bet you would,' I said. 'And you'd have spent the next six months in the Plastic Surgery Unit. So, what did happen?'

'A stroke of luck, and a stroke of genius,' Tom replied. 'Something caught my eye – inside the rear window of the car. A travel leaflet, that was all. It said "Come to sunny Jersey".'

There was nothing written on it. Just the leaflet, with a picture of the sun smiling out of it.

'Well now, I thought; people don't actually go to Jersey for the sun, do they? At least, not people like Joseph Cutler. And that was what gave me an idea. It was an outside chance, but it was worth following up.'

'I don't understand, Tom,' I said.

'Don't you? If you were Mr Millionaire Joseph Cutler, what would make you interested in Jersey? It wouldn't be tomatoes or new potatoes, would it?'

I still had no idea what he was talking about.

'Well, go on!' I said.

So Tom had hailed a taxi and gone straight to his hotel. It was two-thirty in the afternoon. He made a swift phone call. Fleet Street being a discreet kind of mafia, there were certain favours you could always ask a fellow journalist, which of course was why journalists refuse to reveal their sources. Tom wasn't even going to tell me who it was he'd phoned, except that it was someone on *The Financial Times*. The favour was to find out what offshore companies were registered in the Channel Islands in the name of Joseph Cutler, or at least with Cutler on the board of directors.

The man swore at Tom for fouling up his day, but promised to ring him back in an hour. Tom waited in his hotel room for over two hours, while his mind drifted on to Georgina and the amorous ghost of Lord Byron. Tom already had a line on that one, but it would have to wait.

The phone call had finally come through around five. 'How many companies would you like?' the man said. Tom groaned. 'It's all right,' Tom's source went on, 'there are only four.' Then he read them out. 'Abu Dhabi Estates.' That didn't sound like something a man's mistress was likely to be involved in. 'Colombian Textile Company.' Drugs, certainly. 'Pretoria Mines.' Armaments. There was a pause, followed by a laugh. 'You'll love this one – "Full Frontal Productions.".'

'Tell me more,' Tom said.

'The registry doesn't tell you much more,' the man answered. 'Only the date the company was founded – last year. And the directors: just two of them, Cutler and someone else.'

'The someone else being . . .?'

'Brand. H. Brand. Any relation of yours?'

Tom had been too overjoyed to answer.

'Got her!' was all he'd said.

There was just one more favour he needed to ask. And it was a big one. What were the assets of Full Frontal Productions, and what salaries or dividends were paid to whom?

A snort of indignation came down the telephone. This could get him the sack, the man protested. Tom reminded him that he'd have been given the sack years ago if it hadn't been for him.

'You arsehole!' he said.

That meant he would do it, Tom assured me.

I was still finding it hard to take all this in. I took Tom's hands in mine.

'Just tell me what it means – in words of very few syllables, please. I'm a bear of very little brain. You know that.'

Tom laughed.

'Well, it means', he said, 'that I'm expecting a phone call to tell me just how much my lying slob of an ex-wife is secretly receiving as a director of a tax-evasion company appropriately named Full Frontal Productions. That's what it means.'

I felt utterly bewildered. Could that really be it? Was it really all over? The Valkyrie had gone, and might we now actually be able to live a life? Something we could call our own?

'Tom,' I said. And I threw my arms round him. He lifted me in the air and whirled me round and round.

'Haven't we got any more champagne?' he asked.

And this time it didn't go on the floor.

We made love instead of lunch. I hoped Clive's music in the next room was a tactful gesture on my son's part, making up for his behaviour over the French lessons and his treatment of Solange. I wasn't looking forward to telling Tom about either incident, but this was hardly the moment.

I lay curled up against him, my fingers gently combing his chest hairs. He was asleep, letting out little whiffling snorts from time to time, like a dog having a dream – not very romantic. I sometimes wondered if there was something wrong with me, being so wide awake. Shouldn't I be knocked out by all those orgasms, instead of lying here thinking about the building works and my illustrations to Hilaire Belloc? It was scarcely more romantic than Tom's snorts. Ruth, I remembered, always maintained she passed out after sex while her lovers kept prodding her with urgent erections, wanting more.

I propped myself up on one elbow and gazed at Tom. He opened an eye. It blinked.

'Ah! More Full Frontal Productions,' he muttered, reaching up and fondling my breasts.

'Not as full frontal as Harriet's, I'm afraid. What do you suppose her production company actually produces?' I asked.

Tom raised his head and worked the tip of his tongue round my left nipple.

'Not a lot of love,' he managed to say, and transferred his tongue to my right nipple. Then he leant back to contemplate his good work. 'I imagine the company's tangible assets will have fallen heavily over the years, unlike yours.'

I laughed.

'Champagne cups,' I said.

Tom pressed my shoulders back on the bed, and ran his hands lightly over my body.

'I like them. And all of you.'

The telephone roused us with a start. Thank God Clive was there to answer it. Tom was already hurling himself into a dressing-gown.

'Shit!' he said, staggering towards the door.

'It's for you, mum,' came Clive's voice.

Tom looked aggrieved, and slumped back on to the bed. I grabbed my own dressing-gown, trying not to look as though I'd been savaged by a Rottweiler, and stumbled into the kitchen. Clive had a knowing look on his face.

'Don't know why I bother to advertise for French lessons,' he grumbled, holding out the receiver towards me. 'I can have home tuition just by listening through the wall. It's Mr De Vere.'

He pulled a long snooty face as he said it.

De Vere! Who the hell? I thought. Then it came to me. Oh my God – Ashley de Vere!

'I'm lost, darling,' came the high-pitched drawl. 'Sorry I'm so late, but where *are* you? I'm outside some village shop and there's a goat trying to eat my car.'

I'd entirely forgotten – Ashley de Vere, the interior designer Ruth had put me on to. I remembered with horror that he'd said he was coming down this afternoon to look at the mill and bring some suggestions. It was to be my big surprise for Tom. Well, it was going to be a big surprise all right. I cleared my throat.

'Mr De Vere, I'm so glad,' I said. 'I really should have sent you directions. We're the first on the right after the pub, at the end of a long track. You can't miss us – builders' rubble everywhere.'

I broke the news to Tom, who said 'Shit!'

Clive asked, 'Who was the wanker on the phone?'

'Just turn your music down, will you?' I snapped.

Then I tried to prepare myself for one of England's leading interior designers, cursing Ruth for ever having suggested it.

But I was *not* prepared for Mr Ashley de Vere. It wasn't so much the dyed red hair and the heavy make-up, or the perfume, or the ivory-white silk suit, or the shirt-cuffs that looked like tea-roses in full bloom, or the rings that would have cowed a pope. It wasn't even the voice, which soared in bright arpeggios loud enough for John Gant to gaze in wonder from the nearby field.

These I could almost take in my stride after the events of the past few weeks; they felt like normality. No! What threw me was the vision of our house which he'd brought with him, projected on to sheet after sheet of scented paper, and lovingly laid before us.

As I gazed at these creations I found myself wondering if the Prince Consort might have experienced similar emotions when Nash presented him with plans for the Brighton Pavilion.

'Well now, darling,' he began, his hands taking off like a flock of swallows. 'When you told me it was a mill, naturally I thought of France in the eighteenth century.' The great man was continuing to unfold his designs on a large groundsheet provided by the builders, who were standing back in bewildered silence. 'And as you can see, the inspiration is Boucher. Pastoral rococo. Naughty but poetic.'

There was nothing in the least poetic about Tom's expression. He was blinking, and from time to time shooting me horrified glances. Before us lay our future home transformed into a Versailles Temple of Love, the walls alive with frolicking peasants pursuing scantily-dressed milkmaids among forest glades and classical temples; while on the ceiling of what I took to be our bedroom a life-sized image of Cupid, naked except for a quiver of arrows, aimed his bow (and apparently his penis) at our reclining bodies – although maybe the penis was intended for Tom.

'I do the figures myself, naturally,' Mr de Vere assured us. 'My assistant creates the background. Six months will certainly be enough, darling, though I must say the house I've just completed in Palm Springs took rather longer, but then you know how these Hollywood stars change their minds – and their partners. Oh, the things I've seen – you wouldn't believe.'

He gave a little giggle. The builders exchanged glances.

The maestro stood back to allow space for admiration, adjusting his rose-petal cuffs and removing specks from the silk suit. The agonising pause was suddenly interrupted by a distant telephone. Tom made a dash for the cottage as if released from jail, and I was left with the silence of the builders and the genius of Mr Ashley de Vere.

I passionately wished I was elsewhere. Oh Ruth, Ruth, how could you do this to me?

Then he turned to me and in a hushed voice said, 'Such a beautiful man, your husband. Artistic too, I can tell.'

I wished Tom had been able to hear that.

'Yes, quite an artist,' I said, 'in his own way.'

'Lovely eyes.'

I murmured something.

'And hands.'

Any minute, I thought, it's going to be his prick. This really had to end. But how? Here was this man lusting after my lover, proposing to turn our house into a miniature Versailles, and threatening me with a life-sized Cupid hovering over my bed. And *I* was responsible.

I was rescued – bless her! – by Emelda. She'd run out of butter, she explained, and it was early closing. Her eyes grew wider when she caught sight of Ashley de Vere, and even wider when she saw the drawings spread across the floor.

'Goodness, my dear,' she exclaimed. 'You never told me you were opening a brothel.'

Mr De Vere didn't stay long after that. He wasn't accustomed to these 'rustics', he said huffily as he left. I apologised, and assured him I'd be in touch. I didn't tell him that the rustic in question could trace her family tree back to William the Conqueror.

I found Tom reclining in a chair with his feet on the table and a slip of paper in his hand. As I entered he waved the paper in my direction.

'Well, d'you want to know?' he asked. Then, without waiting for an answer, he read out: "'Full Frontal Productions. Registered Jersey, CI, March 1992. Directors J. Cutler and H. Brand. Capital estimated at £1,250,000. Interest – less fees for accountants etc. – payable solely to Coutts & Co., Leadenhall St., London EC3, Special Deposit Account Number 7893618." And would it surprise you to know in whose name that account is held? "Approximate annual income to a certain H. Brand – after deduction of tax and sundry emoluments – £30,000."'

Tom gazed at me with a wry smile.

'So much for "our client's restricted circumstances",' he said. 'Thirty grand a year, tax free!'

I suppose I was relieved. Of course I was relieved. At the same time another thought insisted on floating through my head. Why should Sleepy Joe be committing that sort of money to a vicious slag with a fat arse? Granted that Harriet might not be vicious to him; granted that Joe might have a penchant for generous buttocks; granted that Harriet might possess all kinds of stimulating tricks in bed; none the less, millionaire mafiosi were surely not noted for parting with their wealth so conventionally. Diamonds, yes! Yachting sprees, yes! Furs, fast cars, villas, oceans of champagne, yes! A rapid turnover of bimbos, yes! But an income, albeit modest, payable to one woman on a regular basis from interest in an offshore company: this didn't fit my image of Sleepy Joe at all, and I couldn't come up with the answer.

Tom was far too pleased with himself to care much.

'Oh, just another tax fiddle,' was the best he was prepared to offer. Then he strolled across the room and began to gaze dreamily out of the window.

I decided to join him. It was true – why should I be bothering about such things? The habit of feeding my mind with thoughts of Tom's Valkyrie had grown instinctive over the past months, and now it was time to remind myself that there was a life beyond them. Our life.

It was early evening. The sun was low over the river, painting swathes of orange on the water. Suddenly there was a flash of electric blue.

'Look, Tom,' I called out. 'Halcyon.'

The kingfisher did an abrupt turn in mid-river and disappeared among the alders.

Tom put an arm round me.

'And look there.'

He pointed across the garden towards the little island raised above a delta of streams, with its rustic arbour which the estate agent had been so proud of. I remembered gazing at this same view on the day we arrived, when the entire garden looked like the Ganges in flood and Tom was convinced that 'arbour' in the agents' brochure must be a misprint for 'harbour'. That still made me laugh.

Then I noticed Tom peering intently at something.

'Look, Jan,' he said, pointing. 'The first rose.'

Astonished by this outburst of sensitivity I peered

towards the rose-arbour, but could see nothing remotely resembling a flower. I decided to take his word for it.

'Then why don't we go and sit there?' I answered. 'And you can tell me all the things you promised to tell me, and haven't.'

Tom looked puzzled.

'What do you mean?'

'About Georgina and Byron's ghost. Don't tell me you haven't been investigating that too.'

He laughed.

'All right,' he said, steering me towards the door. 'I'll pick you the first rose, and then I'll tell you.'

Tom's moments of romance are brief. This one was briefer than usual. The 'rose' turned out to be no more scented than one would expect from a clot of bird-lime. The magpies evidently enjoyed the perch. Tom looked at the mess wistfully.

'You see? I try to be a romantic, and what happens? I get shat on.' Then a smile spread across his face. 'Let me try it another way. Close your eyes.'

I did as I was told. I sat on the wooden bench under the rose-arbour with my eyes tightly shut.

Nothing happened. And still nothing happened. I became convinced that Tom had gone somewhere. Eventually I heard soft footsteps on the grass. It was an eerie sensation, and I wanted to open my eyes to make sure it wasn't some serial rapist, or yet another lady offering interesting French lessons. None the less I went on doing as I had been told.

Next, there came a deep sigh close to my ear. I gave a start, and was about to say, 'Tom, for fuck's sake what's going on?' when a hand touched my shoulder and a deep, dreamy voice began to incant:

> 'Remind me not, remind me not,
> Of those beloved, those vanish'd hours,
> When all my soul was given to thee;
> Hours that may never be forgot,
> Till time unnerves our vital powers,
> And you and I shall cease to be.'

There was a pause, then the voice resumed, even closer:

> 'She walks in beauty, like the night
> Of cloudless climes and starry skies;
> And all that's best of dark and bright
> Meet in her aspect and her eyes.'

And as he said 'eyes' he kissed mine very tenderly. I was beginning to feel quite turned on. I was still troubled that it might not be Tom at all, but decided to take a chance on it, and continued to keep my eyes firmly closed.

The kisses were moving downwards to my throat and neck. I was beginning to feel like an adolescent dreaming of her demon lover.

> 'And the midnight moon is weaving
> Her bright chain o'er the deep,
> Whose breast is gently heaving.'

So was mine. Hands were unbuttoning my blouse. Jesus, this was erotic! I no longer knew if it was daylight or dark, or where I was. I only knew where Tom's lips were – assuming they *were* Tom's. And that most of my clothes seemed to have been spirited away. The voice continued, scarcely more than a whisper.

'I enter thy garden of roses.'

And my God he did; or was just about to when a surge of panic overcame me. This was public! What about the builders? What about Clive? What about the entire village?

My eyes snapped open. Spread above me was a rampant ghost!

The transition from lust to laughter took about three seconds.

'Tom,' I gasped, retrieving articles of clothing as I struggled for words. 'The white sheet! . . . Ghosts don't wear them any more . . . And they're spirits; they don't have erections.'

A swirl of the sheet hid the offending member.

'Just testing,' Tom said breathlessly. 'A little experiment, that's all.'

'Experiment!' I said crossly, buttoning up my blouse. 'To prove what?'

Tom threw off the sheet as if it were a toga, and adjusted his clothes.

'That Georgina's lodger could have used Byron's poetry as an aphrodisiac.'

By now, I was sitting upright and composed. Tom was looking unduly pleased with himself.

'It seemed to work rather well,' he said.

'Go on then. Tell me. Another seminar. I'm listening.'

If I hadn't grown accustomed to the lunacy of Tom's women, I should have found it hard to believe his story.

It transpired that the young man who rented a room in Georgina's house was a poet who had remained bitterly unpublished for some years. He possessed three ambitions as yet unfulfilled – fame, money, and sex. Being resourceful by nature, he'd detected in his eccentric landlady a means of achieving all three ambitions at once. Georgina's literary ventures under the imprint of The Afterlife Press had by now become required reading on the wilder shores of scholarship, which were numerous and far-flung. The reputations of Emily Brontë and John Milton were being earnestly revised, and D. Phil. students, many from colleges in the Midwest, beat a frequent path to her door. Georgina herself was already something of a cult figure, and, though scarcely wealthy herself, her authors would certainly be so if they hadn't been long dead. Book sales soared. Post-modernist scholars squabbled with each other in print and on television. A chair in Afterlife Literature had been established at the University of Texas.

As always I never knew at which point Tom's stories were straying into fantasy. And as always he wasn't letting on.

'Well, you can believe what you like,' he said, chuckling. 'But this bit you have to believe.'

Bill the lodger's reasoning, he explained, was simple. The most successful of the 'long dead' in his own lifetime – both as poet and lover – had been Lord Byron. Bill had the good sense to realise that Georgina's recent seances with Milton were unlikely to have left her body as gratified as her mind. And this was where he could come to her aid. His own verse, with a few 'thee's' and 'thou's' scattered here and there, could easily become Byronic. His own physical charms could do the rest.

'Now, do you see? Very clever! Bill the poet got it all ways at once. Nights of carnal bliss with Georgina, combined with the fruitful passage to the printers of *Don Juan*, Canto XVII. Or so he hoped.'

In the gathering dusk of our garden, Tom had the expression of a man who had just politely seen off a delegation of Seventh Day Adventists.

'So, how did you find out?' I asked.

'Simple. I went to see Georgina,' he said. 'She joyfully showed me the scene of creativity. But as I looked around it seemed to me rather unlikely that ghosts – even Byron's ghost – would have left dents in pillows or used Croxley A4 paper. So, I decided to go downstairs and beard the lodger. I never told Georgina, and I never intend to.' Again I found myself touched by Tom's solicitude. 'I merely thumped the guy.'

It was almost dark, and growing cold. I put my arm through Tom's as we walked back towards the house.

'Two phantom lovers in one day, Tom,' I said. 'Not bad. Thank God we weren't observed,' I added. 'I don't fancy the village knowing I'd been seduced by a ghost.'

Tom paused.

'I wouldn't be too sure,' he said, and pointed towards the trees across the river.

I froze. It was Mooncalf. And this time I did feel haunted.

13

TOM greeted the morning with unusual gusto, then announced that a turkey was wandering about in our field.

I grunted something about it being far too early to start thinking of Christmas, and pulled the duvet higher round my ears.

'It's got whiskers,' Tom added.

'How did it open the tin?' I muttered, imagining he was talking about cat food.

Tom's response was to grasp my feet and drag me down the bed, shedding most of the duvet.

'Good legs!' he said. 'The rest of you's not bad either.'

And he ran his hands up my body.

I was about to do something painful to his anatomy when the door burst open and Clive rushed in to announce that there was a turkey in the field. Tom and I both made a hasty dive for the duvet and stuttered, 'Yes, we've seen it.' God knows what Clive had seen. He appeared much more interested in the turkey, though I suppose this may have been out of disgust. Clive's mind is deeply confused. He relishes the conviction that Tom has had just about every woman under the sun, and is determined to emulate him; I, on the other hand, am only supposed to do it under duress in order to keep Tom happy. ('When d'you think he'll find someone else, mum?' he enquired the other day.) I avoid psychiatrists in case they tell me Clive only wants me for himself, or that it's entirely my fault for kicking out his father. Sometimes I think I should have encouraged the French lessons after all. However, at least he's stopped laying plans for Tom to marry Madonna.

Thank heaven he was returning to school tomorrow.

'It's got whiskers, mum. Come and look.'

I realised by now that we weren't talking about cat food, and decided I'd better set eyes on this strange visitor. But I could only have done so in tandem with Tom, shuffling towards the window and grasping the duvet around us.

'I'll see it later,' I said, remaining huddled where I was.

Clive gazed at me thoughtfully.

'Why don't you wear a nightie, mum?' Then he nodded wisely: 'Though I suppose it must make it easier to pee.'

Tom told him to leave the room while we dressed. Clive departed, muttering, 'prudes'.

The turkey was still there after breakfast, and did indeed have whiskers – long white ones like a retired Wing Commander. I came to the conclusion it must be some special breed that John Gant was raising, and that it had done a bolt. I'd phone him when I got back from the station. Tom was catching an early train to London for an appointment with Kyra Vansittart – 'the *final* appointment,' he had said gratefully. They'd spoken on the telephone. Kyra had already phoned Harriet's solicitor with Tom's discoveries about Full Frontal Productions. The effect, Kyra said, was dynamite. Most satisfying; solicitors love drawing blood.

'She complimented me on a good piece of detective work, the patronising bitch,' Tom added.

So today was for tying matters up once and for all, he assured me. He'd be back on the early evening train. 'For good!' Meanwhile I was about to have the first day to myself for nearly a month. Sarum Magna in the spring, and all the Valkyrie gone – it was going to be a truly wonderful day. And later, I'd gut and prepare the river trout Ayrton had sweetly brought round for us. 'Coals to Newcastle, I know,' he'd said. 'I don't imagine your husband's been idle with his rod.' (I restrained myself with a polite smile.) 'But these were such wonderful specimens,' he went on, 'I wanted you to have them – a gift from one angler to another.' I was touched. I'd make a dill sauce, and put a bottle of Pouilly Fumé in the fridge. *Two* bottles – why not? Our life was going to begin. And the summer lay ahead. Summer after summer after summer. I was on top of the world.

When I returned from the station mid-morning the village lay dreaming below me in the sun, curled along the river and garlanded with blossom. From the familiar ridge I realised I could respond to many landmarks which only two months ago had seemed merely objects. Now as I gazed down on the straggle of houses and fields I could attach memories and associations to so many of them: John Gant's farm-gate where he would lean his enormous tattooed arms and talk of women; the village shop where a disapproving face would peer out in search of prey; Winston Cash's garden, waiting for Concha to cushion it with her flesh, and hidden in the bushes Clive's video camera quietly whirring. Then the long gravelled path to Emelda's house, nibbled bare by Lloyd George; and next to the house the patched and venerable church where Ayrton's ancestors measured the history of this place beneath slabs of brass and stone.

And there was our mill – down there – ringed with bright water. Would we always belong there? It was frightening to think of 'always', but 'for now' felt good. I seemed to have spent so much of my life in transit between one hope and the next; here was the first anchorage I felt sure of. I used to think of a John Lennon line: 'I'd give everything I've got for a little peace of mind.' Not any more! Those days had gone. My peace of mind was there waiting for me. It was my life with Tom.

I drove on down the hill and along the village street. It was empty except for an unmistakeably autumnal figure in plus-fours who was peering into the hedge a few hundred yards from our turning. His tweed hat all but hid his face, and the pockets of his Norfolk jacket hung down on either side of him like panniers. I stopped the car to greet him, and to thank him once again for the trout.

Ayrton gave a start, glanced round at me and raised his hat.

'They're late this year, but they've arrived – the whitethroats,' he assured me.

'I'm glad,' I said. Whatever the whitethroats might be put me in mind of our turkey. I told him about it. 'And it's got whiskers,' I explained.

Ayrton stared at me sharply. Then a look of bewilderment spread across his face, and he dabbed his eyes as though to clear them of some error of vision.

'Whiskers?' he repeated. 'What sort of whiskers?'

I flapped my hands about trying to suggest what they looked like.

'Long and white,' I said. 'Like Jimmy Edwards.' I thought that might ring a bell.

But Ayrton was already clambering into the car.

'Show me – if you please, madam,' he said urgently.

I noticed his hands were trembling. As I drove on he sat hunched forward with his nose almost touching the wind-screen, eyes as bright as torches scanning the road ahead.

'Whiskers. Long white whiskers,' he kept muttering to himself. 'Couldn't be. Couldn't be.'

I felt unable to ask what in God's name was going on, and why he should be so excited about a turkey – even a turkey with whiskers. So I kept quiet, glancing at Ayrton in the mirror and wondering what curious thoughts were churning around behind those watery eyes.

I pulled up outside the cottage and he got out of the car as though I'd uncorked it. Then I led him through the garden towards the gate into our field, praying that the creature would still be there. Ayrton's thin legs seemed to bound on springs, and his arms swung like twin pendulums in time with his pockets.

But there it was, our turkey, just standing in the middle of the field, its pale head raised, back bronze and mottled. Long powerful legs. And of course the whiskers, silvery-white.

Gazing at it again, I realised it didn't actually look too much like a turkey after all.

For a few moments Ayrton's hands gripped the gate as though he were trying to crush it, while inarticulate sounds emerged from somewhere below the long blade of a nose. Finally he turned and awarded me the look of a man who has just stumbled upon the Holy Grail. He was shaking his head in disbelief.

'My dear madam – a hundred and fifty years! Just think of that!' he said softly. Then he turned, and in a more brisk voice added. 'This is history! I must phone the Royal Society.'

And with that he hurried away like some urgent insect, leaving me standing there with the mystery of our turkey that wasn't.

I looked at my watch. It was eleven o'clock. What should I do? I felt I ought to guard this whiskered thing, whatever it was. But how? I could hardly catch it – its beak looked formidable enough to take my arm off. In any case it seemed contented enough, taking the occasional stroll and gazing around as if it owned the place. Besides, if it had really taken a hundred and fifty years to get here it was probably in need of a rest. How ridiculous that sounded. What the hell did Ayrton mean anyway? No doubt the Royal Society would know, and suitably advise.

I stayed in the garden for the best part of an hour, enjoying the peace of the place. Eventually I decided to go back to the cottage. In the distance the telephone was ringing. I heard Mrs Teape answer it in that special milady's voice she'd perfected: 'The Brand residence.' (That always made me cringe.) There was a pause, then – 'I'm afraid madam is still in conference with Lord Bustard.' (Oh God!) 'Who shall I say called?' The voice changed dramatically. 'I beg your pardon! Very well, I'll tell Mrs Brand.'

I got there just in time. Mrs Teape was looking ruffled as she handed me the phone. Ruth was laughing.

'I shouldn't have said I was a drunken old slag from Liechtenstein but I couldn't resist it,' she announced. 'And what have you been up to with the peerage?'

I explained about the hundred-and-fifty-year-old turkey. Ruth decided that the English countryside had finally softened my brain just as she'd always predicted. Then she urged me to fly out and join her: it was lonely having a libido in Liechtenstein, she said, and she needed immoral support. What was more, she'd found the perfect man for me.

'If he's so perfect why don't you have him yourself?' I said.

'I just did,' she answered. 'That's how I know he's perfect.'

I side-stepped that one, explaining I already had an *im*perfect man of my own, and that was quite enough.

We chatted on for a while. Ruth explained that she'd really phoned to say she was stepping off the diplomatic carousel for a few weeks and intended to visit us – even the English countryside would be an improvement on Liechtenstein PLC.

I just had time to say 'Great!', when out of the corner of my eye I noticed a white Rolls Royce making its way slowly up the track towards the mill. A white Rolls – that rang a bell. So did the number-plate: A10 DOL!

Sleepy Joe! Oh Christ, what could he possibly be doing here?

With a quick 'Goodbye' to Ruth, I slammed the phone down and rushed to the front door. Mrs Teape barred the way, dithering with excitement and hurriedly drying her hands.

'Don't fluster yourself, Mrs Brand,' she said. 'I'll tell them you'll be ready just as soon as you've gathered up your papers.' She was convinced it was an official car from 10 Downing Street, whisking me off to my first cabinet meeting. 'And do make sure Mr Major looks after you in your condition, won't you!'

'Just be ready to phone the police,' I said, pushing past her.

Mrs Teape thought I meant a police escort.

'Quite right, Mrs Brand. I'll do that. I'm surprised they're not here already.'

I desperately wished they were.

The Rolls whispered to a halt on the gravel, and two men got out. The older one in the camel-hair coat, I realised, must be Sleepy Joe. The younger man with him wore dark glasses and looked as if he'd just walked off the set of *Minder*. He was flexing his fingers with an air of casual menace. Neither of them looked at me as I approached.

I'd only once faced physical danger before, from a lecherous drunk on the Thames towpath. Some instinct in me had turned terror into saccharined charm. 'Good evening, sir! Can I help you?' I'd said with the loveliest smile. He had looked astonished, zipped up his flies, and wandered away.

The same instinct overtook me now.

'You must be Mr Cutler,' I said brightly. 'I'm delighted we've had a chance to meet at last. What a pity my husband isn't here: you have so much in common.'

The minder's fingers stopped flexing, and hung loose. Sleepy Joe shifted his weight from one foot to the other, and looked at me, surprised. His eyes were hard as ice. I managed to keep my smile intact.

'Perhaps some coffee, after your journey?' I went on bravely.

And I gestured towards the cottage.

Joe shook his head as if sweeping my chat aside. I decided to plunge ahead.

'You're a close friend of my husband's ex-wife I believe, Mr Cutler. How very nice. A charming lady – I only met her once.'

Joe continued to look at me stonily, while the minder looked at him, his face expressionless behind the shades, his fingers twitching now and again as if waiting to kill something. I was glad for Tom's sake that he wasn't here.

I sensed that I wasn't exactly winning this contest, but felt I had no viable option but to press on. I decided to double my stake.

'You must forgive me if I'm mistaken, Mr Cutler,' I continued cheerfully, 'but I understand you're likely to be married very soon. You have our warmest congratulations, and I'm sure you'll be extremely happy. I know Tom was.'

294

(I realised I shouldn't have added that, but I was carried away.)

Sleepy Joe's face suddenly changed. He blinked, and for the first time he said something, though I couldn't catch what it was he said. He was now gazing at me with puzzled fascination. And then the most unlikely thing happened: he blushed. And then he smiled. Not a smile to warm the heart exactly, but none the less a smile.

I realised that by an outrageous fluke I'd hit on the truth. And in that same moment it struck me that it also explained the company set up in Jersey, and the director's salary paid into Harriet's bank account. I'd made a discovery every bit as remarkable as anything Tom had managed to uncover. He loved her!

My astonishment was cut short by a further unexpected event. Suddenly and out of nowhere there was pandemonium all around us. Along the track, across the fields, across the little bridge, through the garden, people began hurrying towards us. Joe spun round as if he'd been ambushed. The minder's right hand went automatically to where I'd noticed a suspicious bulge beneath his jacket.

But it was too late. We were surrounded.

'Where is it?' the man closest to me asked breathlessly.

He wore boots, a woolly hat and an anorak that looked as though it would defy the Arctic. A pair of binoculars dangled from one hand, while the other grasped a tripod to which was attached a camera with a lens that could have magnified the furthest star.

'Where is *what*?' I said, bewildered.

A chorus of voices answered me.

'The bustard. The Great Bustard!'

I gazed around me at the sea of earnest and hairy faces. And then I understood. I had encountered that zealous fraternity – the twitchers. The grapevine had clearly been working overtime this morning. And from those three excited words – 'the Great Bustard' – several pieces of jigsaw came together all of a sudden. Our 'turkey' was the very bird that Ayrton's ancestors had mounted on the family crest, having changed their own name from 'Bastard'. It was long extinct in this country, Emelda had explained. And now, it seemed, the creature had returned to its former habitat after an absence (as I realised Ayrton had meant) of one hundred and fifty years.

Well, whatever Sleepy Joe and his minder may originally have prepared for us was by now forever lost. To say that they were mystified would do an injustice to the expressions on their faces. I wondered if they believed that I'd rigged the entire performance for their benefit, or that such events were the customary and time-honoured thing in rural England. But whatever they believed, they were in no position to suggest or do anything. The white Rolls was trapped by a dozen or more mud-spattered vehicles of all shapes and descriptions, each one of them disgorging more and yet more twitchers along with a battery of cameras, telescopes, binoculars and elaborate sound-recording equipment. The army of bird-watchers was on the move. Purposefully and without heed of obstacles they seethed through the garden and across the streams in the direction my outstretched arm was pointing. It was like Passchendaele.

Finally we were alone. I wasn't at all sure what I should do next. It would have been a relief if Joe and his minder had just gone. But they couldn't go; they were stuck here. Conversation didn't seem to be on the agenda either: Joe had barely spoken a word, and the minder didn't look as if he was capable of doing so.

It was then that I caught sight of my saviour. Accompanied by her goat, a round and mauve-clad figure was hurrying down the track, squeezing her bulk between the parked cars and gazing anxiously in my direction. Blessed Emelda!

Out of breath, she hurried up to me with a cursory nod at my visitors and the white Rolls.

'I've come to see if you're all right,' she announced. 'Poor you! So, the family crest has sprung to life – the only part of Ayrton that's sprung to life for years, I assure you.' She gave one of her growling laughs, and then glanced at the goat. 'Lloyd George, leave the Rolls Royce alone; I'm afraid he likes to nibble tyres. But good God, my dear, what an invasion. I suppose we'll have David Attenborough here in no time.' She paused to gaze once again at the Rolls, then at Sleepy Joe and the minder. Her face brightened. 'You must be from the Royal Society,' she said, and shook both men by the hand. 'My husband rang you. You'd better stay for lunch.'

At this point I thought I'd better introduce them.

'Mr Cutler . . . and friend,' I said, 'Lady Bustard.'

Even gangland millionaires are snobs, I realised. The Queen of England couldn't have induced greater deference. Joe even addressed Emelda as 'ma'am'.

I felt I ought to explain that these gentlemen weren't as a matter of fact representatives from the Royal Society for the Protection of Birds, but had arrived on a rather different mission. But I could scarcely announce to Emelda that they'd actually come to beat the shit out of Tom who, thank Christ, wasn't here. So I decided to leave her in ignorance and pursue my previous line of argument.

'Mr Cutler is a close friend of Harriet Brand,' I explained, 'whom you've met on a number of occasions.'

There was a brief pause as Emelda glanced at me, and in that glance I detected her perfect grasp of the situation. Whatever happened, Emelda was going to play this for all it was worth. I decided to give her a lead.

'As a matter of fact,' I went on, 'they're shortly to be married.'

Joe showed signs of uttering something, but Emelda was launched.

'Oh, I'm delighted for you, Mr Cutler. Dear Harriet, such a lovely lady! And when is the happy day, may I ask?'

Joe cleared his throat, and managed to explain that it wasn't actually fixed.

Emelda wasn't having any of that. She glanced at me with a look of the purest mischief.

'Oh, but there's no point messing about, Mr Cutler,' she exclaimed. 'Really! A man of your distinction and mature years.' Joe obviously enjoyed that. 'And where is it to be? A cathedral? I always think one should be married in a cathedral.'

This time Joe could do no more than blink.

Suddenly she clapped her hands, and her eyes grew round.

'I've got a splendid idea. What about our local? Salisbury. Should be big enough, I imagine. D'you have a lot of relations, Mr Cutler – children, ex-wives, mistresses and so on? Most men do.'

I was beginning to wince: this was going too far. Joe was standing there agog. The minder was staring helplessly as Lloyd George continued to chew gently at the car tyres.

'But you don't need to worry about any of that,' Emelda went on. 'Our bishop's very understanding – not one of your evangelical churchmen forever waiting for the stigmata. Besides, the dean owes me a favour or two; I've raised a great deal of money for the spire, you see. Would you like me to give him a ring? Yes, why don't I do just that? I see you've got a phone in your car. May I?'

And with that she wrenched open the door and slumped herself in the driver's seat, half in and half out. Before anything could be said she'd tapped out a number and was shouting: 'Ambrose! Get me Ambrose!' There was a moment's pause, then: 'I don't care if he is in a diocesan meeting: this is much more important. Tell him it's Lady Bustard, and that I can't wait – I'm in a car – or half in a car; my goat appears to be chewing the other half.' She turned her head, holding the telephone away from her. 'Lloyd George, stop it! I am sorry, Mr Cutler, he's badly trained. But I'm sure the Royal Society will give you a new one.'

There was another pause while presumably the flunkey went to fetch the dean from his diocesan meeting. Emelda chose to fill the time by leaning out of the car as though she owned it, and asking Joe some further questions. Was he the President of the Royal Society, or only the Secretary? Wasn't it immensely rewarding to have so worthwhile a vocation? Had he always been involved in good works?

She didn't bother to wait for the answers. Then it seemed to occur to her that there was one vital question she hadn't asked. Her eyes brightened.

'The bride-to-be – where is the lady? She ought to be here. When is she coming down?'

For the first time the minder woke from his reverie. He gave Joe a meaningful glance, and a grin.

'Abart free o'clock, innit Joe?' he muttered. 'To see the body.'

I blinked. That would have been Tom's body, I realised. Or what was left of it.

Emelda ignored the sinister reference, or perhaps she hadn't understood.

'Three o'clock this afternoon!' she exclaimed. 'What could be better? So, you can do it all at once, Mr Cutler, can't you? I'll tell the dean.'

Just then a voice crackled out of the telephone, and Emelda rammed the instrument back to her ear.

'Ambrose!' It was precisely the same tone she used for summoning the goat. 'A wedding for you. Special Licence. This afternoon, about three-thirty. Is that all right? Friends of mine – very distinguished. President of the Royal Society. Will you tell the organist, or shall I?'

If there were objections from the deanery Emelda was in no mood to listen to them.

'Thank you, Ambrose,' she said firmly. Then, turning to Joe she gave a decisive nod of the head. 'That's fixed then, Mr Cutler. We'll have lunch, then meet your fiancée and go straight to the cathedral. Not much rehearsing; I imagine you've been through it all plenty of times before. If you'd prefer something other than the usual Mendelssohn wedding march I'm sure the organist will arrange it; you may not want to be reminded of the last occasion. In any case I'll send for a car: yours is imprisoned, I'm afraid. Besides,' she added, gazing at the Rolls Royce, 'it may not be in the best of health after Lloyd George's attentions.'

On cue, a soft hiss could be heard coming from Joe's car. We all of us turned in the direction of the sound, to witness the Rolls sink before our eyes as one of the rear wheels gracefully collapsed on to its rim. Lloyd George was continuing to chew in a rhythmical fashion, tossing back his head from time to time in an effort to engorge the last fragment of the tyre's valve which still protruded from his lips.

Emelda appeared not to notice. She gave Lloyd George a sharp tug and turned to the two men.

'Right! Lunch! Follow me!'

And they did. Stepping carefully past the potholes the unlikely trio, plus a goat, made its way down the track towards the village.

The Great Bustard flew off, perhaps for another one hundred and fifty years. And with his departure, the twitchers went too. They straggled back across the garden with the radiant look of wise men who had followed their star to Bethlehem, and could now return home with tidings of great joy. They paid no attention to me; I had no role to play in their dreams. They folded their tripods, dismantled their lenses, restored their binoculars to weathered leather cases and stuffed their woolly hats into capacious pockets. Then, like a raggle-taggle caravan of New Age travellers, they moved off. No doubt one of their car-phones was even at this moment relaying the precise whereabouts of some storm-tossed albatross gasping for life at Cape Wrath; and another star was beckoning.

Apart from the builders' truck, only two cars remained on the gravel outside the mill. One was our own, the other a Rolls Royce, now considerably less than white as a result of the attentions of Lloyd George from both ends, and displaying a severe limp.

Mrs Teape was gazing at it with a vexed expression, clicking her tongue at the thought that I'd missed my first cabinet meeting.

'And all those hooligans turning up and tramping through the garden,' she said, jamming in her combs and preparing to leave. 'Disgraceful! I don't know what the world's coming to.'

Neither did I. What I did know was that millionaire gangsters could be putty in the hands of powerful women. I'd also learnt that in the service of British aristocracy goats can be almost as lethal as their owners.

I also reflected on what kind of mangled creature I might now be tending had Tom been here. I shuddered. Then my vision of a pulped lover was dispelled by the sound of a heavy motor. I went to the window, and there making its way laboriously towards the cottage was a breakdown truck, the giant hook of its crane swinging from side to side as it bumped through the potholes. I watched as it managed to reverse painstakingly on the gravel; finally two men in overalls got out and fed a chain round the rear axle of the Rolls Royce, attaching it to the giant hook. One of the men then clambered back into the truck and began to operate a hydraulic winch. The rear of the Rolls began to rise: it looked absurdly like a white arse getting up after a crap, and I laughed. And off it went, very slowly, A10 DOL, bump bump bump up the track towards the road. Why, I wondered, didn't they just change the wheel? Lloyd George must have done his duty extraordinarily well.

At last everyone had gone. I fixed myself a bite of lunch, speculating on how Emelda's guests were faring, and whether Ayrton was at this very moment instructing Sleepy Joe on the mating habits of Polynesian dragonflies. At three o'clock Harriet was due to arrive in the village to receive the biggest surprise of her life since her debut wearing a dustbin liner. No doubt Emelda would arrange the reception committee, Lloyd George included. And then there would be the cathedral, and the happiest moment of a girl's life. I poured myself a drink and raised a toast to the bride and groom, and to the burgeoning fortunes of Full Frontal Productions.

I was still unsure if I was in a state of euphoria or shock. Clive was out somewhere, and I was alone. I thought of phoning Ruth, then decided to keep the events of the morning fresh for Tom. Instead I did the most calming thing I knew, and worked in the garden, repairing some of the damage caused by the stampeds of twitchers. Then I took myself into the field where the bustard had been. Tiny purple orchids were dotted here and there in the grass. Suddenly in front of me I caught sight of a single feather. It was more than a foot in length and golden-bronze with dark veins running across it symmetrically as though a fine brush had been applied to it. I picked the feather up, and it was warm as if it were alive. I looked around me, but there were no others; just this single feather, the only sign that the great bird had ever been here. It was like a signature.

I would give it to Ayrton, I decided. Dear Ayrton – the feather would mean more to him than all the ancient emblems on his family crest. I could imagine him framing it on the wall, reminding him of the day the Great Bustard had come back to where it once belonged.

An hour remained before I was due to leave for the station to pick up Tom. The sun was warm. It was a perfect spring afternoon. Ruth might have found this the dreariest of places to be, but to me it was heaven. I wandered round my patch of paradise, savouring every step of it, making a mental inventory of everything in it that I loved, so that I would always have it with me wherever I happened to be. Then I did the same in the old mill. The builders were gathered outside in the yard drinking tea, and I could furnish the emptiness of the place with everything that our life would soon be – mercifully without the assistance of Mr Ashley de Vere.

Then I returned to the mill cottage. Surprised to find the front door ajar, I walked in with some trepidation. But no one seemed to be there – until I noticed that Clive's bedroom door was open.

'Clive!' I called out. 'Are you there?'

There was silence for a few moments, followed by a long, gentle moan.

I put my head round the door. He was lying stretched out on the bed, gazing up at the ceiling. The expression on his face was one of the purest rapture, and from time to time he blinked as if unable to believe whatever beatific vision hovered above him.

'Clive, are you all right?' I said anxiously.

Could he be stoned? I wondered. Or drunk?

'Clive!' I said again.

Another gentle moan rose from the bed. And still his eyes never left the ceiling.

I went over and sat beside him.

'What's happened, Clive? Tell me.'

This time his eyes wandered from the ceiling down on to my face. Then he gave out a deep sigh.

'Everything!' he said. 'Everything!'

I'd lived long enough to understand that sometimes 'everything' means only *one* thing, and that this was one of those times. It was also one of those times when a mother finds she has absolutely nothing to say, and wishes passionately she were elsewhere. So, what in God's name did one say to one's son who's just made it perfectly clear he's had his first fuck? 'Jolly good show!' didn't sound right. 'Oh, really!' seemed a bit inadequate. 'Well done!' wasn't quite appropriate either. 'Better than masturbating, eh?' was altogether too crude. 'I hope you used a condom' was what I felt like saying, but I dreaded having to follow this up with a stern lecture about Aids.

Simple curiosity won.

'Who was it?' I asked.

I was assuming that one of Clive's little notices about French lessons must finally have found its mark.

He looked at me almost shyly.

'Oh, you know, mum!' he said. 'Her! The one with the artist.'

I blinked.

'You mean Concha? You *asked* her?'

Clive shook his head.

'No! She asked me.'

A little after four, I left for the station. Tom's train was due in half an hour. This time it was with huge pleasure that I caught sight of Harriet's car parked on the verge not far from Emelda's house. They had obviously all departed in the hired limousine Emelda had promised.

From the ridge above the village I could follow the River Avon winding towards Salisbury, and in the distance the slender spire of the Cathedral dwarfing the city. I thought of the ceremony even now taking place within those ancient walls. Had Sleepy Joe managed to slip away and buy a ring? I wondered. Or had Emelda thought of that one too?

Tom was smiling broadly as he made his way down the platform. He was brandishing a bottle of champagne. It was all done, he said. Wrapped up. And he lifted me up and carried me past the barrier, the champagne dangling. The ticket collector, accustomed by now to our displays, waved us through without a hint of surprise. And at that moment a joyful peal of bells began to ring out from the cathedral, muffling the sound of traffic and sending a flock of pigeons swirling round and round above the roofs of the city.

'You see, I arranged everything,' Tom said coolly, still carrying me.

'Indeed,' I answered. 'What a lovely surprise. And now I've got one for you. In fact I've got two surprises for you.'

I made him put me down before I told him.

'The first surprise is that Clive is no longer a virgin.'

Tom merely smiled.

'And you call that a surprise?'

'All right, Tom,' I said. 'If that's how you feel, how about this one?'

Then I told him about the events of the morning, and what was at that very moment taking place only a few hundred yards away.

Tom stood in the car park like a man who was witnessing a miracle.

'And to think,' I added, 'if only you'd caught the earlier train you could have given the bride away. After all, you've been trying to do that for years.'

The bells rang on and on. I thought I'd better do the driving in case the next request to the dean was for a funeral. From time to time I caught a glimpse of Tom's face in the driving mirror, and it was as though the minder had been to work after all. He said nothing until we reached the ridge overlooking the village. Then he cleared his throat meaningfully.

'Sweetheart, why did I ever imagine the country would be a peaceful place to live?'

I laughed.

'Look!' I answered. Sarum Magna lay below us like a toy village. 'It is!'

The trees along the river were filtering the last of the sunlight as we pulled up outside the cottage. The builders were loading their gear into the truck; and they waved as they drove off. Another couple of weeks and we could move in, they'd already assured me. The summer would be ours. Meanwhile we had the weekend ahead of us. No builders. No Clive. No Mrs Teape. And – I sincerely hoped – no twitchers. My feather lay on the kitchen table, the only visible proof I could offer of all the bizarre events of that day.

'We've survived, Tom,' I said. 'And we're alone. Come and enjoy the evening.'

It was that moment before the day dies when the dusk is luminous, and the stillness seems to be waiting for the night. The garden was rich with the scent of spring, and we walked round it as though it were ours for the first time.

It wasn't.

Tom pointed her out, as he had before. She was standing on the little bridge, barely visible in the half-light, and gazing at us. Mooncalf.

For a moment I was frightened. Then outraged. And finally calm. This was to be it! I'd had more than enough. I wasn't sure what precisely I would do, but it would be final. 'Mooncalf,' I said to myself, 'none of your earth goddesses, your star signs, your summer solstices or your druidical mumbo-jumbos are going to come to your aid now. You can dress in a white toga, pray to the dawn, eat bats for breakfast or whatever it is you do with your bloodless self: forget it! This is going to be your moment of truth. Zap!'

I waved frantically and ran towards her. At first she seemed about to slip away as she had so often before. But then she hesitated, her hands gripping the rail of the bridge as if any minute she might jump in.

Suddenly I realised she was terrified; her face twitched and her body shook as I came up to her.

I stopped, and without thinking put out my hand. She took it as if it might burn her. It felt like a little claw.

'I'm . . . I'm sorry,' she said. 'Forgive me, but . . . I've been wondering . . . I've been wanting to ask you, but I've not liked to . . .'

I waited. What was to be the long-awaited message from the Druids?

'It's just that I . . . I believe I knew your mother.'

I don't know what she made of my face. I hope she wasn't offended by my laughter. I wanted to hug her. But she'd gone.

And so the night fell on the strangest of days.

'Tom,' I said after I'd returned to the cottage. 'For God's sake open that champagne. I intend to get extremely pissed.'

'Well, you certainly managed it,' Tom announced as he brought me breakfast.

I groaned. The light was unkind.

'Did I?' I murmured.

I took a sip of orange juice. My mouth was like a sea-cave.

He was laughing.

'What's funny?'

'You.'

'Why?'

He was still laughing.

'You don't remember ringing your mother?'

'No!'

'You don't remember ringing the Dean of Salisbury?'

'No!'

'You don't remember ringing Clive's headmaster?'

'No!'

'You don't remember cooking the trout in a kettle?'

'No!'

'You don't remember asking me who I was?'

'No!'

'You don't remember saying you never allowed strange men to undress you?'

'No! Oh God, Tom, what else don't I remember?'

'Not a lot. You were very funny. You made a speech as I put you to bed.'

'What about?'

'Well, the main drift seemed to be that men who are circumcised do it better than those who aren't; but you fell asleep before you could explain why.'

'Oh no! I'm never going to get drunk again. Tom, why weren't you drunk?'

'I was. But I'm more used to it than you. Besides, your performance was too good to miss.'

'Bastard! . . . Tom, do you still love me?'

Making love did wonders for my hangover. By mid-morning I was feeling frail and happy. I'd managed to move on to coffee.

'Tom,' I said, feeling serious. 'What d'you think you'll do, now it's all over?'

He pulled a chair up to the table and rested his chin in his hands.

'I've been thinking about that,' he said. 'You know, all the years I've worked there've been things I've dreamed of doing when I didn't have to work. Little things. Romantic things. The trouble was, I was always so busy getting divorced I could never imagine doing them with the person I loved.'

'What sort of things?' I asked.

Tom looked reflective.

'I suppose always having a project which would keep me anchored. A book to write – *not* Byron's biography. A language to learn. Or whatever. But then making lots of trips on the spur of the moment, at just the right time. You know, waking up one morning and deciding to go and wander through fields of alpine flowers. Or go to Florence. Or Burgundy – a walk among the wine labels. Or go up the Nile on a felucca. Or to tell the winter to fuck off and go to Australia. To be able to afford to live on impulse, I suppose.' Tom paused for a moment; then without looking up at me said, 'And now you're with me, all that's not just a dream any more.'

There were tears in my eyes. There was nothing to say except, 'Thank you'.

Tom got up and gazed out of the window.

'But there's one thing I'm going to do first,' he said.

I was about to ask what when there was a ring on the doorbell. Tom let out a groan, and got up.

'Oh shit!'

I followed him.

There have been bad moments, but this was one of the worst.

Neither of us said anything for a moment, and nor did the woman standing at the door. She was youngish, dark-haired, petite. Not exactly pretty. And dressed rather dowdily. But she was smiling. She was smiling at Tom. And in her arms she held a young child.

I didn't need to be told anything. I knew straight away. A picture came into my head from my art school days. It was a Victorian painting – I couldn't remember who the artist was – but it depicted a young woman with a naked child in her arms, and she was holding it out with a fraught expression. The title I recalled only too clearly – *Take your Son, Sir*. I always loathed the picture without ever thinking of it as a dark omen.

And here it was, come to life.

I was too muddled to know who she might be. I only knew that she was holding Tom's child. I also knew that this was one shock too many. Everything we'd been talking about only a few minutes earlier – everything we'd planned and promised ourselves over so many months – suddenly I could feel them all dying inside me. There would be no future. I would leave tomorrow – today! I would pay back the deposit on my little house in Chiswick. Perhaps I'd take up Ruth's long-standing invitation and fly out to Liechtenstein; I might agree to meet her 'perfect man', and get fucked stupid.

It felt like an hour just standing there on the doorstep. Probably it was five seconds: the imagination works like lightning in emergencies. And even when Tom spoke I barely took it in.

'Sarah!' he said.

I noticed that his voice quavered, the bastard. Was he going to have the cheek to introduce her to me? Should I hit him now, or later? Perhaps I might just scream.

At last she said something.

'Tom, I'm sorry.'

(I bet you are, cookie. Sorry you ever met the arse-hole.)

'I was just passing. I knew you lived here.'

(You mean he even gave you our address!)

'It's lovely here. Really lovely. I'm so happy for you.'

(Jesus, you've got a bloody nerve, you bitch!)

'And this must be Janice.'

(So he actually talked about me while screwing you!)

'By the way, this is Adam.'

(Son of the old Adam. Well, at least Tom now knows the name of his little bastard.)

'He's just two months.'

(That means Tom was screwing her all the time he was trying to seduce me, the rat fink!)

'He's so wonderfully well-behaved.'

(Which is more than could ever be said of his father.)

'I'm just on my way to my in-laws. They haven't seen Adam yet.'

(I'm now puzzled. Tom's mother's been dead for over

fifty years, and his father for forty. So what's this 'in-laws' bit?)

'John's joining me tomorrow.'

(John?)

'It's our wedding anniversary. Listen, I won't keep you. But I've got some things of yours in the car. I've been meaning to return them for ages. This seemed a good opportunity. I shan't be a minute.'

She walked back towards her car. I gazed at Tom, bemused.

'Sorry!' he said, turning to me. 'I wasn't able to get a word in edgeways. It's Sarah – my ex-wife. Remember? Well, she got married about six months after we parted. Nice girl.'

'Oh!' was all I said.

And I put my arms round him.

Sarah was returning with a large package. She'd left the baby in the car.

'I'm so glad you're happy,' she said, smiling. 'Here you are. All your Le Carrés. And now I must fly. I'm due there for lunch. Lovely to meet you, Janice. Bye bye.'

I couldn't say anything at all. So that was Number Five. The last one.

And I started to laugh.

'Tom, you've no idea what I thought.'

As I said it a look of astonishment came over his face.

'You didn't think that, did you?'

I nodded.

'Jesus Christ,' he said. 'How could you? A pillar of virtue like me.'

He hugged me. I ran my hands through his hair.

'Tell me, Tom. Why did you marry her?'

'Because she's nice,' he answered.

'Then why did you leave her?'

'Because she's nice.'

'What a good thing I'm not,' I said. 'Tom, I love you.'

He gave me one of his mischievous smiles.

'I'm beginning to get that way with you too.'

And we agreed to drink to that.

It was warm in the garden, and we sat there watching the swans on the river.

'Tom,' I said. 'Before your last and nicest wife appeared, you were telling me all the things you wanted to do. We got through alpine flowers, and Florence, and the Nile, and Australia. But you said there was one thing you were going to do first of all. What?'

He looked at me gravely, and I wondered what grand project was about to be revealed.

'Well,' he said. 'I thought I'd learn to fish.'

I realised Tom would always surprise me; and I loved that. We took our glasses of wine down to the river, and gazed back at the old mill. Already it looked like the place we had dreamed it would be.

'Happy?' Tom asked.

I nodded.

'Extremely.'

A flash of blue cut across the surface of the water into the alders.

'You'll have competition,' I said, laughing. And I raised my glass. 'But to you, Tom. And to us. Halcyon days!'

Primula

Forrestii

Act India. (Ivy)